# JOURNEYS

JOHN CARSTENSEN

Ark House Press
arkhousepress.com



The characters in this novel are fictional, except those whose names are recorded in history.

Cataloguing in Publication Data:
Title: Journeys
ISBN: 978-1-7645620-9-6 (pbk)
Subjects: [FIC014000] FICTION / Historical / General; [FIC145000] FICTION / Places / Australia & Oceania; [FIC032000] FICTION / War & Military.

Design by initiateagency.com

To Miep and Sharon, whose critiquing helped bring this project to fruition.

# INTRODUCTION

This novel is set in New Zealand between 1863 and 1918, a period marked by profound political and social upheaval. Its historical backdrop includes the New Zealand Wars of the 1860s, and their aftermath, notably the invasions of the Waikato and Parihaka.

The central characters are fictional, but the historical setting, events, and many of the figures who appear in the background are real and presented as accurately as possible. The narrative begins with the protagonist's involvement in the wars, then follows the life he makes for himself in colonial Auckland, with the story continuing into the next generation.

An understanding of the historical and political forces at work during this period is important to appreciating how modern New Zealand has been shaped, particularly in relation to The Treaty of Waitangi and the political issues that continue to arise from it.

# JOURNEYS

# 1

Private Finbar Kelly dug up the basalt and scoria with a pickaxe and Private Michael McCann smashed the lumps to pieces with a sledgehammer. He shut his eyes with each blow to protect them from the flying shards. The birdsong of the morning had died with the noise of nearly two thousand workers hacking a road through dense bush, over steep hills and through swamps. The sun beat down relentlessly from a cloudless azure sky. Cicadas grated incessantly in the heat of the day. It was hard, sweaty labour to be sure, but less of a strain for McCann, by Kelly's reckoning. Kelly was tall and lean, whereas his mate was a stocky, barrel-chested young bullock of a man, built closer to the ground, with short limbs and a thick neck. He'd been brought up in a cob hut and he seemed like a creature of the earth.

McCann had been a tenant farmer in Ireland, but Kelly was not of peasant stock, nor was he of landowner or merchant class. He had worked as a clerk for an Irish manufacturer, but he'd lost his job when the factory closed down. Kelly and McCann both aspired to be landowners, not as landlords in Ireland—that would be impossible—but as farmers in New Zealand, with a military land grant when they finished their service in the

British Imperial Army. When the recruiting sergeant came to town, Kelly and McCann both turned up at the same time and, agreeing the time was right for a grand adventure with good prospects at the end of it, they signed up together. However, their military service thus far fell well short of their expectations of action and adventure.

"This is prisoners' work," Kelly said. "I didn't join the army to smash rocks and build roads."

"Right," McCann agreed. "Give us some good honest fighting."

"Well, it's grand to hear the voices of the home country," said an older Irishman on a horse-drawn cart, "even if they're only whining and complaining." His ruddy, bearded face and stout frame were a stark contrast to the lithe young soldiers with their neatly clipped regulation moustaches.

"And who are you?" said Kelly.

"Patrick Quinn's the name. I'm what you might call a merchant, from County Armagh, late of Auckland town, bringing this here load of banjos for the work," by which he meant the big round shovels for shifting the dirt. "Keep working boys. You'll be glad of the road when it comes to moving supplies and big guns."

"A shopkeeper, from Armagh," McCann said. "Private Kelly here has a sweetheart back in Armagh, name of Annie Gallagher."

"I knew a Thomas Gallagher of Armagh. Maybe her father or an uncle."

"Not that I know of," said Kelly. "Gallagher's a common name in Armagh."

"Aye, well, I'm a shopkeeper all right and before that a soldier like yourselves."

"Serving here in New Zealand?" Kelly asked.

"Aye boys, fighting the Māori in the North in '45 and '46 under Colonel Despard." The merchant climbed awkwardly off the cart and limped to the back. His jacket caught on the rail of the cart and lifted to reveal a revolver tucked in his belt, an Adam's five-shot of the type carried by officers.

The quartermaster came with his inventory and checked the load. He gave Quinn his instructions and went back to his station.

"All right then boys," said Quinn, "give us a hand to unload these shovels—just the shovels, mind, not the boxes." He carried on with his story. "It was a musket ball in the leg that finished my soldiering days. We were attacking the Ruapekapeka Pā, rooting old Kawiti out of his Bats' Nest, where he'd been digging in for six months. We could have done with a road there, I can tell you. We dragged thirty tons of heavy artillery uphill through thick bush at the rate of a mile a day."

"And you took the pā," said Kelly. "I've heard of it. The last battle in the north and a victory for the British."

"Ruapekepeka wasn't much of a victory, really. We bombarded the pā with cannon fire for ten days and breached the palisades. When we stormed the pā most of the Māori had left for the day, for Sunday prayers, so they say. They were a Christian village, except for Kawiti himself and only he was still in the pā. We caught them unawares outside, behind the pā and we shot a few but most of them escaped into the bush, including Kawiti. A few of our men were killed chasing after them into the bush. So we captured a deserted pā in the middle of the bush miles from nowhere. For what? What sort of a victory was that?

"Now, Ōhaeawai, there was a battle." Quinn leaned with his back against the cart and lit a meerschaum pipe of tobacco. Through a cloud of smoke he regarded the pair of young soldiers, who sat on the ground, in the meagre shade of the cart, and drank the warm water in their wooden water bottles. They were glad of a break from their back breaking labour and listened to the old soldier's tales.

"The Ōhaeawai pā was like the one at Ruapekapeka but the Ōhaeawai battle was six months before. We set up all the cannon on the hills surrounding the pā and pounded it every day for a week with six pound, twelve pound, thirty-two pound round shot. We moved the guns closer and closer. We couldn't miss. The poor devils in the pā must have thought all hell had come down on them. At the end of the week we moved in to finish off the survivors—250 of us handpicked for the job. About fifty paces from the pā we were cut down in a fierce volley of shots. In ten minutes half our number lay dead or dying on the ground and the rest of us retreated for our lives."

"How did the Māoris survive the shelling?" Kelly asked.

"They were all huddled safely in underground bunkers and tunnels. Then they were waiting for us in trenches, stepping up and firing under the palisades: two rings of fences, the outer one to slow us down and fire on us. A few days later we took the pā because the Māori just abandoned it and disappeared. In that fortress were defences the likes of which we'd never seen. Despard drove us into the traps, not just once, but twice. The old fool refused to believe the Māori could have built it themselves without European military engineers. Governor Fitzroy reported it was a victory but we were soundly beaten by a bunch of so-called savages we outnumbered six to one. The Māori are masters of garrison warfare and a fearsome enemy. Don't expect an easy time of it in the Waikato."

"And what of our new governor and our new general?" Kelly said. "Do you think they're up to the job?"

"It was Governor Grey, just arrived in the country, ordered the attack on Ruapekapeka after he got reinforcements from Sydney. Grey is a cunning devil and I believe General Cameron is a good soldier and he'll do his master's bidding. Grey's determined to 'smash the Kīngitanga rebels'. He's going after the Māori King, the new one, Tāwhiao, and that trouble maker Rewi Maniapoto, who went down to the Taranaki with his Kingite warriors to help fight the British. Cameron's of the same mind. He says the Māori can't set up a king of their own race. They have to acknowledge the Queen as their sovereign. They signed the Treaty."

"I hear we're all under threat from the Kingites," said McCann. "They're planning to attack Auckland. If we can put down the Kingite rebels…"

"Why would they want to attack Auckland?" Quinn interrupted. "They'd be killing the goose that laid the golden eggs. They're coming and going in and out of Auckland every day in their canoes and ships with goods for trading: flax, produce from farms and orchards, animals, grain, not just wheat, but flour from their own mills. They're even exporting to Australia and America."

"What are they getting from the trade?" Kelly asked.

"Benefits of our civilization: tools, the machinery of agriculture and the machinery of war. Muskets are in great demand and so is flax, for rope, for ships' rigging. It's one musket for a ton of dressed flax. The wāhine are busy stripping flax with mussel shells all the day long. The northern tribes got muskets and decimated the Waikato tribes in the twenties and thirties, so of course the Waikatos were keen to gain the upper hand in the arms race. They trade for other goods too like cloth and liquor. Māori and settlers both been prospering from trade. And we been under the protection of Te Wherowhero and Tāmihana. No other tribes would attack us. Auckland is a peaceful town, or at least it was till it filled up with more and more of the drunken rabble of Her Majesty's Imperial troops."

"Then why is Grey saying the Māoris plan to attack Auckland?" said Kelly sceptically.

"He's put the rumours about and the report to London to get more troops for the invasion."

"But why?" Kelly persisted, "if we have peace?"

"Land, boys! Men will fight over women and land. This one's all about the getting of land. They've got it and we want it. All that fertile Waikato land. We've got more and more land-hungry settlers and the Kingites are refusing to sell more land, and the so-called rebels will pay with their lives and their land."

The Commander of the Imperial Engineers, doing his rounds, shouted at Quinn, “Move along and deliver the boxes to the quartermaster’s stores.” And to Kelly and McCann, “Enough shirking you two. Get back to work.”

Quinn tapped the pottle from his pipe on the cart wheel and hoisted himself up onto the seat. “Keep building that road, boys,” he said as he set off to complete his delivery, “and good luck with the good, honest fighting. But how do you feel about dishonest fighting?”

Kelly got to his feet and stretched his lanky legs, raising his right leg to the side to unstick his scrotum from his groin, and he and McCann resumed their digging and smashing. At the end of the day, Kelly’s hands were blistered and his face was burnt, as the pork pie hat of his uniform gave it scant protection from the sun. Back in the barracks in Ōtāhuhu, Kelly was mulling over what Quinn had said about the invasion. “What do you think he meant by dishonest fighting?” he asked McCann.

“I don’t know,” was the reply. “Let the governors and the generals worry about the politics. We’re just soldiers taking orders and doing our jobs.”

Kelly sat on his cot and, bending down awkwardly with his aching back, he liberated his feet malodorously from his boots.

“Well, that takes me back,” McCann remarked. “Back to the pig shite in the sty.”

Kelly drew a knife from his kit and, ignoring McCann’s nostalgia for the croft, he concentrated on sharpening the pencil he still carried from his time as a clerk. He put the pencil to the paper he also carried and wrote a letter.

*My dearest Annie*

*I hope this letter finds you well. I find myself transported to a strange country at the end of the world, a country of untamed beauty, a land with green hills, as in Ireland, but with tall trees and thick bush, full of birds calling out day and night. In the night sky the stars are all wrong, upside down, as if the sky itself has lost its way. I am grieved at the vast distance between us now and I wonder if I have made a mistake in coming here but I shall make the best I can of it. It is a troubled country but I think it has great prospects for the future, once the fighting has ended. I still hope to send for you if I can make a life for myself here, hopefully as a farmer, with a military land grant after my time as a soldier. Just think of it. We could live on our own land with no landlord demanding rent. That's what I dream of, but if it doesn't work out I can still return home to you. I miss you so.*

*All my love,*
*Finbar*

He folded the sheet of paper into an envelope and wrote a letter also for McCann, who, like many of the foot soldiers, could neither read nor write.

Annie Gallagher rose before dawn and lit a candle. She did her morning ablutions with the porcelain basin and pitcher of water at the washstand as quickly as she could in the chill air of her bedroom in the basement. She dabbed her armpits with vinegar and dressed herself also in haste, tied on her apron, and went from room to room, drawing the curtains open. When she'd let in the light of the new day, she went about getting a fire going in the fireplaces. Young Brian brought the coal in and Annie banked up the fires to where she could safely leave them for breakfast of porridge and milk, with the other staff. She'd started as a scullery maid, scrubbing pots in the kitchen, in 'the grand house', on the Richardson estate and then moved up to housemaid.

Mrs Percival, the Protestant English housekeeper, made sure Annie was occupied with other duties about the house as well until it was time to draw the curtains closed for the night. Mrs Percival kept a close eye on all the staff beneath her and any whose work did not meet her standards would get a harsh rebuke from her sharp Cockney tongue. She took Annie to task early on when she'd let the fire go out in the drawing room. It was no use protesting that the room was not in use on the day or that she thought it was the responsibility of Moragh, the parlour maid. Mrs Percival enumerated Annie's duties for her, since she had been so negligent, and added to her tasks by having her relieve Miss Bridged of her chamber pot duties for the week.

There was just one other English woman on the staff and that was Mrs Theobold, the governess. Mrs Theobold took a liking to Annie as much as Mrs Percival took a dislike to the young housemaid and the other Irish servants. Mrs Theobold was more kindly disposed and was good enough to help Annie with reading the few letters she received, with writing replies, and even helped her with learning to read and write. Annie admired the matronly governess with her education and her refined English speech, and her position as the private tutor for Lord Richardson's grandchildren.

Annie was tending to the fire in the drawing room when Lord Richardson's son Robert entered the room. Annie knew not to speak to Mister Robert unless he spoke to her. She'd cleared the ash from the grate and got the fire started with the kindling. She was building up the fire with bigger bits of split wood while Robert walked about the room. He came and stood by the fire.

"Just checking the arrangements for this evening. As you know we're having guests for dinner today and we'll be withdrawing in here afterward."

"Yes Sir." Annie looked up briefly from the fire. She was still kneeling at the hearth and her eye level was no higher than Mr Robert's waist and he was standing uncomfortably close.

He held his hands to the fire and Annie stood aside from it. "It's a cold winter's day all right," he said. "But you'll have the room cosy and warm by dinner time."

"Yes, Sir."

"And I'm thinking there's a bit of warmth to be had here." He put his arm around Annie and drew her close.

"Please don't be so familiar, Sir." She pulled away from his embrace. "I'm engaged to be married."

"Is that so? And where is your betrothed?"

"He's in New Zealand, serving in the army."

"New Zealand! My goodness! Away at the ends of the Earth. It must be lonely for you here."

"My family live not so far from here."

"I hear our army is having a tough time of it fighting the Māori." Mr Robert chuckled as he left the room. "Let's hope he doesn't get eaten, eh."

At staff briefing a few days later Mrs Percival informed Annie that she would be responsible for an additional room, as per the master's instructions. "You'll do the curtains and the fire in Mr Robert's room."

At the end of the meeting, Annie asked if Brian could tend to Mr Robert's room as he brought the coal up anyway. "And I don't think it's proper for a young lady to go into a gentleman's bedroom," she added.

"A young lady, indeed," Mrs Percival scoffed. "Carry out your duties as instructed."

Annie found Brian in the coal cellar and asked him if he wouldn't mind taking charge of Master Robert's room.

"And what will you do for me?" he said slyly.

"I'll tell your Ma what a good boy you are," she said, just as slyly.

So Annie didn't come to warm Mr Robert's room or warm his bed, as he'd hoped, and she carried on with her usual duties. She avoided him as much as possible and never had much contact with the Lord's family anyway. But Mr Robert found her in the grounds one day and asked her if she knew Miss Enid would soon be leaving.

"Yes, Sir. We all know she's getting married."

"Perhaps you'd like to replace her as the nanny for my children."

"I'm happy with being a housemaid."

"Perhaps you'd be just as happy as a scullery maid again."

Annie ignored his veiled threat and carried on with her duties without any change. She had a trusted friend in Molly, the laundry maid, and she confided in her when they attended Mass together on Sunday. "Mr Robert suggested I could be a nanny for his children, when Enid leaves, and sure I would like to, but I don't want to be beholden to him, not after what she's told me about him, so I said I would just continue as the housemaid."

"I think you're right to be wary of him," Molly said. "Mister Robert does have a reputation. They say he takes after his father."

When Enid left there were some staff changes and Annie was reassigned to scullery maid duties.

Mrs Theobold commiserated with Annie about her demotion. "There must be some mistake. I'll have a word to His Lordship about it."

"It'll be Mr Robert's doing." Annie told the governess about what had led up to it. "It might do more harm than good to take it up with his father."

Annie usually met with Mrs Theobold in the governess' room on Sunday afternoons, both still wearing their church-going Sunday best. Annie's dress, which she had sewn herself before leaving home, was tailored to fit snugly over her modest bosom and narrow waist. Mrs Theobold's dress was made of a good deal more material to cover her greater girth and extra gathered in flounces at the back. The two ladies would chat about this and that and Annie would get a reading and writing lesson, with children's books and her catechism.

"I do appreciate you taking the time to help me with reading and writing." Annie said.

"I enjoy the time I get to spend with you, Annie dear, and you're certainly quicker on the uptake than those children I'm teaching. And my goodness, I get to read your letters from your beau in New Zealand. There's only so much you can read about the colonies in the newspapers." Mrs Theobold handed back the letter Annie had entrusted her with. "And such a romantic story. What an adventure it would be to start a new life in New Zealand!"

She poured them both a cup of tea and asked Annie, "And where did you meet this Finbar Kelly?"

"Well, we first met at school."

"Ah, childhood sweethearts."

"No, not really. I didn't even like him much when we were at school. My parents couldn't afford to keep me and my brother and sister at school so I didn't stay long. It was a mixed school and my parents also thought it was too anti-Catholic and pro-British. Even so, my brother stayed on till he turned twelve. My da didn't think it was important for a girl to have an academic education and I could just as well learn needlework and weaving at home."

Mrs Theobold fingered the string of pearls that hung around her neck, below her double chin, as she listened to Annie's story. "So did you just stay at home?"

"For a time I did, and I helped my ma with all the chores. But then I got a factory job working the looms, ten hours a day at the linen mill and it was there I met Finbar again. He was working in the office. He'd stayed on at school and got a job as an accounts clerk. He took a great deal of notice of me and I thought him quite handsome then. We saw each other every day, until the mill closed down. He was kind and friendly and we went out walking together. We fell in love and after a time he asked me to marry him."

"And you said yes."

"Yes, I said I would, but it didn't feel like a proper engagement. My parents said why was I running around after an unemployed Protestant boy when I could have my pick of any of the good Catholic boys with good jobs. In fact they had chosen one for me but I was only interested in Finbar.

"You say he was unemployed?"

"We were both unemployed when the mill closed down."

"And what about Finbar's parents?

"They didn't approve either."

"It's so ridiculous. You're both Christian, for goodness sake. It's not as though you were wanting to marry a heathen."

"So I stayed at home for a time, until I came to work here and I was one less mouth to feed at home. Finbar wanted me to go with him to Belfast."

"To elope with him?

"Yes, but I couldn't do that. I couldn't run away from my family. Finbar said we should just run further away."

"To New Zealand."

"Finbar was so fed up with our families refusing to accept us getting married and fed up with being out of work—"

"—that he joined the army." Mrs Theobold had a habit of finishing Annie's sentences.

"—and went to New Zealand." Annie continued. "He said he would send for me when the time was right. He made me promise I would join him... if he survived, and he got a piece of land of his own that we could farm. So I'll stick it out here for now and hope that things work out for us in New Zealand."

"You'll not have to worry about Mr Robert again, for a while at least. He's soon to leave for Italy and won't return until the spring."

"Will he be taking the children?"

"Oh no, the children would just be an encumbrance. They'll be left in the care of their nanny, their grandmother and me, just as they are now. He hasn't shown much interest in his children since his wife died and now he cavorts about like a bachelor." Mrs Theobold shut her eyes and sighed. "His poor wife died of the small pox, you know, but no one speaks of it."

The months passed and the road from Auckland grew longer, pushing on and on toward the Waikato River. The Great South Road, now also known as the Road to the Devil's Nest. Kelly and McCann marched side by side in a file of hundreds, along the hot, dusty road, bearing knapsacks, haversacks, muskets and water bottles slung from their shoulders and jostling off their right hips. The army camped at Drury, then finally at Pōkeno, where they built the Queen's Redoubt close to the Mangātawhiri River and the Waikato River into which it flowed. Alongside the road a telegraphic line was strung from Auckland to Pōkeno.

Then the days grew colder and an ominous war machine rolled along the road: legions of soldiers, horses, heavy artillery, supplies to the burgeoning chaos of the military headquarters at Pōkeno. Even boats were conveyed overland to the Mangātawhiri River. The Mangatāwhiri was the great demarcation between Auckland province and the Waikato. All natives who had not sworn an oath of allegiance to the Queen and surrendered their arms had been forced by decree out and beyond this Rubicon. Kelly had seen groups of Māori leaving their ancestral homes, trudging miserably southward along the road. Some remained unseen to ambush the supply line from the forested margins of the road. Troops and settlers looted and destroyed abandoned Māori property.

The officers and men of the 18th Royal Irish Regiment had landed in Auckland aboard the Elizabeth Ann Bright and marched from Ōtāhuhu to Pōkeno. Kelly and McCann welcomed their countrymen to the camp and shared a sly rum with a few of the new arrivals and went about getting what news they brought from home. The poor tenant farmers in the counties were still doing it hard with ever smaller plots of land. The landlords had been dividing up small holdings since the famine, as a way of collecting more rent. Families were increasing but the land was not. However, things were looking more hopeful of late with the Fenians demanding political reforms and a fairer distribution of land.

More rum appeared mysteriously in the camp with inevitably ensuing drunkenness and ill-discipline. An officer of the 18th confronted an obviously intoxicated foot soldier who responded rather foolishly by confronting the officer back and punching him in the face. The unfortunate reprobate was court-martialled and singled out for exemplary punishment. He was stripped to the waist in a chilly July breeze and lashed to a wooden frame in a position that afforded his fellow soldiers a good view, while a leather scourge flayed the skin from his back in bloody stripes.

And still more troops arrived at the camp. "I've never seen such a massive army in one place," Kelly said.

"Or such massive piles of shite," McCann added, leaning on his shovel. "I think I preferred working on the road to digging feckin latrines."

"Would you look at all the men coming in," Kelly continued. There can't be this many Māoris in all the Waikato. More of us here than anywhere else in the world. I wonder if there are any troops left in England to protect the mother country."

"Well, we're here to protect the colony from invasion."

"But why would the Māoris attack Auckland? If it's true what Quinn said, they'd lose all their business. They'd be cutting their own throats. It doesn't make sense."

"No it doesn't," McCann agreed. "Ours not to wonder why."

There could be no doubt that an invasion was imminent and indeed the soldiers did not long have to endure the boredom or the mud and squalor of the Queen's Redoubt camp before the army advanced into the Waikato. General Cameron marched 550 eager men of the 65th regiment across the Mangatāwhiri River to attack the first line of Māori defence at Koheroa.

A band of musket-wielding warriors emerged from the bush and fired off a volley of lead shot. A ball whizzed past Kelly's head, followed by bits of shattered skull and splattered brain of the soldier in front. The primitive savages could handle a musket all right. Kelly returned fire and felled one of the warriors who stood their ground in a wedge formation. He began reloading frantically while he remained exposed. Powder down the muzzle. Powder in the pan. Cartridge of ball and wadding down the muzzle and rammed home. Ram rod replaced. With trembling hands, he was losing the race to reload to the warrior at the apex of the wedge and he could not have covered the ground with his bayonet in time. His bowels were suggesting that he could run faster if he lightened his load. The warrior shouldered his weapon and took aim at Kelly. Kelly prayed for a miss or a misfire from the deadly but unreliable smooth-bore Enfield musket. The shot came not from the enemy in front but from McCann at his side and the warrior was blown off his feet by a lead ball smashed into his chest. The British attackers were joined by the 2nd Battalion 14th and the Māori fled the overwhelming force across the Maramarua River, leaving several dead on open ground. British soldiers also lay dead on the battle field but General Cameron declared it a gallant and decisive victory to start the Waikato campaign.

Meanwhile the supply line was harassed and attacked from out of the bush fringes of the Great South Road and Cameron would not advance till sufficient reinforcements arrived to secure the road and build more redoubts. The troops advanced no further than Bluff Stockade still to the north of the Waikato River and they were stalled in the mire again for another three months.

The Kingites had constructed a heavily fortified pā upriver at Meremere and in the spring Cameron was preparing an assault overland and by river. The colonial steamer Avon, freshly armoured in iron plating, had been slugging its way up the river and was joined by the naval steamer HMS Pioneer, wielding two large gun turrets. Grey and Cameron were taking control of the waterway with a small flotilla of gunboats. They shelled the pā from the river and brought cannon ashore to fire on the fortifications. Kelly and McCann joined a combined force with the Royal Irish regiment and landed upriver of the pā to attack the fortification from the rear. They advanced warily past the rifle pits up to the stockades only to find the pā deserted. The enemy had fled.

Again a great victory, according to Cameron, but not the decisive blow they'd been hoping for. The troops erected tents on the site and raised the Union Jack, but with a mood of sour disappointment. Was this the Kingite strategy? They had succeeded in delaying the army for three and a half months. How long would this war drag on? Where would they make a stand?

Reconnaissance further upriver revealed another fortification of earthworks, trenches and parapets running eastward from the river at Rangiriri. It was seen to be vulnerable to enfilade from the river and Cameron expected Rangiriri to fall as Meremere had, opening the way to the King's capital at Ngāruawāhia.

The steamers proved too cumbersome to attack from the river and the Avon ran aground and blocked the Pioneer from firing on the garrison. But the steamers did manage to land 300 troops to the south of the pā. They were joined by a force of 900 attacking overland from the north, including a militia corps, recruited from Auckland. The 65$^{th}$ attacked the central fortification and came under heavy fire. Kelly and McCann took cover amongst a stand of mānuka to reload, as did many of their fellow soldiers.

"Look at this," Kelly said, clutching a branch of mānuka. "The seed capsules. Five-pointed stars. I'd never noticed it before."

McCann glanced at the capsules and glared at Kelly, "This isn't a feckin picnic, man. Keep your eyes on the fight." He raised a hand to give him a slap.

There was a sudden barrage of fire to their right as several of their countrymen of the 14th went down. Urged on by their enraged commander, Lieutenant Hill, they advanced again toward the fortification. The Imperial troops retreated, regrouped, attacked again and were repulsed again. Kelly and McCann stayed close together and alternated their firing and reloading. The barrels of their muskets grew hotter and hotter. Many of the Māori warriors were quickly swapping muskets with women reloading them in the trenches. Kelly had struck the targets accurately enough in the drills, but these were not painted boards. They were human beings, like himself, and they were trying to kill him, to defend themselves. They were elusive targets within their defences. Still, a few of his shots found their mark.

General Cameron had the battle he wanted but it wasn't going his way. He was furiously determined to take the pā despite the heavy losses suffered in the attempts. At Cameron's command, Captain Mercer led an assault of the Royal Artillery and he and his men were all killed or wounded as they made their way through a narrow opening in the earthworks. The Royal Navy fared no better when Cameron drove ninety sailors over a front rampart into a trench late in the day. Those that survived the gunfire cowered in the trench all night. The rest of the troops also spent a miserable night, sleeping on the cold, damp ground.

"What was going on with you back there?" McCann asked Kelly. "Were you trying to block out the battle?"

"I just got distracted."

"Are you going to be all right? We need to depend on each other to get through these battles."

"Don't worry about me. I'll be all right, and I'll have your back," Kelly assured McCann.

At first light in the morning, they were again in a labour force digging a sap to break through the defences of the pā, but everything halted just after dawn when the defenders hoisted a white flag. The diggers climbed out of the sap and followed the group of soldiers who entered the pā, also carrying a white flag, ahead of General Cameron and an interpreter. As they mingled and shook hands with the defenders, Cameron commended the natives for their bravery, accepted their surrender and ordered them to give up their arms. Their chief protested that their flag signalled a truce to talk terms for peace, as they had done at Taranaki, and not to surrender. In the event the defenders remaining in the pā were taken prisoner.

"Is this a misunderstanding," Kelly wondered aloud, "or British treachery?"

"I think the latter," McCann muttered.

General Cameron claimed the Māoris had surrendered unconditionally because the pā was completely surrounded, but there were no wounded among the prisoners, no King Tāwhiao, no Tāmihana, nor other high ranking chiefs. They had evacuated the pā during the night and left a rear guard.

One of the chiefs of the rear guard claimed he had seen a white flag first on one of the British boats on the river.

Kelly and McCann found themselves again with shovels in hand, this time burying the dead, roughly equal numbers of dead on both sides, from their reckoning. A grave for each of the soldiers and a mass burial pit for the Māori dead. The glazed eyes of warriors glared accusingly at Kelly as he dragged their bloodied bodies to the pit and threw them on the heap of lifeless flesh. The pile of bodies grew till it looked like they were in the pit of Hades. Kelly was relieved but still nauseous when the garish sight was finally covered over. He tried to rid the image from his mind by turning his thoughts to home, to the village, to the girl he'd left behind. That evening he wrote a letter to Annie, which he hoped he'd be able to post. He wrote with some difficulty at first, as his hand was unsteady on the paper. He began with the usual endearments and told of yesterday's battle.

> *. . . This day I surely earned my meagre pay in the Queen's service. We were in a fierce battle and I owe my life to my good friend Michael McCann, who shot a warrior who was about to shoot me. I think your prayers for my safety are working and the Good Lord is looking out for me.*
>
> *I must confess, the more this war goes on, the more respect I have for the enemy and the less for the British Army. The Māoris are an intelligent and fearsome race, not the primitive savages we were told to expect. Some of our own officers have sorely underestimated our enemy. Some are just toffs who bought their commissions and some are old soldiers who should have retired years ago. The Governor and the General are saying they've 'broken the back of this unhappy rebellion'. Their*

*words, not mine. Rebellion or not, I hope this ghastly war soon comes to an end ...*

The troops occupied a deserted Ngāruawāhia and removed the King's flag from the flagstaff and hoisted the Queen's flag in its place. The most substantial building in the pā was King Tāwhiao's residence, measuring twenty by ten yards. This was taken over by the officers. The other whare served as temporary barracks for the troops.

"So this is how the Māoris live," McCann remarked. "It's not so bad. It's warm and dry."

The raupō whare, with its packed earth floor, apparently compared not unfavourably with his dwelling in the croft. "How's your bed?" Kelly asked McCann, as they settled into their home for the night.

"Comfortable enough with all the ferns and the mat, but I don't care for the wooden headrest."

"Me neither. I've rolled up my jacket for a pillow." They lay awake and discussed the state of the war and the way ahead.

"Looks like the Waikatos and Maniapotos are on the run," McCann said.

"They say they're asking for peace and waiting for the Governor's terms."

"Grey's terms will be unconditional surrender."

"Aye and all the Māoris will have to sign an oath of allegiance."

"And give up their land to the Crown."

"All of it?"

"Some will be set aside for them to live on. It's what the colonists in Auckland have been demanding."

"The Māoris will never agree to that. The fighting will go on."

"If they do agree they won't be taken prisoners... except any who committed murder."

"But is it murder when you kill in warfare?" Kelly said. "And are we not also murderers then? And are we not more culpable as invaders than those who are defending their homes? Are they not fighting in self-defence?"

"We're soldiers, Finbar," said McCann. "That's our lot. It's kill or be killed. That's the way it is here. Don't be wringing your hands about it. Just thank God you're still alive."

"What of the families killed in their own homes? Women and children hacked to death."

They'd all heard the reports of Māori attacking farmers in their homes. Settlers on disputed land. Casualties of war. But killing women and children, killing innocent non-combatants in their own homes? "Yes, that was murder."

"You know the Māoris attack the farms to draw troops away to try to protect the settlers. Military tactics," McCann explained. "There's always civilian casualties in war. And what of the nine soldiers killed at Ōākura? It was an ambush. It wasn't a proper fight. It wasn't self-defence."

"True. But we're still at war in the Taranaki. There's no peace declared. It's still soldier against warrior in a war zone. And yet Grey is calling it murder. It's just another pretext for the invasion."

"Anyways, no point in getting all philosophical about it." McCann yawned and farted and pulled his mat snug around his body. "It's the natural order of things: struggle and conquest and survival of the strongest. A superior race conquering one less civilised."

"So, might is right? And what of the Treaty? Might it not be more honourable to just declare a war of conquest, as you say, rather than make a treaty and break it?"

"The Treaty means nothing," McCann said dismissively.

"Apparently so," Kelly agreed. "Enough said. Let's get some sleep."

# 4

The sun rose on a fine December summer's day and shimmered on the river at the doorstep of the whare. At morning assembly, General Cameron delivered a state of the campaign briefing to the troops.

"It seems we've put the enemy to flight after the battle at Rangiriri. Here we are at the Māori King's fortress, deserted. The Waikato Chief Wiremu Tāmihana is calling for peace. He called for Governor Grey and his ministers to meet here at Ngāruawāhia to negotiate a peaceful settlement. But it seems the Governor has decided not to come to the party."

"The General and the Governor look to be disagreeing with each other," McCann whispered. "What do you think Grey's up to?"

"The cunning old bugger doesn't want to make peace," Kelly whispered back. "He wants to destroy the Kīngitanga completely."

"This will be our headquarters for the time being," the General continued. "Starting today we shall convert this pā into a proper military encampment and construct a redoubt. The Pioneer will be bringing us another 500 troops of the Fortieth Regiment."

After breakfast, Kelly and McCann were again drafted into a shovel-wielding work party digging trenches and fortifications. In surveying the site, a commander of the militia broke into the tomb of the first Māori King Te Wherowhero, searching for greenstone treasures reputed to be buried within. But he came away with nothing; in fact, less than he'd entered with, as he came away cursing the loss of his sheath knife.

No peaceful settlement having been reached, at the end of the year the troops were ordered to push deeper into the Waikato and Maniapoto and establish a frontier line from Raglan on the west coast to Tauranga on the east coast, dipping south in the interior into the economic heartland of Kīngitanga territory. The troops now included many kūpapa, so-called loyalist Māori, fighting on the side of the British. The kūpapa had more disdain for the British officers, than respect, as far as Kelly could see. It was for opportunities to settle scores with tribal enemies, rather than loyalty to the Crown, that they had joined forces with the British Imperial Army. The government was also offering land grants as rewards to 'loyal' Māori.

Ngāruawāhia was a strategic location at the confluence of the Waikato River and the Waipā River, which was the route into the richly cultivated, thriving settlements of Rangiaowhia and Te Awamutu. However, the army's advance was blocked at Pāterangi by the most formidable fortifications they had ever encountered.

"Would you look at that," said McCann, gazing into the distance, "There's at least four pās and palisades as far as the eye can see."

"And swampland on either side," Kelly added. "What are we supposed to do with that?"

General Cameron concluded that he could not storm the pā, much to the relief of all the troops. The advancing army came to a halt and set up camp at Te Rore, which was as far as steamers could go up the Waipā River. Here the troops enjoyed a month's respite and recreation. Field rations continued to arrive on the steamers Pioneer and Avon, courtesy of the British Treasury and the troops queued for their rations.

"What have you got?" McCann asked Kelly.

"Same as you: a pound of bread and a pound of pork." Kelly screwed up his nose. "The bread smells of vinegar and the pork smells of fish."

"Ugh. Pigs fed on fish, I suppose."

"I got an extra four ounces of rice for twopence."

"I got a pound of potatoes and half an onion for mine."

They queued again for their daily ration of beverages: a sixteenth of an ounce of tea, a third of an ounce of coffee, as well as sugar, salt and pepper, and a gill of rum.

The troops were flush with soldiers' pay but had little to spend it on and some passed the time gambling at card games.

"Not for me," Kelly said. "I'll not be throwing my money away."

He and McCann, instead, joined some of their cohort in a cricket match against the blue-jacketed sailors. It was an improvised game with a roughly hewn bat and a ball of tightly wound leather strapping. Kelly, in the field, chased after a well-struck boundary that landed in the river. He stripped off to retrieve it, threw it back to the pitch, and dived back into the river. It was late January, the height of summer, and all the players abandoned the match and joined Kelly to cool off in the river. Kelly luxuriated in the cool water and rubbed his body vigorously with kumārahou, as the Māori soldiers did, to rid his skin of the lice that had been plaguing him. He felt almost carefree briefly, until the pale bodies of the bathers were fired upon by Waikato snipers; after which any excursions into the river were undertaken more cautiously with scouts and armed guards.

Governor Grey arrived by steamer at Te Rore and angrily ordered General Cameron to attack Pāterangi immediately, which the General refused to do. Here were two titans of political and military might facing off against each other, two men of a similar age and similarly lofty bearing, though the General had the greater physical stature. After a brief standoff, Cameron went to his tent, followed by Grey. Grey continued, in rising volume and pitch, to insist on the attack. Kelly and McCann and many others were close enough to the tent to hear Cameron tell the Governor to "Go to hell!"

Cameron decided instead to outflank Pāterangi. With the aid of two half-Māori kūpapa, who knew the terrain, the army marched by night quietly past the fortifications, skirting the swamp, into the deserted settlement of Te Awamutu and on to the nearly deserted Rangiaowhia. Grey had been very critical of Māori bringing women and children into defensive pā to become victims of warfare and both sides had agreed that non-combatants should go to places of refuge for their own safety. Pāterangi was a fighting pā manned by warriors and Rangiaowhia was a virtually undefended refuge for women, children and the elderly. Under Cameron's command, the 65$^{th}$ attacked the soft target of Rangiaowhia to draw the warriors out of the impregnable fortress of Pāterangi to defend the settlement. The attack began early on a Sunday morning with a cavalry charge led by Colonel Nixon. The terrified villagers scattered and fled for cover and fired on their attackers. The troops rounded up prisoners and pursued others who had fled into the two churches and thatched raupō whare. Six men and a boy were seen running into one of the whare, where they lay on the sunken floor below the bullets fired through the thin cladding of the walls.

McCann was at the front of a phalanx of soldiers firing at the whare and Colonel Nixon ordered him to get the fugitives out and take them prisoner.

*I'm glad he didn't order me to get them out,* Kelly thought. *Well, I wish he hadn't ordered McCann to go either. I don't like the look of this. There it is. A muzzle out the window.* Kelly shouldered his musket to fire into the window. *But oh God! Too late. The flash. The crack.* McCann went down.

Kelly had no appetite for attacking a peaceful village and had, up until this point, not fired a shot. However, with the shock and grief at McCann's death, he found it easier to kill and he joined the other soldiers firing more volleys, reloading and firing, like an automaton, into the whare.

More troops arrived on the scene, including General Cameron, whereupon Nixon joined in the attack and was also shot from the doorway of the whare. Finally the whare was set alight and one elderly Māori walked out with his hands raised. Some of the officers shouted to spare him but this did not prevent some of the men from shooting him. Naturally, the remaining occupants of the whare were not then inclined to surrender and perished in the flames. The air was full of smoke and noise: musket fire, women wailing and children screaming, and the smell of burning thatch and burning flesh.

Other whare were also on fire and villagers were fleeing, some into the Catholic church and some into the Anglican church, from where they fired at pursuing soldiers through the windows. But the thin wooden cladding of the churches gave no more protection from the musket balls than the thatched walls of the whare and those that survived the attacks on the churches fled into the nearby swamp or escaped on horseback.

Kelly knelt by the lifeless body of his mate and uttered a prayer—words he'd recalled from his grandfather's funeral—*into your hands Lord, we commit his spirit.*

Regimental stretcher bearers arrived, but an officer ordered, "Leave him, for now. Tend to the wounded." It was Captain Inman of the 18th Royal Irish. To Kelly he said, "It's all right, son. We'll give him a proper burial at the Anglican church there," pointing with his chin. "Get back to your regiment."

Kelly trudged off through the carnage, past another burnt out whare. Something in the smouldering ruins caught his attention. He bent down and picked up the charred remains of a portrait of Queen Victoria with Prince Albert and their children. *And what is this on the reverse side? A message of thanks to the two chiefs who had sent a gift of bags of flour from their own mill at Rangiaowhia to the royal family.*

The Imperial troops withdrew from Rangiaowhia to Te Awamutu and the following day marched with reinforcements on Hairini, where Maniapoto and the defenders of Pāterangi took up position on an old pā site on a ridge to block the way back to Rangiaowhia. General Cameron had succeeded in drawing his enemy out of their fortification and finally had the advantage of fighting on open ground. His army broke through the Hairini defences with the aid of Armstrong guns and cavalry charges and on again to Rangiaowhia and back to Kihikihi to plunder the farmland, which had been the food supply of 'the rebels'. From across the Pūniu River, the Kingites watched the troops fell their flagstaff and burn their treasured Ngāti Maniapoto meeting house.

The troops marched back to their base camp at Te Awamutu with all the food they could carry for a grand feast. Kelly had his fill of potatoes, kūmara, pumpkin, chicken and pork. At first it satisfied, then it began to cloy and finally he went outside and vomited.

*Aye, I'm sick, all right. I'm sick of this war. I'm disgusted with the army. Disgusted with myself. I've had enough. If I had ten pounds I'd buy my discharge. How about you, McCann? Too late now, mate. I was too late. I'm sorry. So much for the grand adventure.*

Nor was Kelly alone with such sentiments. Some of the regiment were happy to go on killing more 'savages' but many others were grumbling and disillusioned. The whole sorry war must surely soon come to an end. The screams of women and children in Rangiaowhia still rang in Kelly's ears and in the fading light of dusk, he gazed at the dark clouds glowering on the horizon over the smouldering ruins of the village.

*So the mighty British army wiped out a virtually defenceless village and smashed through the Māori making a stand to defend their home turf. Why Hairini? Why that place? Why that name? Hairini, so named as the Māori translation of Ireland. Ireland, which has suffered centuries of conquests and confiscations by British forces. And how like the Irish are the Māori, in their villages, with their crops, their potatoes, their fish, their few farm animals, and their children.*

# 5

General Cameron left for the redoubt at Pukerimu, leaving Brigadier General Carey, of the $18^{th}$ Royal Irish Regiment, in command to secure the area around the army's base at Te Awamutu and reconnoitre the surrounding area. It was a misty autumn morning when the bushy-bearded Carey addressed the assembled troops.

"More Māoris are moving into our area from other parts of the North Island to support Maniapoto and the Kīngitanga. So we can expect to come under attack."

*Other tribes probably fearing they'll be invaded next,* Kelly thought.

"Reconnaissance shows combined Māori forces constructing a pā only three miles from Kihikihi, at Ōrākau. It is a hastily constructed fortification and not a strong defensive position. Our scouts report it is quite exposed, lacks a water supply and lacks the usual escape route for retreat. We shall seize the opportunity to attack the unfinished garrison without delay." Carey raised a clenched fist. "We should be assured of an easy victory."

*He probably wants to attack the pā before Cameron returns.*

General Carey divided his force of 1,100 troops to completely surround the pā in readiness for the attack. He kept the cavalry in reserve. The pā was not as weak as it first appeared and the initial assaults were easily repulsed. Kelly was ordered to the front of the third assault and he advanced without any regard for cover. A shot from a rifle pit struck him on the upper arm. It tore into the flesh and fractured the bone. The pain of the wound surged through his body and his legs became unsteady. He did not regret being sidelined with the wounded, but continued to observe the progress of the attack, or rather the lack of progress.

General Carey ordered a change of tactics to siege warfare, artillery fire and sapping. The siege began to bite after a couple of days as the defenders were running out of food, water and ammunition. They had begun firing bullets of carved peach stones and plugs of branches. On the third day the British commanders called on the Māoris to surrender, but the response from within the pā was that they would continue to fight forever. "E hoa, ka whawhai tonu mātou. Āke! Āke! Āke!" Even the request to send the women and children out of the pā, so that they at least might be spared, was defied. A woman's voice shouted, "Ki te mate ngā tāne, me mate ano ngā wāhine me ngā tamariki. (If the men die, the women and children will die with them.)

*Poor beggars. They don't want to be taken prisoner to Auckland like the defenders of Rangiriri. Or more likely they fear a worse fate if they surrender, like the victims of Rangiaowhia.*

In the late afternoon the defenders emerged from the pā in one group, with Rewi Maniapoto and women and children in the centre, and advanced calmly toward the cordon of dumbfounded British troops. There were fewer defenders of the pā than they had supposed, and certainly fewer men, as many of the women had put on the clothing of men who had been killed.

The troops recovered from the shock of the sudden appearance of the enemy as they dashed toward the Pūniu River. Soldiers gave chase and fired at the fugitives from behind and on either side to prevent their escape. Many of the men, women and children were shot and some fell to the swords of the pursuing cavalry. Some of the pursuing soldiers were killed by rear-guard defenders and by the crossfire of their own flank attacks. One of the warriors held off pursuing soldiers for a time by kneeling and taking aim with his rifle but he never fired a shot, as he had run out of ammunition.

One zealous foot soldier ran about bayoneting the wounded men and women as they lay on the ground until Captain Mair caught up with him. "We spare the wounded women."

The soldier protested, "If they survive they'll breed sons to continue to fight."

Mair said no more but struck the man and knocked him to the ground.

A few Forest Rangers protected most of the women from the slaughter, but one lay dead on the ground clutching a Bible to her breast. Thirty-three prisoners were taken, nearly all of them wounded. None of them was Rewi Maniapoto.

Captain Inman had left the Officers' Mess in the redoubt and was walking past the huts where the enlisted men were sitting outside eating their dinner. He stopped in front of Kelly, who was sitting on his own on a log, with his arm in a sling, eating his boiled beef, with his good arm, off the tin plate on his lap.

"You, Private. "What is your name."

"Private Kelly, Sir."

"No need to get up or salute, Private Kelly. Carry on with your dinner." Captain Inman crouched down by Kelly. "I see you took a bullet to the arm."

"Yes, Sir."

"And the Surgeon has taken care of it?"

"Yes, Sir. He removed the bullet and dressed the wound."

"Good. You'll be evacuated back to Camp at Ōtāhuhu, to the infirmary."

"Yes Sir." Kelly took another spoonful of beef.

"Sorry about your mate getting killed back there at Rangiaowhia. What was his name?'

"Private Michael McCann, Sir. May I ask Sir, has the Kīngitanga been defeated now? Has Maniapoto surrendered? Have we taken the Waikato?"

"Maniapoto and all the Kingites have retreated down south of the Pūniu River. No surrender yet. As for the Waikato…" Captain Inman broke off here and said, "Can you read Private Kelly?"

"Yes, Sir."

"Well then you can read about what's happening now for yourself. You finish your dinner and I'll fetch you a copy of The Daily Southern Cross. I've finished with it."

"Thank you Sir."

The Captain returned from the redoubt with the paper and left it with Kelly.

According to the correspondent, Charles Williamson, the 'obstinate rebel' and the remnants of the Kīngitanga retreated south of the Pūniu River, just as the Captain had said. Emissaries had reported to Grey that Rewi Maniapoto and all the Kīngitanga were anxious to make peace, but they would not surrender their arms lest they all be taken prisoner and lose their liberty forever.

*So Governor Grey has still not succeeded in destroying the movement. Still unsatisfied.*

The Pūniu River has become the new Rubicon and General Cameron will not prosecute the war beyond it.

*The morale of the troops is so low it's unlikely that they'd respond to such a call in any case. Let Grey and the government ministers argue over the extent of the land to be confiscated from the 'rebels'. It looks like they want all of the Waikato as far as the Pūniu River, and more.*

According to Williamson, the ministers are keen to expand the area of confiscation beyond Waikato and Taranaki.

Conflict erupted to the east at Tauranga, where General Cameron landed a garrison of troops on the Te Papa Peninsula, which was occupied by the Church Missionary Society. Kelly read the account of the Battle of Pukehinahina, also reported as the battle of Gate Pā, in *The Southern Cross* and *The New Zealand Herald*.

'Tauranga Māori, the Ngāi Te Rangi, led by Chief Rāwiri Puhirake, had built a pā less than three miles from the British garrison and goaded the British troops into a battle, even offering to build a road to the pā for the convenience of the troops. General Cameron responded by landing 1,700 troops mostly from the Waikato and seventeen cannon at the port. The heavy artillery included an enormous Armstrong gun that fired 110-pound shells. The big guns fired over the pā initially as the gunners took their range from the flagpole, which the defenders had moved some distance beyond the pā.'

*How can the British Army have learnt so little from their experiences of Māori garrison warfare? It's all so familiar and predictable.*

'The British troops attacked the pā at dawn with an unprecedented bombardment of heavy artillery, each of the big guns firing off a hundred rounds. At four o'clock in the afternoon, Colonel Greer was satisfied that they had blown the pā to the devil and sent in a storming party. The advancing soldiers met with only light fire, as expected, and easily made their way into the main part of the pā.

'All of the above ground defences were blasted away, but most of the 230 Māori within the pā had survived the bombardment by sheltering in deep underground bunkers and emerged through tunnels into concealed rifle pits to fire on the British troops at close quarters with muskets and shotguns. Some of the soldiers were killed with blows of tomahawks and mere, flat clubs with honed edges, like tomahawks. One had the top of his skull removed like a boiled egg, when the mere sliced into it and prised off the dome.'

*The poor blighters would have rushed into a maze of trenches like sheep into an abattoir. They would have had their skulls split open with mere in hand to hand combat. Deadly weapons in the hands of the warriors. The mere are beautifully carved whale bone and greenstone artifacts. Not that that would be any consolation to the victims.*

'The British soldiers that survived ran away howling. Thirty-five were killed, including ten officers, and a further eighty-three wounded. The Māori defenders suffered relatively few casualties from the shelling and storming of the pā and they evacuated during the night, taking a hundred British rifles with them. The British Imperial Troops suffered a humiliating defeat at the hands of half-naked, half-armed savages.'

An additional note of interest in the report recounted the actions of Hēni Te Kiri Karamū, who risked her own life in going out of the pā to give water to Colonel H. J. P. Booth and two other wounded soldiers. Rāwiri Puhirake and Hēnare Taratoa had drawn up a code of conduct before the battle in accordance with Christian principles. 'If your enemy thirsts, give him water.'

General Cameron finally concluded that 'it is not generally desirable to attack such positions' and he returned to Auckland, leaving Colonel Greer to hold onto the Tauranga territory. Colonel Greer received intelligence that Puhirake and his warriors had retreated further inland and begun constructing another pā at Te Ranga with reinforcements from other tribes. Greer seized the opportunity to storm the unfinished defences and the 43rd and 68th regiments under his command killed a great many of the unprepared Māori defenders.

*Just like at Ōrākau,* Kelly recalled. *Well, General Cameron is at least partly avenged for the ignominious defeat at Gate Pā.*

Fighting ceased in Tauranga, as it had in the Waikato, but it could not be said the country was at peace. Premier Domett and government ministers still wanted a 'conclusive' war that would secure a lasting peace, punish the 'rebellion' in the Waikato and deter other tribes from rebelling. The colonial government had concocted the Settlements Act and the Confiscation Act to provide for large scale land seizures and General Cameron was being urged to expand the area of conquered territory to see the confiscation policy 'enforced to the fullest extent'. The disaffected General, however, refused to continue with more military operations, to the relief of the troops, many of whom were also by now disgusted with the war. Nor was the British Colonial office willing to continue 'funding a war to satisfy settler demands for wholesale confiscation of Māori land', an expensive war that would bankrupt the colony if it continued. The New Zealand Parliament planned to defray the expenses of the war from the sale of confiscated land.

The troops still stationed at Te Awamutu, still on full pay and rations, eventually returned to camp at Ōtāhuhu. Private Kelly was evacuated with all the other walking wounded from the field dressing station at the Te Awamutu Redoubt and received treatment for his arm, which had become infected. The treatment consisted primarily of applying maggots to the wound to consume the suppurating flesh, hopefully leaving vital flesh which would heal cleanly. The infirmary and the camp were quite basic and the water supply was polluted. Flies swarmed and had constantly to be brushed off the patients. Illness flourished in the unsanitary conditions.

It was fortunate for Kelly that he received a letter from home delivered in person by a courier for the commissariat, one Patrick Quinn, who was delivering medical supplies, candles and oil and a mail bag to the Ōtāhuhu military camp. Quinn had recognised the name on an envelope as one of the two young soldiers he had met on the Great South Road construction and decided to see how the pair were getting on.

On hearing that Michael McCann had been killed in action, he told Kelly, "I'm sorry to hear you lost your mate, but that's the way of it. That's always the risk when you enlist in the British Army—well, in any army." He inspected Kelly's arm. "You need to get that wound cleaned up and get the bone properly set. Some of these fellows here will lose a limb to gangrene. If you survive, they'll have you back in the wars with a rifle in your hands."

Patrick Quinn, the merchant, had prospered and expanded his business interests. The war was good for business. He had a proposition for Kelly. "I'm looking for a worker I can trust. We can get you out of here quick smart with a discharge by purchase. We'll get you proper medical treatment and I'll employ you when you're fully recovered. You can repay me from your earnings."

Kelly scratched the back of his hand against the stubble on his chin and considered Quinn's proposal. "A kind offer but if I don't serve my full three years in the army, I won't be eligible for the military land grant."

"You still want to be a farmer then. You might end up a one-armed farmer. And what sort of land would you get? Fifty acres of swamp or rock or some rubbish. The officers will get four hundred acres each of the best land. You want to save that arm, lad. I'm going to see your Commanding Officer now."

As soon as Quinn left the tent, Kelly tore open the envelope he'd been holding. The date franked on the envelope showed it had been on a four-month journey. It was from Annie and of course he was anxious to read it.

*My dear Finbar*

*I miss you so and I hope you are still all right. You are always in my prayers. I hope you can quit the army and come home.*

Then there was news of her older brother and her younger sister.

*Sean got involved with the Republican Brotherhood and he was betrayed by an informer. He fled to America to avoid arrest and to join the Fenians there to attack the British in Canada. Lizzie and I are still at home with Ma and Da...*

Quinn returned to the tent. "News from home, from your sweetheart?"

"Yes, she wants me to quit the army and come back home."

"Well, you could be the first Irishman to go back since I left there myself during the Great Famine."

"I'd rather bring Annie out to New Zealand. Either way, I could work and save the fare."

"Indeed you could. Come with me now to get this discharge sorted with the adjutant."

Quinn's influence and his money had bought possibly the quickest discharge in the history of the British Army. Kelly's wound did eventually heal in a proper hospital, with the bone set by a surgeon and the wound healed with the aid of bromide treatment.

Quinn came and fetched him to his home, where he met his wife, Āwhina, a striking Māori woman with a distinctive moko kauae, a chin tattoo, signifying her high status in her hapū of the Ngāti Hauā tribe. Also, their son, Rāwiri, a fine looking boy of about fourteen, with the dark skin of his mother.

Quinn poured two glasses of celebratory fine Irish whisky. He raised his glass and toasted, "To your good health Finbar."

"I'm grateful for your kindness, Sir," said Kelly and they drank together.

"Don't be thinking I rescued you from that hell hole just out of the goodness of my heart. I'm a businessman and I intend to recoup my investment in you."

Quinn refilled their glasses and put a newspaper on the table. "Here's a copy of the *Irish People,* since you're so interested in what's happening in the home country. Personally I'm more interested in what's happening right here in New Zealand. And don't you think it's interesting how history repeats?"

Kelly sipped his whisky and turned the pages of the paper as Quinn elucidated. "New Zealand is just the latest in centuries of British colonies. Ireland was the first. Oliver Cromwell invaded to take our land and our sovereignty and the Brits ensconced themselves within the Pale, their boundary line in the East. Now here in New Zealand they've pushed a boundary line down through to the south of the Waikato, the aukati the Māori call it. There's more Waikato Kingites than Maniapotos behind the line. They're refugees in their own country and they're starving and dying of disease: the typhus, measles, whooping cough."

"And this is what we're fighting for," said Kelly ruefully.

"And look what the *New Zealand Herald* is saying." Quinn placed another newspaper on the table. "*The Māoris are dying from their own filthy habits and we should harass them day and night to hasten their extinction.*"

"Is the government really saying kill them all off?"

"Well that's the settlers saying it but there are those in Parliament who agree. And look," said Quinn, jabbing at the article, "They're criticising the Governor's 'mistaken leniency'."

"Really? Grey is not noted for his leniency, although over in Tauranga after the Māoris were soundly beaten at Te Ranga he ordered that the survivors be given supplies so they wouldn't starve."

"I heard that was because he was having an affair with a Ngāi Te Rangi woman."

"He does have a reputation as a philanderer."

"And they quote Grey here", said Quinn, pointing again at the article. 'He desires for the two races to live in peace.'"

"Yes, but on his terms."

"You know Grey served in the British Army in Ireland too. Then in Cape Colony killing Kaffirs. He's made a career of British colonising and confiscating land for the Crown. And it's always punishment for rebellion. Defending your home becomes rebellion. It's legalised theft," said Quinn, referring to the Suppression of Rebellion Act and read aloud from the *Herald* article, '*The Kingites had rejected the Queen's sovereignty... The government has suppressed insurrection amongst the evil disposed persons of the native race that had caused great injury, alarm and intimidation of Her Majesty's peaceable subjects of both races.*'"

"So we were not fighting against enemy combatants. We were suppressing an insurrection."

"Exactly so and rebels have no rights. I tell you the treachery of this government knows no bounds. Drink up lad," said Quinn, refilling his own glass.

But Kelly was not a seasoned drinker and was getting a bit giddy. "Why is Grey so determined to smash the King Movement? Why could the Māoris not govern themselves and still recognise the Queen as the Scots do?"

"Why not indeed. Treachery and pretence to justify the great land grab for the benefit of Auckland businessmen and land hungry settlers."

"Auckland businessmen," Kelly echoed thoughtfully.

"I'm not in the land business," Quinn hastily replied. "I'm not a farmer and I don't have any ambitions to own more land than my own home here in the town."

"But you do supply the ploughs."

"Aye and I'd supply them to Māori farmers again if they still had farms in the Waikato, or if I could do business in the King Country, as they're calling it now. But as things are now I'd be shot on site if I went past the aukati."

"The government needs military settlers to protect all the land they've conquered and they're not farmers either."

"True," Quinn agreed. "Soldiers don't always make good farmers, from my experience. Still there's plenty of soldier farmers for the Auckland province. But now they're being imported from Australia to take up farming the Waikato."

"What about the ordinary British settlers?"

"There's plenty of land over to sell to the settlers to pay for the war. We're talking about over three million acres of land, good fertile farmland too. You've seen it for yourself."

"Aye," Kelly said, with a yawn. I'm ready for bed now, after that night-cap. Good night to you both and thank you for welcoming me into your home."

# 7

On the first morning in his new home, Kelly woke to a chorus of birdsong. When he joined the family for breakfast Quinn greeted him with a cheery "Good morning," and asked, "How did you sleep, son?"

"I slept well, thanks. It's a comfortable bed." He made no mention of the nightmares that disturbed his sleep.

Quinn and Rāwiri went off to work after breakfast, leaving Āwhina and Kelly at home. His new home was a solid kauri house with matai floorboards, rimu wainscoting and a bay window at the front, mullioned in solid rimu. The front door opened onto a veranda, shaded by four peach trees that grew between the house and the road. Behind the house were stables and storerooms and a well-tended garden.

Kelly was in the sitting room later in the morning, arm in a sling, standing before the tall rimu bookcase, reading the titles of the books: classic and popular English literature.

Āwhina appeared suddenly at his side, having padded quietly into the room in her bare feet. "Feel free to borrow any of the books."

"Thank you, but I'm not much of a reader. What would you recommend?"

Āwhina took a Bible out of the bookcase and handed it to him. "I would recommend this. Do you read the Bible?

"No."

"I read it every day."

"Well, I wouldn't want to deprive you of it." He handed it back to her.

"Oh, I have my own Bibles, one in English and one in te reo Māori. This is a spare one." She handed it back to him. "You're welcome to it. If you've not read it before I suggest you start in the New Testament. The book of John is my favourite Gospel."

Kelly accepted the Bible and continued to scan the bookcase. "I wouldn't have taken Patrick for a fan of Shakespeare."

"Oh, Patrick is not much of a reader either, really. Most of the books are mine."

Kelly coloured with embarrassment at the assumptions he'd made.

Āwhina smiled and said, "I was educated at a Church Missionary School in Peria. It was there I learned to read and write in te reo Māori and English and there I discovered a love of literature. I'm reading John Milton at the moment. I enjoy his epic poems, *Paradise Lost* and *Paradise Regained*. They don't accord exactly with the Bible but they are interestingly and vividly conceived."

"How did you meet Patrick?" Kelly asked.

"It was the first time some of our iwi took produce to Auckland to sell. I went as the interpreter. We would have been cheated at the market if Patrick hadn't intervened. He was an honest trader. He was very helpful to us and then we dealt with him each time."

"I'm looking forward to working with him. Now I think I'll go to my room and write a letter to my fiancée."

"Ah, yes, Patrick told me you have a young woman back in Ireland."

Kelly's room at the back of the house was furnished with a bed, a wardrobe, a wash stand, a desk and a chair. He sat at his desk and wrote:

> *My dear Annie*
>
> *I hope this letter finds you well. My life here has changed for the better. I have left the army, just as you wished, discharged thanks to a Mr Quinn, an Ulster man, who wishes to employ me in his business. I now have room and board in his home, in exchange for indentured labour. Quinn has a Māori wife, who is a devout Christian and is very kind. This is what I think you would call divine providence.*
>
> *I suffered a wound to my arm, which is healing now, thanks to good medical treatment. The invisible wounds I carry may take longer to heal. I have better prospects now than in the army or going farming. If things go well for me here, as I think they will, I shall be able to send for you. I yearn for us to be together again...*

It was a quiet household, especially during the day. Āwhina had a bearing of serenity, which was remarkable considering the turmoil the country was in and the extremity of her people. And Rāwiri was usually sullen and taciturn. Quinn, on the other hand, could be quite boisterous, especially when he was drinking.

Kelly was permitted a brief period of convalescence during which he lounged on the veranda, helped with chores that he could manage with one hand, and walked about the town. He had politely accepted the Bible Āwhina had given him, and left in on his desk. Having little else to occupy his time, he began to read it, starting in the book of John, just as Āwhina had suggested. He continued to write letters to Annie, encouraging her to agree to come to New Zealand when the time was right. Her replies had always been that her parents would not agree and she was loath to leave against their will.

On his first day on the job, Kelly took the horse and dray down the rutted, muddy Queen Street to Commercial Bay, with Quinn and Rāwiri on the horse and cart. At the Queen's Wharf they loaded some farm machinery and commissariat supplies, including some barrels bearing a WI stamp: hogsheads of West Indian rum for the British Imperial Army. They also loaded crates of clinking bottles onto the cart. Quinn had branched out into a lucrative sideline of importing and distributing non-commissariat fermented and spirituous liquors: rum, brandy and whisky. There was a ready market for the imports and the Auckland Provincial Government were happy to collect the excise on alcohol, although they probably didn't collect any tax on the moonshine packed in cream cans. Rāwiri was conspicuous among the workers on the dock as by this time there were not many Māori in the town.

A youth in a gang from the disreputable Freemans Bay called out, "This is our land now boy. Get down behind the line with the rest of the niggers."

Then the ruffian brazenly took a crate from the cart and started walking off with it. But he didn't get far before he was stopped in his tracks. A gun shot rang out. A spray of gravel struck his legs, where the bullet struck the ground at his feet. There was a lull in the bustle of activity on the dock and all eyes turned to the boy holding the crate of bottles. Quinn pointed his revolver at the would-be thief and then waved it in the direction of the cart. The crate was returned to the cart without a word and everyone went back about their business.

Quinn and Kelly shipped all manner of nonmilitary supplies along the Waikato River and the Great South Road to the military settlements at Hamilton, Cambridge and Alexandra (Pirongia). Kelly became acquainted with another Auckland merchant, Ralph Simpson, as they kept his military camp canteens regularly supplied with liquor. There were lots of deliveries to grog shops and it soon became apparent that liquor was not so much a sideline as the mainstream of the business. It was certainly in more demand than farming equipment.

Kelly and Quinn sat side by side on the seat of the cart as it trundled along the road through the Waikato. "It's sad to see so much of this land covered in fern and scrub," Kelly remarked. "Where are all the wheat fields and kūmara gardens? Where are all the crops? Why isn't the land being farmed?"

"It's the military settlers. They're mostly men with no farming experience and no desire to be subsistence farmers. They're given uneconomic plots, in what's potentially still a war zone, no road access, far from markets and they've got no capital. They come off army rations and they're desperate so they sell their bit of land. Some are heading off to Thames and the South Island to try their luck in the gold fields."

Quinn flicked the reins to keep the horses from dawdling. "The rich speculators buy up lots of land cheaply: ten pounds, twenty pounds. The speculators aren't farmers. They're not interested in developing the land. They're land banking. They'll sell it off in bigger parcels when the price goes up. Wait till we get the railroad through the Waikato and all the way to Wellington. The land will be worth a fortune."

"Why doesn't the government buy some land back? They're supposed to grant some land back to Māoris, at least to the ones who were loyal to the Crown."

"There's plenty of land they could buy from the absentee landlords, the wealthy investors and speculators in London."

"How did they buy land here?"

"Just paper transactions. They bought land from Wakefield's New Zealand Company while it was still owned by Māori. And they bought land in Auckland from the Crown. The government could buy some back but they don't seem to be interested in buying land back just now. Mind you, some of the ministers are buying land privately. The likes of Russell and Whitaker are doing all right out of it."

Quinn trusted Kelly to conduct more of the business on his own and he was soon delivering orders on the river steamers and barges. Quinn always reminded him to never take his eyes off the cargo, especially the rum, and especially the sailors. Theft was a constant threat.

On returning from one of his trips to the Waikato, Kelly found only Āwhina at home, and not with her usual calm demeanour.

"Patrick's in jail," Āwhina informed him. "He says you and Rāwiri carry on the business. You do the selling."

"What's happened?"

She was clasping her hands and pacing the floor.

"Rāwiri got into a fight with a pack of youths at the dock. One came at him with a knife. So Patrick shot him."

"Dead?"

"Yes."

"Where's Rāwiri now?"

"In his room, in bed."

"Is he all right?"

"He's battered and bruised but Patrick prevented him from being stabbed."

"So what'll happen now?"

"There will be a trial. He'll probably get off. He has a good lawyer. Meanwhile he is remanded in custody."

Kelly, Āwhina and Rāwiri rose on the day of the trial to steady rain falling from a darkly brooding sky. In the carriage Kelly had rented for the occasion they headed up Queen Street, which, fortunately had been freshly gravelled. Muddy water gushed along the open drains on either side of the street and past the courthouse.

They made their way into the leaky wooden building, negotiating a path through the buckets placed at several strategic points to catch the rainwater that dripped from the roof. The atmosphere was close and fusty with the smell of damp woollen clothing. When all were seated in whatever dry spots they could find, they rose again to the orders of the bailiff as the judge entered, wearing a black robe and white wig. The judge himself was obliged to sit at a desk brought in for the purpose, as the magisterial bench was getting a drenching. He apologised for the state of the building and assured the gallery that a new courthouse was soon to be built. He had seen the plans himself for the splendid new courthouse of brick and imported Bath stone.

A constable led Quinn into the courtroom to the dock and remained to guard the prisoner. Quinn stood stoically in the dock and scanned the crowded gallery. His morose countenance brightened to a reassuring smile as he spotted Āwhina, Rāwiri and Kelly in the gallery.

The clerk of the court read the indictment of murder against the accused, to which Quinn pled not guilty. Counsel for the prosecution, robed and wigged, rose from behind his table and outlined the case for murder. In essence, he said, it was an egregious case of man with gun versus boy with knife. He called Mr Smythe, the father of the victim, to the stand, as well as a few other witnesses to the incident on the wharf. All swore on the Bible to tell the truth.

As the trial proceeded, Quinn's barrister, Mr Pugmire, also forensically attired, refuted the charge of murder on the grounds that it was actually a case of justifiable homicide. He argued cogently that the defendant had had to use immediate and necessary force to protect another for whom he was responsible. More eyewitnesses to the incident were called to give corroborating testimony.

The prosecutor argued that it was a case of culpable homicide, as the defendant unreasonably used lethal force to protect another who was not certainly in mortal danger. He added that in any case the life being protected was of lesser value than the life taken. Pugmire objected on Quinn's behalf before he could say anything.

Āwhina sat impassively at Kelly's side, but the movement of her lips testified to her silent prayers. The jury of twelve Pākehā men, sitting on benches behind a rail, followed the proceedings attentively. A few of them glanced at Quinn and one, apparently an acquaintance smiled and nodded. At the conclusion of proceedings, the judge delivered a summing-up to the jury.

The court clerk announced: "Gentlemen of the jury, you will now retire to consider your verdict."

The judge then announced, "The Court will stand adjourned while the jury deliberate."

A constable led the jury to an adjoining room and stood guard outside the door. There was a palpable tension in the court room and a buzz of urgent conversation. Smythe glared at Quinn, but Quinn kept his composure of equanimity. There was much coming and going amongst the gallery, to the toilet and walking about outside, as the rain was letting up.

The court eventually reconvened. The jury returned to their places and the clerk called the court to order. The judge returned to the makeshift bench and addressed the jury. "Gentlemen of the jury, have you agreed upon your verdict?"

"We have, Your Honour," the foreman replied. "We find the defendant not guilty of the charge of murder."

Voices were raised in anger, but they had been raised from the start anyway above the noise of the rain on the tin roof. The verdict was greeted with cries from the gallery of *Murderer* and *Bastard* directed at the defendant and the judge. The judge banged his gavel and demanded order in the court. Quinn left the court and stood outside, relieved the trial and the rain had ended. He was joined by Pugmire and they both filled and tamped their pipes. All around was soggy and carriage horses stood by dropping dung onto the muddy ground. Mr Smythe approached Quinn and struck him across the face with an open hand and challenged him to a duel.

"I'm sorry your son died," Quinn said, "but I was protecting my own son. I will accept your challenge, if you insist, so that your honour may be satisfied."

As the offended party, Smythe set the terms. "Pistols. At dawn. On the shore of Freeman's Bay. Three days hence."

The court gradually emptied and people picked their way through the mud and made their way home in carriages, traps and on horseback. For the Quinn family the gloom of the trial had lifted but now the dark cloud of a duel was filling the horizon. Āwhina had seen the challenge and knew what it meant.

"Well, I have to go through with it but I'll be all right," Quinn said, trying to reassure Āwhina. Little else was said as the carriage rolled down Queen Street past the 'street Arabs' who had come out from the slums of Shortland Street and Chancery Street to play and make mischief. The whores would soon be out as well from over the back of High Street when the evening grew dark and the new gas lights were lit.

The Quinn household rose before dawn on the day of the duel. Āwhina prayed for divine protection in the name of Jesus Christ, for 'the covering of the blood of the Lamb' and committed her husband to the care of her God. It brought to Kelly's mind the times he'd faced death as a soldier on the battlefield. At the prospect of meeting his maker he never failed to utter a quick prayer. As muddled and inarticulate as they may have been, they were prayers born not just of fear but also of faith.

Kelly accompanied Quinn as his second and they met the challenger and his second at Freeman's Bay. The sun rose in a clear sky and the only sounds in the still morning air of the deserted beach was of the waves slapping and hissing on the mud and gulls screeching overhead. The seconds loaded the single shot pistols and the duellists faced each other at twenty-five paces. At the signal given by Smythe's second, Smythe fired quickly and missed. Quinn held his aim without firing. Smythe shifted his stance to full front, raised his arms from his sides and awaited his fate. Quinn had already established his prowess as a marksman.

Kelly stood by nervously, but was then relieved when Quinn raised his pistol and fired into the air. *So honour is satisfied without the shedding of more blood.*

Āwhina's relief at the safe return of her husband soon turned to consternation when Quinn celebrated the occasion by pouring three glasses of whisky. "We are all survivors," he declared, and toasted his survival, Kelly's and Rāwiri's.

"It's still early morning," Āwhina reproached, "and it's the Sabbath. We'd all do better to go to church and thank God for answering our prayers." She then left for church, with Rāwiri.

Christmas was approaching and it was a busy time for the business. Kelly and Quinn were often on the road and on the river. At a time when Quinn was delayed in Hamilton, Kelly returned home and found two extra horses tethered at the back of the house. He hadn't been expecting visitors. Āwhina met him at the door and introduced her brother Hāmana and sister Pania. Hāmana had the look of a Māori warrior with his tattooed face—a tā moko of blue-green whorls on both cheeks and either side of his nose and stripes ascending to his hairline. He also had the unnerving, hostile look of the Māori for whom he had been the enemy.

Pania looked like a younger version of Āwhina. She had virtually the same features: the same dark eyes, black hair, though longer than Āwhina's, the straight, snub nose and plumpish upper lip. Unlike her elder sister, Pania's lips and chin were unadorned with moko kauae.

A family reunion for the Christmas season, perhaps? They had just had a meal and Pania and Rāwiri were clearing up and washing dishes. Āwhina was making tea and poured a cup for Kelly.

"We are going to Peria together," she said. "I'm glad you've come home before we left. We're going to a tangihanga, the funeral of Tarapīpipi Te

Waharoa, the great rangatira of my iwi, Ngāti Hauā. You may know of him as Wiremu Tāmihana."

"Yes, they call him the Kingmaker. I didn't know he had died."

"He hasn't died yet. He will die in five days."

"How do you know when he will die?"

"He has said so himself."

"Is he also a prophet then?"

"Yes, and a great man of God and a man of peace. When he became a Christian, he was baptised and given the name William Thompson. Hence the name Wiremu Tāmihana. He was my teacher for a time at the mission school. He established a Christian community at Peria, named after the biblical Berea, with a mission statement of 'King and Queen together with God over both'. Life there was based on the Ten Commandments."

"Why is he called the Kingmaker?"

"It was his influence that brought the leaders of the many iwi together to agree on who would be our King. At the coronation, Wiremu anointed Pōtatau Te Wherowhero as King by placing a Bible above his head."

The siblings discussed the journey, with Āwhina taking the lead, as the organiser. They would take the coastal steamer to Thames with their horses on board and the river steamer to Te Aroha, then ride overland to Peria. They spoke both in English and te reo Māori, except for Hāmana who spoke only in Māori. Even Pania's voice was similar to Āwhina's, though she didn't have the same easy command of English.

They had already packed and Āwhina packed more of the food for the journey and left some for Kelly: bread, cheese and slices of mutton. The four departed on horseback, leaving Kelly to look after the home and business.

"Where are Āwhina and Rāwiri?" Quinn said when he arrived home and found only Kelly in the house.

"They've gone to Peria with Pania and Hāmana," Kelly said. "Āwhina got news that Tāmihana was on his deathbed. Āwhina asked that you wait here for her. She said she'd return after the funeral."

Quinn frowned. "Tangihanga go on for three days."

"Looks like just you and me for Christmas."

Quinn set the kete he was carrying onto the dining table. "Merry Christmas," he said, still frowning, and slumped in his chair at the table.

Kelly drew a Christmas ham and a bottle of wine out of the kete, which brought a smile to his face. He prepared a meal with potatoes and peas he'd harvested from the garden. While the pots were boiling on the stove, he carved the ham and set the table with plates, cutlery and glasses.

Quinn uncorked the bottle of Hermitage and filled the glasses. "To Tāmihana," he said, raising his glass. "May he finally rest in peace."

Together they consumed the wine with the meal—Kelly's two glasses to Quinn's three—not that Kelly was counting, and Quinn probably wasn't. Quinn laid the bottle on its side to settle the dregs and poured the last few drops into his glass. He thanked Kelly, scraped his chair back from the table and belched.

"Very satisfying. And now, time for a whisky." He fetched the bottle and shot glasses from the sideboard.

He'd quaffed a few glasses while Kelly sipped his way through one. They talked about the business Quinn had done in Hamilton and Kelly had done at home. "All good then," Quinn said. "I know I can always rely on you."

As Quinn's mood had lightened, Kelly judged it was time to broach the subject that had been at the forefront of his mind of late. "The business is all going well, and I reckon I've cleared my debt and will now be entitled to draw a decent wage, with my board deducted of course. I should be able to save the price of a ship's passage to New Zealand for Annie."

Quinn's face was a study of serious consideration, but only briefly. "Right you are," he declared, grinning as if he had just received good news. Putting down his glass, he shook Kelly's hand. "This calls for a celebration." He poured Kelly another shot and they clinked glasses. "Onward and upward! Drink up lad. It's the good stuff."

And indeed it was quality single malt Irish whisky imbued with the smoky, peaty tastes of the land where it was distilled.

Quinn fetched a small wooden box from the sideboard and offered Kelly a cigar. "Oh, that's right. You don't smoke. Never mind. I'll have one anyway." He lit a cigar from the candle on the table, puffed and savoured the musky smoke.

Kelly had a night cap and went to bed, leaving Quinn to continue indulging his vices on his own in the gloom of the dining room. Without a woman's touch about the house, dust had settled in the rooms and spiders had spun their 'Irish curtains' in the corners.

Quinn resumed pining and fretting in the morning and for another week till Āwhina and Rāwiri returned home from Peria, travel weary, saddle sore and careworn.

Āwhina spoke with great sadness of the settlement and the tangi. "Most of Ngāti Hauā land has been confiscated. The church at Peria is destroyed, the meeting house, the school, the flour mill, the post office, all are gone. Wiremu's house is in ruins. Many houses broken and deserted."

She was resting in the armchair and appeared to be dozing off but she collected herself and continued. "Wiremu died with his Bible in his hand to the end, two days after Christmas, just as he had foretold. His last words were, 'Obey the laws of God and man.' Hundreds of mourners on the marae were weeping and wailing."

Āwhina's own eyes filled with tears as she recounted the scene. "On his last day he called his two sons to his side and asked them both how they would respond to the Pākehā, the Tauiwi. Hoto, the elder said he would continue to make war. Tupu, the younger was for peace. 'That is well, Tupu,' Wiremu said. 'You shall be the head of the tribe, to follow after me.'"

There followed a long pause and Quinn and Kelly left Āwhina to rest. "Wiremu Tāmihana is a great loss," Quinn said to Kelly, as he fetched a bottle from the cupboard. "A lot of fighting and bloodshed could have been avoided if the government had listened to his proposals. Instead they called him a rebel and a murderer. It broke his heart to see so much of the Waikato confiscated and he tried repeatedly to negotiate the return of the land. He took a petition to Parliament for an enquiry into the true causes of the war and to clear his name of the false accusations of evil deeds against him. Grey insisted he come to Wellington in person. That would have been in the last week before Tāmihana went home to Peria."

Quinn paused to pour two glasses of whisky. "Well, Grey showed him the land had already been covenanted to military settlers. Two thousand men are already settled on it, he said. Tāmihana said at least let the land be given back as promised to those who did not fight. But all that land was kept to pay the cost of the war. 'Well,' Grey says, 'Is there any piece of land you really want in the Waikato?' 'I want it all,' says Tāmihana."

"Appeasement and division," Kelly said.

"Aye. It's a tactic the British employed in Ireland and Scotland. Redistribute tribal land into individual titles and create new landowners who help to put down rebellion. But Tāmihana couldn't be bought.

"You know what the feckin ministers did then? They put on a special reception to honour Tāmihana, to finally treat him with some respect. He'd been treated so shamefully on his first visit to the Native Office in Auckland. He was kept waiting for two days, while all the Europeans who came and went were attended to. He finally left in disgust and said, 'We are treated like dogs.'"

Quinn paused to sip and savour his drink. "So, they got James Osgood to cater this grand banquet. After all the feasting, Tāmihana says, 'I would like to reciprocate your hospitality gentlemen but I am now very poor and my people have to borrow money to buy food.' Then Tāmihana challenged Whitaker to a game of draughts for the Waikato. Whitaker laughed off the proposal of the Waikato as the stakes for the game, but played him all the same. Tāmihana beat him and then proceeded to beat the other superintendents, Featherston and McLean." Quinn laughed despite the tragedy of the situation.

While it could not be said the country was at peace, there was less fighting and life was becoming more settled, at least in Auckland province, and Āwhina continued her habit of attending Saint Mark's Anglican Church in Remuera.

She had also become involved with several other Christian women devoutly dedicated to campaigning against the evils of alcohol. Whether it was the work of the devil, as they claimed, was debatable but alcohol was undeniably causing grievous social problems in the fledgling community. It was a great embarrassment to Āwhina that her husband provided for his family by dealing in alcoholic beverages, but what most concerned her was that Rāwiri was now also partaking of the demon drink. She had accepted that Quinn had no interest in attending church but could not continue to tolerate all the liquor in his business and in their home. Quinn's drinking had increased to where he was seldom completely sober.

Tension simmered in what had previously been a haven of tranquillity in troubled times and things came to a head when Āwhina presented Quinn with an ultimatum. "You can be an honest merchant without the trade in liquor and you can moderate your own drinking. But I will not have you corrupting Rāwiri with alcohol. I would rather leave and return to my own people in Peria, or what is left of it, and take Rāwiri with me."

"You'd be better off staying here but go if you must," said Quinn solemnly, "but the boy can make up his own mind as to what he wants to do."

"I have," said Rāwiri. "I'll go with her."

It was no great surprise to Quinn that Āwhina was ready to leave but he hadn't expected Rāwiri to join her. He sank into despondency after they left and drank himself into a stupor. Kelly was left to run the business on his own, which he did quite capably, but there was little else he could do for Quinn in his present state.

As Kelly took on responsibility for the work, he necessarily learned the true nature of the business, which was that Quinn was employed by one James Dilworth, a wealthy farmer, businessman, and banker. Dilworth held commissariat contracts for the provisions of the British Imperial Army in New Zealand, and Quinn was a subcontractor, which allowed him to pursue other business interests, like the importation and sale of liquor. Kelly recalled meeting the middle-aged, lanky Irishman with the gruff manner when Quinn introduced him as a business associate, while they were picking up a shipment of goods at the dock. He never gave the man a second thought till he discovered he was working contracts for him.

The business thrived under Kelly's management and much of his time was spent travelling and making deliveries. But disaster struck at home. On returning from a trip to Alexandra he arrived back in Auckland to find the Quinn home completely destroyed by fire. By the time the volunteer fire brigade had arrived the house was well ablaze. The firefighters had managed to pump water from the Waipapa stream at the back of the property and prevented the fire from spreading to the stables and storage shed. But the kauri house was razed to the ground and Quinn had perished in the flames.

Kelly made arrangements with Reverend Heywood for Quinn's funeral and made the four-day journey to Peria to inform Āwhina. He found, to his dismay, that the village still lay in ruins, and a remnant of Ngāti Hauā were rebuilding some dwellings. One, an elderly man spoke to him in te reo Māori and a boy was able to tell him many of their iwi had gone to join Te Ua Haumēne and his Pai Mārire. Āwhina? She has gone to Tokangamutu (Te Kuiti) to join Tāwhiao in the Rohe Pōtae. Kelly would have continued on to the King Country, despite the dangers of crossing the aukati into the hostile territory, but that was a journey of another four days overland and the time for the funeral would have passed.

Instead, he returned to Auckland in time for the interment of Quinn's charred remains in the cemetery of Saint Mark's Church. Many of Quinn's friends and business associates were at the funeral. Dilworth was there with his young wife, whom he introduced as Isabella, and he invited Kelly back to their home after the service. Kelly was happy to accept a ride in their carriage to the Dilworth estate in Remuera, at the foot of Mount Hobson, to the grandest house he had ever entered. Such a large house, Kelly observed, for just two people, as there were no children. Isabella served tea in the drawing room and left the men to discuss business. So it was to be a business meeting, and Mr Dilworth did not take long to get down to business after a few pleasantries and condolences about poor old Quinn.

Dilworth was an Irish immigrant from County Tyrone and always happy to do business with fellow Ulster men, like Quinn and Kelly, and while he had always been very fond of Quinn, he was aware of his recent circumstances and his decline. "Liquor never did anyone any good," Dilworth said, though he conceded it did make Quinn a lot of money. He said he was also well aware that Kelly had been running the business and Quinn had been fortunate to have him in his employ.

"Business is not just about money and goods. It's about people and in business I've learned to be a good judge of character. It is my observation, Master Kelly, that you are a young man of ability, integrity and ambition."

"Thank you, Sir," Kelly managed to reply. "It is my ambition to make a go of it here in Auckland and become a family man when my fiancée can join me here."

"Ah yes. Quinn told me of your plans. You should soon be able to send for the young lady as you'll now be paid for contracts, not for wages, if you're willing to stay on in the business. I'll pay you a retainer if you'll agree to manage a warehouse for me. You may have seen the building under construction now in Customs Street."

Kelly was very happy to accept Dilworth's offer and assured him he had every intention of continuing in the business. "But first I have to attend to another matter," he said. "I still need to find Āwhina and inform her of Quinn's death."

"I suppose you'd be the man for that mission," Dilworth agreed. "Aye, you'd better take care of that first." He shook Kelly's hand to seal the business agreement and wished him well for the journey to the King Country.

Kelly returned to his makeshift home in the storage shed and immediately penned a letter to Annie and took it up Shortland Crescent to the post office on Princes Street.

*Dearest Annie*

*Much has happened since I last wrote. I am well, but saddened by the loss of poor old Quinn. He died in a fire that destroyed the house. Only he was at home. Āwhina and Rāwiri had gone away and I was away on business. However, now it seems I have a new employer, another Ulster man, who has made his fortune in New Zealand, though I think he already had family money. I am sure I have greater prospects here than I would ever have back home. I am not dreaming of becoming rich, but dreaming of making a life here together with you. I am sure I will soon have money enough for your passage to New Zealand and a home for us here. Please say you are ready to come.*

*With all my love, Finbar*

Kelly rode south along the Great South Road to Mercer, boarded the river steamer to Alexandra and continued by horseback into Ngāti Maniapoto territory, across the aukati. At Te Kuiti he dismounted and approached a group tending a large garden. Here he was accosted by two tattooed warriors, one of whom he recognised immediately as Āwhina's brother.

"Now you are in my territory," Hāmana said, "You remember seeing me in Auckland, but you don't remember seeing me at Rangiriri. I remember seeing you there, in your red coat, carrying your musket. With the musket a slave can kill a chief. Different when it's hand to hand."

With that he thrust his taiaha into Kelly's hands and took up that of his companion. He then postured and grimaced, hopped from one foot to the other, deftly twirling the fighting staff, whooping and yelping. He struck Kelly a stinging blow to the side of the head. Kelly was dazed but parried the next strike and then took a blow to the thigh. He managed one or two blows himself but he was no match for the skill of the warrior. Hāmana raised his taiaha above his head to strike another blow and Kelly struck him on the forehead with the butt of his taiaha, as he would with the stock of a rifle. Hāmana fell onto his back and sprang back to his feet, stung by the humiliation of being struck down by a Pākehā with a taiaha. He attacked with a flurry of blows, high if Kelly defended his legs and low if he defended his head, to the same thigh until the muscle spasm crippled the whole leg. A thrust of his taiaha struck Kelly in the groin, tearing the crotch of his trousers. A swiping blow struck the side of his head again and he fell to the ground.

Hāmana pinned him down with the point of the taiaha against his throat and said, "Now you are my slave."

"Then you'd better finish me for I will be no man's slave."

"An honourable answer," said Hāmana. He stood over Kelly, then withdrew the taiaha. He walked off with his fellow warrior, laughing scornfully.

Kelly lay on the ground bruised and grazed, but the worst of his injuries were a gash on his thigh and a torn scrotum. Blood was soaking his trousers. Āwhina rushed to his side and was joined by Rāwiri and two other women, one of whom he recognised as Āwhina's sister, Pania.

"Āwhina, you're a sight for sore eyes," Kelly declared, with a weak smile that was more of a wince.

Āwhina and Rāwiri helped Kelly to his feet and to Āwhina's whare, where she tended to his wounds. He gritted his teeth as she stitched the tear in his groin and applied a poultice to the wound to prevent infection. He felt exposed and vulnerable but appreciative of Āwhina's ministrations. Her gentle touch might have aroused feelings of a different nature in different circumstances.

"You look well, Āwhina," he said, *but you're looking thinner and your hair has gone grey*, he thought.

"I'm sorry this has happened to you Finbar, but why have you come here?"

Kelly broke the news to her of Quinn's death.

"Aue! Kua mate tōku tāne aroha," she cried. "He should have had a tangihanga."

"At least he had a decent Pākehā funeral," Kelly said.

"We will tangi for him here."

Rāwiri hugged his mother and said, "I should have stayed with him."

Āwhina wiped tears from her eyes and introduced her other companion, now also embracing her. "This is Te Paea Tiaho, Tāwhiao's sister. I'm serving as interpreter for Tāwhiao," Āwhina said, "and helping him compose petitions to Parliament and to the Queen. The government has confiscated our Waikato land and the Native Land Court is stealing more, ever closer to our King Country. The Queen says she cannot force our government to honour the Treaty and we have to deal with the government ourselves. But we get no justice from Governor Grey and Minister McLean."

Kelly saw King Tāwhiao himself during his brief sojourn at Te Kuiti. He certainly had a striking visage with his full face tā moko, not just inked into the skin but carved and contoured into his face. He was a man of quite short stature but still had a regal bearing, though his mana was rather diminished when he indulged his fondness for alcoholic beverages.

Āwhina proposed that Kelly buy the section of land in Auckland if he wished to stay there and rebuild. The community supporting the King in Te Kuiti were hard pressed for resources and she wished to contribute the proceeds of what was now her land to her new whānau, to ensure their survival and fund political action. Kelly gave her £20 on the spot and promised another £200 for the purchase, which Āwhina said was quite acceptable.

She gave him his trousers, stitched and washed, and said, "You should leave here as soon as you are fit to travel. I cannot go with you. I'm needed here and I'm in mourning here on the marae. But Pania can go. She is a healer and will take care of you."

"I'm sure I'll be all right now thanks to your first aid, but I'm not up to riding again just yet."

"We have a light cart you can take, you and Pania."

"Our family should do this for you because of what our brother has done," Pania insisted.

"Besides, my home is not much more than a shed at the moment," Kelly said.

"You've seen how we are living here," Āwhina replied.

"I'll return the cart with Pania and goods for the whānau when I'm fully recovered."

Āwhina began each day with a dawn prayer meeting, attended by most of her whānau, and by Kelly on the day of his departure. She concluded the meeting with a New Testament benediction: "Kia tau ki a tātou katoa, te atawhai o te Ariki o Ihu Karaiti, me te aroha o te Atua, me te whiwhingatahitanga o te Wairua Tapu. Āke, āke, āke. Āmine."

Then privately to Kelly, she said, "How is the Bible reading going?"

"Um, good," he replied. "I'm enjoying the beauty of the language."

"Ae, the grand language of the King James Bible. And what of the content?"

"Well, I'm still digesting it."

She didn't press for more response, but said, "Haere tonu. Keep reading it. And pray. You know, you can talk to our God."

She prayed the same benediction over him, in te reo Pākehā: "May the grace of the Lord Jesus Christ and the love of God and the fellowship of the Holy Spirit be with us all."

Āwhina gave Pania a hug and said, "Return to us as soon as he is recovered."

Kelly and Pania sat side by side on the seat of the cart, Kelly on a cushion for the journey and he winced with each jolt of the cart over holes and rocks in the tracks. He was relieved to transfer to the steamer at Alexandra and spend a day meandering along the Waikato River. The paddle wheels propelled the boat past thick bush, farmland and swamps, with stops at villages en route, and at the town of Ngāruawāhia.

"Te Kuiti is Āwhina's home now," Pania said. "Ngāti Maniapoto is not our iwi, but they have adopted her and she's adopted them. She's a great help to them. She says iwi doesn't matter. Tribal divisions have held us back. Māori must work together to get justice. Mahi tahi."

The country was no longer being torn apart by war but there were still localised conflicts arising from disputes over land, attacks on settlers, surveyors and soldiers. Māori throughout the country were ravaged by war, disease and starvation. There were many voices in the press predicting the inevitable extermination of the Māori race, colonists' voices, emboldened by Charles Darwin, who had visited the colony, declaring that it was a matter of the survival of a superior race. There was much grief and bitterness among Māori throughout the land, but there was also hope.

Kelly had witnessed, in Te Kuiti, a people defeated but not broken. They were angry and grieving, but clinging to hope for the healing of the wounded land, hope for injustices to be righted, even for reconciliation of peoples divided: the Kingites and the Queenites, the Tauiwi invader colonisers and the tangata whenua dispossessed colonised. That was a longer journey.

Kelly was anxious to return to Auckland to start rebuilding, to get a new home ready to receive his bride and start a new life together in a new land, a land still troubled and divided, but a land with a hope and a future.

His journey with Pania, back to Auckland was an uneventful return to his makeshift home in the storage shed of the fire ravaged property. After he'd settled in and rested from his journey, he reported to Dilworth.

"Yes, I see you've met with a bit of misfortune," Dilworth commiserated. "But we can still do business, as agreed, when you're fit to work, if you're still willing. Get yourself checked over by my doctor first."

Which Kelly did and it was the doctor's opinion that he could have done no better than the treatment he was already receiving and there was no sign of infection, but that was still a risk. Pania continued to be an angel of mercy. She tended to his wounded groin every day with a warm poultice until one day his anatomy betrayed an ardour he could not conceal. His swelling member and then his face became flushed with blood. Pania, for her part seemed unperturbed.

"He tohu pai," she said. "A good sign." She deferred to Kelly's modesty and withdrew to the other side of the curtain, which had become her bedroom, and left him to finish tending his wound. Kelly gazed at the curtain and mused: *A good sign? A sign of healing, returning health and vigour? Does the good sign portend something other than my health?* It became apparent that it did when that night his angel of mercy slipped quietly, nakedly, irresistibly, into his bed, and ministered to a need long suppressed.

"For your wairua," Pania whispered. "For healing your spirit."

In the light of dawn, Kelly's conscience pricked him. *What of Annie? She is still my fiancée. Pania is a temporary affair, nothing binding—she understands that. A soldier's dalliance—like so many others, even the married officers. Sowing wild oats, McCann had called it.*

Kelly thought of Āwhina whenever he looked at Pania. "What would Āwhina say?"

"Āwhina would not approve," Pania said. "But she's not here. I'm here. Do you want me to go?"

"No. Yes, before Annie arrives. No. You can stay a while longer if you want."

"Don't worry. You're still a single man. When you're married I'll be gone."

He decided to try to be as casual as Pania. He found himself with a live-in housekeeper, lover and gardener, as Pania restored the gardens that Āwhina had planted and tended.

Kelly was soon discharging his assigned duties, carting goods to the warehouse and sales deliveries. At the warehouse he was also supervising another worker Dilworth had recently hired, another Irishman by the name of

Francis O'Neill. O'Neill had sold up the military allotment he had been granted on being decommissioned from the British Imperial Army and taken lodgings in Auckland. His money had run out. He was looking for work and he had the good fortune to be hired by Dilworth, who, as always, favoured fellow Ulstermen. Kelly and O'Neill worked together in the warehouse, hoisting sacks of grain and produce onto the mezzanine floor for storage and bringing them down for deliveries. O'Neill took on more of the shipping of goods, leaving Kelly to spend more time on administration. Dilworth entrusted Kelly with more of the commissariat business, leaving himself free to concentrate on his various other business interests.

James Dilworth was a man of considerable means and was much higher up the commissariat food chain than Quinn had been. He tendered on large and lucrative contracts directly to Deputy Assistant Commissary General J. Leslie Robertson.

Dilworth called Kelly into the warehouse office, opened a newspaper on the big kauri desk and pointed to an ad in the public notices. "It starts here, Finbar."

Kelly read the call for tenders for the supply of a large quantity of 'beef of the best marketable quality'. He could read proficiently and had a good head for numbers so why should he not learn the business? Dilworth commended him for his aptitude and diligence and himself for exercising good judgement in hiring him.

Kelly accompanied Dilworth to One Tree Hill Farm where they walked along the ridges of ancient pā terraces and took in the view. To the north lay the town and farmland and beyond, the harbour, ships at anchor, and the islands: the cone-shaped Rangitoto, Motutapu and Waiheke, visible in the distance, as it was a clear day. To the west lay swampy ground and tidal creeks feeding into the Manukau Harbour.

But enough of sightseeing. There was a herd of steers to inspect. Dilworth negotiated a price with the amiable merchant farmer, John Logan Campbell. From there it was a visit to the Hellaby brothers to negotiate the slaughtering and butchering. The tender was submitted in duplicate in a sealed envelope and the contract was duly won and expedited with good profit. Strong demand continued while Her Majesty's troops remained in New Zealand. Other lucrative contracts followed and Dilworth continued showing Kelly the ropes.

There were no more Māori merchants supplying farm produce and the Treasury continued to divert British tax revenue to feed the troops still stationed in the Albert Barracks and around Auckland province. The commissariat was also supplying Taranaki, where renewed fighting had broken out, instigated by Tītokowaru, and in Poverty Bay where troops were pursuing another 'troublesome rebel', Te Kooti.

Dilworth was hurriedly preparing a bid for a contract including the supply of a large quantity of flour. He was, at the time, preparing to meet with Deputy Commissary General Humphrey Stanley-Jones in Alexandra and left Kelly to finalise the tender. Kelly studied Dilworth's calculations. *Thirteen pounds, nine shillings per ton of flour. This is just a purchase price based on previous transactions. But there's been a very large increase in the price of flour on the open market. This won't be enough to win the tender.*

Kelly's doubts were confirmed upon visiting Mr McFarlane, named on the tender document as the miller. McFarlane was happily selling flour at thirty pounds a ton on the open market and had to be persuaded of the wisdom of continuing to deal with Dilworth and the commissary. Kelly hurried back to Dilworth with a negotiated price of twenty-four pounds, eight shillings per ton, which, on Kelly's advice would still win the contract and return a good profit. Kelly's analysis proved to be correct. He had, in fact, saved the deal and Dilworth rewarded his protégée a bonus payment in recognition of his acumen and stewardship of the business.

Dilworth was busily buying more land, in addition to his three hundred acres in Epsom, and investing in various business ventures. He was well aware that the commissary economy would likely have a limited future. On his desk, among various newspapers was a copy of *The Times of London*, open at an article which questioned:

> *... how long the lives of 10,000 English soldiers and over £1,000,000 of money raised by taxes in the United Kingdom annually have been, and will be, under the control of the Legislature of New Zealand, which contributes not one penny to our taxes, which gives not one soldier to our army, which makes and unmakes its own ministers, passes and repeals its own laws and pursues its own policy, without the least references to our wishes, our conveniences, or our interests. We doubt if the whole history of the world can afford a parallel to this portentous phenomenon.*
>
> *We have lost all imperial control in this portion of the Empire and are reduced to the humble but useful function of finding men and money for a Colonial Assembly to dispose of in exterminating natives with whom we have no quarrel, in occupying lands from which we derive no profit, and in attracting to their shores a vast commissariat expenditure, which we have the honour to supply out of the taxes of the*

> *United Kingdom and from which they derive enormous profits. The next Maori war must not be fought with British troops nor paid for out of British taxes.*

Kelly found himself again an office worker, but not in the office of the old mill back in the home country, reeking of boiled flax, when he was a callow youth in a scratchy shirt made of coarse linen from the seconds pile. He'd sat at his desk then, writing up the accounts with ink stained fingers and stolen glances out the window to the factory floor at the girls working the clattering looms—one girl in particular.

Annie was never far from his thoughts, but this was no time for daydreaming. *Focus on the work here and now,* he reminded himself. *Responsibilities to the company. Administrative duties to attend to. A means to an end. Make the future happen.*

He had just received the paperwork on a consignment of rum to the Hamilton military camp, and was concerned to see that a considerable sum of money had been deducted from the sale owing to a shortfall of two hogshead barrels, amounting to over one hundred gallons of rum. He questioned O'Neill on the matter, as it had been one of his deliveries. O'Neill assured him he had delivered the full load to the dock and the barrels must have been stolen overnight.

"And where were you when the rum was stolen?" Kelly asked.

"Well, I wasn't out on the dock freezing my arse off all the night," was O'Neill's reply.

It didn't take much sleuthing to get to the bottom of what had happened; just a few enquiries and some time spent in the field—time that would have been better spent carrying on the business. The quartermaster at the Hamilton headquarters confirmed that there were two barrels missing when the consignment was uplifted in the morning and the shortfall was later made up by another merchant, a Mr. Slater. Kelly inspected all the barrels and found that the two late arrivals bore the same barrel batch numbers as the rest. O'Neill had sold off two barrels to Slater, who watered down the rum and on-sold it to the quartermaster. Kelly confronted O'Neill about the theft.

"Will you tell him?" O'Neill asked.

"No. You will."

"He'll fire me."

"You've brought it on yourself. You shouldn't have bitten the hand that fed you."

"It's all right for you. You're his blue-eyed boy, getting a share of the profits."

"Well, I started off on wages, the same as you and worked my way up."

O'Neill didn't stay to hear any more but left and was never seen again. Dilworth could not abide disloyalty and yet he showed some concern for O'Neill. "Where do you think he's gone?" he asked Kelly.

"I don't know, Sir. Maybe to the goldfields. Do you want to prosecute him?"

"No, no. I'll just write it off as a business loss. Good luck to him."

Kelly had engaged a carpenter, a Mr. Reginald Jackson, to begin rebuilding the home the fire had destroyed and now, with his hard work and good fortune he was assured of completing the build. Under the burnt rubble the charred kauri piles were still firmly anchored into the earth and most were still serviceable for the foundations of the new build. Jackson arrived with a cart load of rough sawn totara and proceeded to lay four by three bearers and joists of the red wood for the subfloor. The proposed floor plan was almost identical to the original building and Kelly was gratified to see his former home gradually taking shape as the carpenter erected the rimu framing. Jackson was a Samuel Parnell man and would not work more than eight hours a day, six days a week, so the building work progressed slowly.

Pania kept Jackson fed and watered and often served as a builder's labourer.

"He thought I was your wife," she told Kelly. "He thought you got a piece of Māori land by marrying me."

Kelly was eventually able to shift his camp from the storehouse into the shell of his new home and he tried his hand at building a table, bookshelf, a double bed, and a few fittings, with a bit of help from Jackson. The whole interior of the house had a pleasing fragrance of rimu, kauri and matai, cleanly cut and dressed, and treated with flaxseed oil. His first employment of his new table, before he'd set any food on it, was to sit and write another letter to Annie, in which he said:

> *Annie, dearest, our new house awaits you and will be empty until you arrive. I have prospered and advanced so well in my employ with Mr Dilworth that I will be able to book a first-class passage for you to Auckland. Just say the word I long to hear and I will send you a remittance certificate, which you can present at the Shaw Saville office in Belfast for a ticket for a steamer to London, that is to say, to the Gravesend dock, and a ticket to board the Mary Shepherd bound for Auckland. There is a sailing at this time next year. We can get married as soon as you arrive. You may tell your parents that I have*

*become a man of means with a fine home. I hope that this will persuade them to let you go.*

Dilworth was a devout Christian and who strictly observed the Sabbath, so no work was done on a Sunday. Kelly and Pania lay languorously together in bed on a Sunday morning.

"So your Irish girl is coming soon?" Pania said.

"Soon? It could be a whole year from now."

"What is she like, your Annie?"

With some mental effort, Kelly shifted his thoughts again from the present Pania to the absent Annie. "She's sweet and kind and hardworking."

"Is she pretty?"

"Yes."

"Prettier than me?"

"Just in a different way."

"In a Pākehā way."

"I suppose so, but Pākehā or Māori—it doesn't matter. Race doesn't matter."

"What matters?"

"Character."

"Character." Pania considered this word. "So Annie is a woman of good character?"

"Yes."

"What about me? Bad character?"

"No."

"Why so few words for me? What kind of character?"

"You? You are also kind." Kelly thought for a moment. "And spirited."

"Ha, spirited, like a wild horse?"

"I wouldn't compare you to a horse."

"Why not. I am your mare. You are my stallion." Pania giggled at Kelly's discomfort with her questions.

*Shall I compare thee to a horse? Shall I compare thee to a summer's day?* There was a dim memory of a Shakespeare poem from Kelly's school days.

"What about Ireland?" Pania asked. "What is Ireland like?"

"It's a good land of green hills and good people, but poor people."

"Are all the people poor?'

"The landowners are rich. And the people are oppressed by the British."

"Just like here. Just like New Zealand. Why are the British so greedy? Bad character?'

"There are good and bad everywhere."

"And the bad are greedy for land and money and power."

"Just so".

On his day of rest Kelly would often ride out along the coast with Pania, past Point Britomart to Mechanics Bay and along the shoreline to Hobson Bay and onto the beach at low tide. Pania often rode to the coast on her own, fishing and foraging, and returned with kaimoana. She always rode astride her horse, as Āwhina did, unlike the Pākehā ladies, who demurely rode side saddle. It would be unseemly for a Pākehā lady to spread her legs over a horse. Kelly was pleased with the way Pania cared for the horses and exercised them with her riding.

"I like riding," she said. "I like the feel of the beast between my legs when I gallop along the beach and the wind in my hair."

She also just liked getting out of the town. She never accompanied Kelly in town and she understood the reason for that. Nor did she go there on her own, not after the day she went to the grocery store. Kelly kept the larder well supplied but Pania was at home making bread and had run out of sugar. The shopkeeper had refused to serve her. "I got money," she'd told him and put the coins on the counter.

At first she stood her ground but the shopkeeper threw the coins on the floor and shouted, "Get out of my store you black whore."

Other customers in the shop complacently watched the performance, adding to the humiliation. Pania felt the eyes of the townsfolk on her still as she walked down the road. Back at home, she went first to the stables and lay on the hay in the company of the horses till the rage in her gut subsided. She never went back to the shops and never told Kelly of the incident.

# 11

The winter in Ireland had thawed to a mild spring, but for Annie Gallagher there was still a chill in the air, with Robert Richardson's return. She had continued working at the grand house as the scullery maid, and while she had the friendship of some of the other servants, the drudgery of her chores was relieved only by time spent with Mrs Theobold, her confidant and tutor.

The sun rose earlier and cast a thin shaft of light through her window. She woke to a dawn chorus of blackbird, thrush and robin and allowed herself a brief morning devotion before she left the warmth of her bed. She never failed to include Finbar in her prayers and never lost the hope of being reunited with him.

Once washed and dressed, she went about her regular duties. The kitchen smelled of soap and ashes as she bent over the scullery sink, with the black coal range spitting at her side. She worked briskly, scrubbing grease from the breakfast pans, the lye stinging her hands raw. As she went about the house carrying out her other chores, she moved quietly and furtively, keeping her head low, lest she encounter Mr Robert.

After her lunch time duties, Mrs Percival ordered her to polish the brass sconces in the corridor leading to the library and in the library itself. The long passage was lined with portraits, faces of Richardsons past, staring down in gilded frames, cold-eyed and self-assured. She was working in the empty library, rag and polish in hand, when the door creaked open and the ominous bulk of Mr Robert filled the doorway. Annie's stomach turned as he entered the room with a glass of brandy in hand.

"Ah, Miss Annie," he slurred. "How nice to see you again. Still hard at work, I see. Not too busy for a friendly chat, I hope."

Annie bowed her head. "Begging your pardon, Sir, I have my duties to attend to."

"Duties can wait." Robert stepped closer, the smell of spirits heavy about him. "It must be lonely for you here, away from family and your fiancé away at the end of the world, if he is still alive. I, on the other hand, am very much present and ready to give you the special attention and comfort you're missing."

Annie's hand tightened on the rag. "I've no wish for any 'special attention', Sir."

Robert set his glass on a desk and grabbed Annie's arm. "You are only a scullery maid. You're nothing, Annie Gallagher, from a poor family, with a criminal brother, run away to America and a fiancé, who has abandoned you and run off to New Zealand. You are nothing, unless I make you something."

He moved to kiss her but she turned her head away and tried to break free of his grasp. Her heart was hammering as she struggled to get away. They both looked to the door as Mrs Theobold entered with an armful of books.

"Mr Richardson! Let the girl go at once." The governess' normally gentle voice was harsh and cutting.

Robert's hand froze, then dropped. His smile flickered. "You mistake me, madam. We were only conversing."

Mrs. Theobold advanced and placed her books on the desk. "I've seen enough. You dishonour your father's house and disgrace yourself. Leave Miss Gallagher to her work, or I shall take this matter to your mother." They knew that his father would just turn a blind eye. They were cut from the same cloth.

"By all means, take it to Mother. I shall tell her how Annie has been flirting with me and leading me on." So Robert had decided to brazen it out. "The upshot will be that Mother will dismiss her to remove the temptation. She so dislikes to see me getting involved with peasant girls."

"And I will tell her the truth of the matter," Mrs Theobold said.

"Mother knows you have a soft spot for the girl and you will stick up for her. She will believe my word above yours."

"That is your hope. Shall we put it to the test?"

"Even if Annie is not dismissed, things will become rather unpleasant for her here when the other servants hear of how she has been getting notions above her station and playing up to me, especially Miss Bridged. She is such a gossip."

"You sir, are a lying scoundrel," Mrs Theobold hissed.

"And proud of it," said Robert airily and then added a parting shot before he left the room. "Your own position here is not guaranteed. I'm sure we could find a new governess more suited to our requirements."

Annie stopped trembling and drew a steady breath. "It was none of my doing. I gave him no encouragement."

"I know. Your mere presence here entices him. Beauty is a blessing but also a curse when it attracts the wrong sort of attention."

"I do try to avoid him."

"Mr Robert is a spoilt man, accustomed to thinking he can do as he pleases. I know you are not to blame for his conduct."

"I thank you for taking my part, Mrs Theobold. You've been a dear friend to me. But Mr Robert is determined to make my position here intolerable and now he even threatens yours."

"Don't worry about me. That's just a bluff. Come straight to me if he troubles you again."

Robert did not make any physical advances on Annie after the confrontation in the library, but it quickly became clear that he had carried out his threat to spread a rumour among the servants that it was she who was making advances on him. Her former friends among the staff were looking at her differently and she encountered tense silences when she entered the kitchen. But none of this mattered now because she had just received Finbar's letter. She shared the letter, as always, with Mrs Theobold.

"See how he says he's prospered so well that he can get me a first-class ticket to New Zealand and we can have a good life together there. I think that now even my parents will agree."

"Oh Annie dear, I do hope so for your sake."

"They must. I'll tell them why I can't stay on working here and why I won't get a reference. They'll see it's for the best."

"I must say it's good to see you smile again."

"To be honest, I'm tired of the drudgery of being a servant. I'll stop at home until I leave for New Zealand. I'd rather work for my parents."

Mrs Theobold gave Annie a hug. "I'll be sad to see you go, dear, but perhaps it is for the best. It's a brave move. I'll pray for you for a safe journey and a happy married life. You certainly deserve it."

"I'm sad to leave you too. I shall always treasure our friendship. And I'll write to you. Thanks to you I can write."

It was a fine spring day when Annie walked off the estate carrying her carpet bag with her few belongings and the precious letters from Finbar folded neatly in the pocket. She looked back one last time at the grand house, like a foreboding fortress behind her. She walked, almost with a spring in her step in the fresh air of the countryside, along the road and the hedge rows, despite the gravel biting through her thin shoes. She was buoyed by a sense of freedom, but then her mood was tempered by a feeling of trepidation as she neared her home and the uncertainty of the reception that awaited her. She went first to the byre when she saw her sister Lizzie milking the house cow.

Lizzie, sitting on her low stool at the cow's flank looked up from her task. "Annie, what are you doing here? Why are you not at the Richardsons?"

"I've left that cursed place for good."

Lizzie frowned. "Da'll not like this. He counted on your wages. He can't go on working as he has. He's getting old and tired."

Inside, their father sat hunched by the hearth, pipe in hand. He looked up, his face weathered and lined from years of toil in the outdoors: farming and the heavy labour of turf cutting.

Annie set down her bag. "I'm sorry Da. I couldn't stay there, not with the way I was treated by Mr Robert. It wasn't safe for me there."

"I suppose you've left without a reference then. A servant girl quitting without a reference. Who'll hire you now? What shame have you brought on us?"

"None," Annie cried, close to tears. "He was molesting me and he lied and blackened my name."

Annie's mother had come in from the kitchen, where she'd been making cheese. She stood silently while her husband had his say and then embraced her daughter. "You poor dear. It's all right."

Then turning to her husband she said, "Don't be harsh on her, Da. She's done the right thing."

"And what'll you do now?" Annie's father persisted.

"I'll help out at home until I leave."

"Leave? Leave for where?"

Annie drew Finbar's letter from her bag and read it aloud.

Her parents and sister were surprised, first of all that she was able to read it, and then by the contents of the letter.

Her father broke the silence that ensued with the comment, "A man of means he says." His tone was more thoughtful than scornful, as previously.

"Ooh, first-class eh. La de da," said Lizzie.

"You've no shortage of other suitors," said her mother, "but you've turned your nose up at them all, as though you'd rather be an old maid. So it's Finbar Kelly or none at all, is it?"

"There are plenty other folk hereabouts would seize the chance," said Lizzie. "You'll still have me at home."

Her mother began to cry. She had lost a son and now she knew she was soon to lose a daughter.

Annie wasted no time in writing a reply to Finbar to go out in the next post. That night she climbed the ladder to the loft, under the thatch of the roof, to her straw mattress bed next to Lizzie's. The smell of peat smoke from the hearth that warmed the cottage wafted into the loft. It was the smell of home.

Annie turned to her sister and said, "Thank you for what you said," and they spoke in whispers of what she'd endured at the Richardson manor and about the new life that lay before her. She lay awake long after Lizzie had fallen asleep, with the excitement and trepidation of the journey ahead. She felt the gulf of distance and time more keenly than ever.

After the first day at home, Annie relieved Lizzie of the milking and took her turn at churning butter and making cheese. She was gratified to also be working out of doors in the garden, planting potatoes and other vegetables. She even helped her father turn the peat turf for drying and stacking up the turf rick. She also resumed her needlework and weaving indoors on wet weather days and in the evenings. Keeping busy helped the time to pass and contribute to the family income and put some money in her purse. Market day in the town was a family enterprise, selling produce and craft work.

When the halcyon days of spring and summer had passed into the autumn days of harvest, Annie began a daily vigil for the post to arrive. The long awaited letter from Finbar with the Shaw Saville remittance certificates would get her the tickets that would transport her far across the seas to a new life that was never far from her mind. The postman rode out from town on horseback with a saddlebag of mail, never stopping at the Gallagher home, until the day he did stop. It could only be Finbar's letter.

It was a dull grey morning, in early November, when the Gallaghers set off together to the Armagh Ulster Railway Station, on the same road they had so often walked to Mass and to the market, with Da pushing a hand cart of produce. Today he carried a single case of Annie's belongings and the bread and cheese her mother had wrapped for the longer journey. There was a chill in the air, a harbinger of winter approaching, and Ma wrapped her shawl close about her against the damp air. The boreen was muddy underfoot from the overnight rain and a drift of mist hung over the low fields. Crows lifted noisily from the stubble of the wheat fields. The family walked together as quietly and sombrely as if they were going to a wake.

Past the neighbouring cottages, with their peat smoking chimneys, and closer to town the road widened and gave way to cobbles. The spire of Saint Patrick's cathedral appeared on the horizon, pointing into the sky, then the rooftops of the town. A smudge of coal smoke marked the railway station, as did its acrid smell as the family approached the stone station building. Inside the echoing bustle of the station hall they sat and waited and prayed. Ma prayed to Our Father in Heaven, to Mother Mary and to Saint Christopher. She fretted and fussed over Annie, and Annie did her best to allay her fears about the dangers of a young woman travelling on her own and her worry of losing contact altogether.

"Yes Ma, I'll guard my case. I won't let it out of my sight. Yes, I'll write letters, but who will read them?"

"Father Ward will read them for us."

"And don't worry Ma. I'll have a first-class cabin on the ship and servants looking after me."

"Well, isn't that a turnaround," Lizzie remarked.

The train arrived with a hiss of steam and clanking steel and a few passengers disembarked. Most were bound for Belfast. The guard's shrill whistle signalled it was time to board. Annie hugged her parents and sister for the last time. It was an emotional farewell. Even her stoic father was teary-eyed. Annie boarded the carriage and went straight to the window to keep her family in view. They stood waving on the platform as the train jolted and pulled away and Annie disappeared into the distance and into the future.

# 12

How the garden had flourished under Pania's care. Flowers and shrubs: the purple hebe at the front, the white clematis twining round the veranda. The vegetable garden: kūmara, cabbages, beans, tomatoes. The plants were living, accusing proof of all the time Pania had been staying in Kelly's home. Āwhina would be rightly concerned about his failure to follow through on their agreement to return Pania to her home in good time. It had been weighing heavily on his conscience. He knew he should have made the return journey to Te Kuiti with Pania as soon as he was fully recovered and fit to travel. He also now had a sum of money to pay Āwhina for the land, having secured a bank loan. He had been preoccupied with the business and with the building of the new house, and he would likely be away from home and from the business for six weeks. But there were other reasons for his delay. It was such a long and arduous journey, especially the overland leg from Alexandra, with the cart. Truth be told, he had also become too comfortable with having Pania stay on as his housekeeper and lover. He finally resolved to face his responsibilities and delay no longer.

He would need to meet with Dilworth to make arrangements for taking leave from work to go back to Te Kuiti. Dilworth hadn't said anything about Pania but Kelly was uncomfortably aware of his disapproval on moral grounds. Mr and Mrs Dilworth attended Saint Mark's Church in Remuera every Sunday and were respected pillars of the community. Kelly had declined their invitation to join them. He had attended church with his family when he was younger but he decided church wasn't for him when he was old enough to have his decisions respected. He had seen enough of religion in Ulster, where Catholics and Protestants were tribally pitted against each other in a divided community. He believed in God, the God of the Bible, and he would say, if he were pressed, that he was a Christian, but not a Protestant or a Catholic. The Dilworths were Anglican and didn't care for all the popish pomp and ritual of Catholicism and actually did not care about denominations either: Catholic or Protestant or whatever. For them there was but one Church, the Church of Jesus Christ. From his recent reading of the Bible, Kelly had come to the same conclusion. He concluded also that he was accountable to God for his conduct.

He went to work early in the morning, as usual, and awaited Dilworth's arrival, with some trepidation, this day, to discuss arrangements for taking Pania back to Te Kuiti.

Dilworth agreed quite readily to Kelly's request for leave from work and said, "I thought you would have taken the girl back sooner."

Dilworth also said that he wished to make a contribution to Āwhina's whānau. Kelly hadn't realised that Āwhina and Dilworth had been attending the same church and had developed a close friendship.

"Take an extra horse and bring Rāwiri back with you," Dilworth added, "if he wants to come and Āwhina is willing to let him go. I wish to offer him a job."

"Well, I'm sure he'd be a better prospect than O'Neill," Kelly remarked.

"Āwhina foresaw the day when Rāwiri and you and I would work together when the time was right. Yes Finbar, there's more to Āwhina than meets the eye, more than Quinn ever knew, or you for that matter, I'm guessing.

"You know the Māori are a deeply spiritual people," Dilworth continued, "and when they turn from their pagan gods to Christianity, to the one true God, some, like Āwhina, become filled with the Holy Spirit. She was well schooled in the Word of God and often, during worship in the church, prophecy would flow from her lips and she would describe visions she saw when the Spirit was on her. She prophesied in Māori and English and in some unknown language. And she saw herself in the future returned to her own people, but it was a future without her husband. She had already grieved for Quinn before he died."

"Are you saying she's a prophet?"

"Yes, a prophetess, if you like."

This was beyond any conception that Kelly had of religion and he had always associated spirits with primitive superstition, but Āwhina didn't fit that mould. "But then I also see many Māori are suspicious of 'the white man's religion' and many who are very anti-Christian."

"Āwhina and many other Māori converted to Christianity as a result of transformational spiritual experiences. But then there are those who see the Church as just seeking to recruit converts to join a denomination. And once committed, more amenable to exploitation. That's the cynical view."

"The churches have acquired a lot of land, one way and another," Kelly said.

"Usually willingly given, but in some cases by devious means, it must be admitted. There are also many Māori now who are grateful to the missionaries for transforming their language into writing and for the gift of literacy. And for brokering peace between some warring tribes."

"What of the Māori prophets like Te Ua Haumēne and Tītokowaru and the Pai Mārire, the Hauhaus who killed the missionary Völkner. He was a

Christian missionary, a man of God. The Hauhaus hanged him from a tree outside his church."

"A man of God he may have been," said Dilworth, "but they hanged him for a spy."

"A spy?"

"He was an informant on the side of their enemies, the British."

"They didn't just hang him," Kelly continued, "they cut off his head, drank his blood and smeared it on their faces. The Hauhau Kereopa ate Völkner's eyes and said, 'This one is Parliament and this one is the Queen and English law.' Pai Mārire is supposed to mean Good and Peaceful. They don't sound very good and peaceful. Are they also Christian?"

"Yes, we've all heard the reports of the gruesome killing in Ōpōtitki." Dilworth sighed. "Your scepticism is understandable. Well, in essence, yes, they are Christian but in some such cases you see a mix of Christianity and elements of traditional Māori religion, which can muddy the waters, and besides, they're still at war in the Taranaki. Kereopa was at war with the British also because his wife and two daughters were killed in the raid on Rangiaowhia and his sister was killed the next day at Hairini.

"But, anyway, I believe Āwhina is a pure spirit, at least I hope she still is. They've gone through a terrible ordeal with the war and I fear they're suffering great deprivation and hardship. By all means, go to the King Country before your fiancée arrives."

And indeed they were hard times in Te Kuiti and throughout the King Country. They were times of hunger, disease and death. But the remnant in exile grew stronger again as the land was cultivated and brought forth food.

As Kelly and Pania entered the village, Āwhina and Rāwiri came out to greet them.

"I've been expecting you for some time," Āwhina said.

"It's been a busy time with work and building the new house," Kelly said.

Āwhina was unconvinced but welcoming nonetheless.

"Pania has been so helpful. I'm very grateful to her and to you for letting her stay.

Oh, and Dilworth sends his greetings to you both and to you Rāwiri, a job offer. He wants me to bring you back to Auckland to work for him."

"How much would I get paid?"

"Fifteen shillings per week to start with, plus accommodation."

Rāwiri looked to his mother.

"A good offer." she said.

Rāwiri nodded thoughtfully. "I'll think about it."

Tāwhiao and his whānau of supporters were campaigning for the return of Waikato land. There were many hui to plan strategies, to take legal action, to get justice. A hui was convened in the wharenui to draft a petition to Government while Kelly was staying with Āwhina. Among the kōrero there were some dissenting voices, none louder than Hāmana's. He sprang to his feet, clutching his taiaha, to address the meeting.

"You waste your time with petitions," he shouted. "Why do we beg the thieves to return our property? The government will not return any land they have taken. They say it is settler land now and cannot be returned. You petition the Queen and she says she can do nothing and it is a matter for the colonial government. They have stolen our land and left us here to starve. They will come after our land here in the Rohe Pōtae too. There is no end to their greed. They will not rest till they have all our land."

Hāmana was taking a stand against Tāwhiao on the issue of land and government. That was all that Kelly could discern of his tirade. That word *whenua* recurred. Rāwiri at his side provided translation.

"We will protect what remains," Tāwhiao insisted, "and we will not give up our fight for justice."

"They confiscate our land to punish us for our rebellion," Hāmana continued, pacing back and forth in front of the assembly. "Why are we rebels? Because we would not give up our land and we try to protect our homes. And because we have a King they say we rebel against the Queen, the Queen who promised to protect us. What of the kūpapa who fought with the government against us, the 'loyal' Māori?" He was gurning with contempt. "The government has taken their land too. The government and the Treaty that made us subjects of the Queen and promised to protect us and protect our ownership of the land. The Treaty is a lie. I say we have no use for Queen or King."

"We cannot fight them anymore," Tāwhiao said. "They are too many for us. We can only fight them in the courts."

"The courts!" Hāmana hissed. "The Land Court is a monster they have created to devour more land."

"What would you have us do?"

"You can write your petitions. I will not lie down and wait for the government to take the last of our land. I will fight. Ka whawhai tonu ahau, āke, āke, āke." It was the same defiant boast of Rewi Maniapoto at Ōrākau.

"That will justify the government taking the land," Tāwhiao said, glaring at Hāmana.

"They will take it anyway."

"So you will fight them by yourself," Āwhina said.

"I will join Tītokowaru at Te Ngutu o te Manu and others will follow."

Āwhina feared for her reckless brother but feared more for her son. Rāwiri looked up to his uncle and she feared he would follow him. He wanted to have the mana of a warrior.

"Do not follow Tītokowaru. He has lost his way. He has given up on Pai Mārire, the way of Righteousness and Peace. He has given up on Christianity and gone back to the old ways of heathenism, utu and cannibalism."

Hāmana responded: "Yes, Tītokowaru tried Christianity but the so-called Christian colonists were the thieves that Jesus warned had 'come to steal, kill and destroy.' Tītokowaru tried peace, even giving up some land and still the government sent McDonnell and the dogs of war to kill and rape and take more Ngāti Ruanui land and raid his village.

"It was Tītokowaru's utu to kill settlers and soldiers and he boasted he had eaten their flesh, like the flesh of a cow. Then he said, 'I shall not die. When death itself is dead I shall be alive.' He attacked the garrison at Turuturumokai and cut the heart out of the body of the commander, an offering to the god Tūmatauenga. Tītokowaru strikes fear throughout Whanganui and all of Taranaki. Why should we live in fear?" Hāmana challenged. "Let the Pākehā fear us!"

"Does he think he will live forever?" said Āwhina, scornfully. "Has he become a god? He is only a man and he will die like all men." She spoke with authority and was obviously accorded great respect in the community. She stood tall in a long skirt, blouse and shawl, all in black, in mourning for her husband, and likely for the many of her whānau who had perished in the fighting. Kelly's heart went out to her. She was careworn and thinner, but otherwise little changed in appearance, but he was aware of the regal bearing she carried here and of deeper dimensions that Dilworth had intimated.

# 13

Hāmana and Ngārimu journeyed to Taranaki, to Hawera, then Okaiawa and finally to Te Ngutu o te Manu, Tītokowaru's fortified village of many whare and a large marae. After they had undergone the protocol of the wero, they were admitted into the pā. They joined Tītokowaru in the wharenui, just rebuilt after it had been burnt down by Pākehā militia. The villagers had been driven out in the raid and the people not long returned. Hāmana and Ngārimu were immediately drafted into preparing for an imminent second attack.

"They will come again," Tītokowaru said, "the white soldiers, Mc Donnell, Hunter, Manu rau and the kūpapa traitor, Te Keepa."

"I know of Te Keepa –Major Kemp," said Hāmana, "but who is this Manu rau?"

"Manu rau, Major von Tempsky, a foreign Pākehā soldier, so named Hundred Birds for his great skill in flitting quickly about in bush combat."

A day passed with fighting drills on the marae under the watchful eye of Tītokowaru. Hāmana and Ngārimu joined Tītokowaru's warriors in a fierce haka taua in front of the pā. They shouted 'Kia kutia!' Draw together! and they barked, 'Au! Au!' They were the dogs of war. They did not fear death. They were invincible. With powerful incantations they would raise their hands and ward off bullets. 'Hapa! Hapa!' Pass over! 'Pai Mārire!'

Tītokowaru stood before warriors assembled on the marae, a commanding figure, despite his unremarkable appearance: average height and build, but wiry with muscle. His face was plain, not even a tā moko, but battle scarred with a wound from a shell splinter that took out his right eye at Sentry Hill. He raised his tokotoko, wizard-like, and cast his one good eye over the men. He passed Hāmana by, a newcomer, but the tokotoko, would not pass over him. It returned to him. It lighted on him. It chose him as one of the Tekau mā rua, of the Hau Hau, 'the Twelve' of Tītokowaru's inner circle. The twelve disciples of Tītokowaru.

Tītokowaru sat in the wharenui in the evening, praying and chanting and saw the coming evil. "Prepare for battle in the morning!"

Tītokowaru was well prepared this time. He had envisioned the arena of the coming battle and set his defences, concealed in front of the pā. Hāmana waited within a hollow tree. He gathered more strength from the embrace of the tree, the strength of Tāne Mahuta and Tūmatauenga, Tū of the angry face, Tū of hunting and killing. Quietly he chanted:

*Taku uaua ko te rangi e tū nei*
*Taku uaua ko Papa e takoto nei*
*Whiri kaha, toro kaha te uaua.*
*My sinew is like the sky above.*
*My sinew is like the earth below.*
*Let my sinews gather strength and exert strength.*

Nearby, Ngārimu, and forty others in trees and pits, at one with the rākau, the trees, and Papatūānuku, the earth. Another twenty in the pā. They all waited. Hāmana thanked the gods who led them there, he and Ngārimu; led them from the defeated refugees in the Rohe Pōtae to the undefeated warriors of Tītokowaru in Taranaki, led them there for such a time as this, to stand with Tītokowaru at Te Ngutu o te Manu against the invasion of the Pākehā soldiers. To defend the pā with their lives.

The white soldiers came just as Tītokowaru had said. Birds rising from the trees heralded their approach and then the waiting warriors heard them bashing the bush. Mc Donnell and his men appeared in the clearing. The soldiers saw only trees and the pā beyond. They did not see the rifles in the loopholes of the trees and the crossfire from the pits in the ground. The warriors cut down many soldiers and rushed out to attack the rest. Ngārimu was at Hāmana's side and he fell as a bullet passed through his upraised hand and through his neck. Did he forget his incantations? Hāmana avenged his comrade with a blast of his tūpara and killed another soldier with the other barrel. The breach loading carbines of the white soldiers were faster than the muzzle loading muskets of the defenders, but not fast enough. Hāmana drew his pātītī from his belt and rushed a soldier before he could get his rifle to his shoulder. This was the bloody handed, head slashing killing he relished.

The white soldiers were in confusion. Hunter shouted to attack the pā. McDonnell ordered them to fall back with the wounded. Manu rau ordered his Forest Rangers to take cover and he openly stood his ground. Did he think he could ward off bullets with his curved sword? It did not take long for a bullet to find him. One of his men rushed to his dying leader and was also shot. Then another and another till they were lying in a heap. Hāmana finished Manu rau himself with a blow of his patītī. Now he had his sword and revolver. The white soldiers fled into the bush. The warriors gave chase and killed more.

Many lay dead on both sides but only three of Tītokowaru's own. The warriors laid the white bodies on the marae. Tītokowaru called out, "Fetch my Pākehā, Tu-nui-a-moa." They brought the white slave from the hut where he had been incarcerated for his own protection. He walked along the line of corpses and stopped at the feet of one wearing long leather boots. He looked into the pale face shrouded in long, curly hair, matted with blood, and declared, "It is Major Von Tempsky."

Hāmana jumped to his feet and shouted, "Yes, it is Manu rau!" and he fired the Major's revolver. Tītokowaru had taken away his sword.

"Let us cook Manu rau," someone shouted.

"Let us eat his heart," another shouted.

But Tītokowaru forbade it. Manu rau's mana was too great for such indignity. "But feast on these others," he said. "Take one body for each iwi. Consume them. Excrete them from your body. Destroy their mana. Remember your first king. Remember his name: Pōtatau Te Wherowhero Kai Tangata. Kai Tangata, Man Devourer. Forget his son, Tāwhio. Forget the Kīngitanga. They have lost their appetite for fighting."

Two Ngā Rauru warriors dragged a body to the hāngī pit and cooked it on the hot stones. They served the meat in flax kete. Some ate the man meat. Some did not. But the whole body was consumed. Hāmana ate one of the hands, with its fingers clawed from the roasting. Tītokowaru did not partake. His mana was too great to be defiled by human flesh. They piled the other bodies into a heap, starting with Manu rau, and burnt them. The air was filled with smoke and the aroma of cooking and burning flesh and bodies exploding in the flames.

With the white soldiers gone back to Whanganui, the Tekau mā rua spread out on the land and raided the settler farms. They were the twelve tribes of Israel, repossessing the land. They were the scourge of Taranaki. Governor Bowen placed a bounty of a thousand pounds on the head of

Tītokowaru. Tītokowaru placed a bounty of two shillings and six pence on the head of Governor Bowen.

Tītokowaru's mana increased and he was joined by more warriors: the fearsome Big Kereopa and more Ngā Rauru warriors. He abandoned Te Ngutu o te manu and built a new pā at Moturoa. He commanded all the Taranaki grassland to the coast and drove the Pākehā settlers off his land. McDonnell came from Wairoa with his soldiers and Te Keepa with Whanganui Māori. Tītokowaru defeated them again as he did at Te Ngutu o te manu.

The Pākehā of Whanganui lived in fear of Tītokowaru. McDonnell had failed them. Major General Whitmore came to defend Whanganui and defeat Tītokowaru—the Whitmore who failed to catch Te Kooti in the Ureweras. The soldiers of Whanganui grew stronger with more officers: Lieutenent John Bryce, Captain Newland, and Sergeant Maxwell, a farmer whose house the Tekau mā rua had burnt to the ground.

The tribe did not remain at Moturoa to be attacked again. They moved to Taurangaika and built their greatest pā yet. They cut and set poles upright in a trench and lashed them together for a palisade. Tu-nui-a-moa, wearing only a loincloth, was working alongside Hāmana. The sun had darkened his skin but it was still the skin of a Pākehā. There were stripes and welts across his back.

"I see you have the scars of a slave," Hāmana said.

"It's true, I am a slave," Tu-nui-a-moa said, "but Tītokowaru treats me kindly. I got my lashings from my masters in the Queen's army for being a deserter."

"You want to help us kill Pākehā?"

"I don't want to help them kill more Māori to take more land."

"Don't you want to go back to your own people?"

"You are my people now. If I went back, they would kill me for being a traitor."

"Better to be a live slave, eh," Hāmana said. "You are a Pākehā but you speak te reo Māori and you have a Māori name. What is your Pākehā name?"

"Kimble Bent. I was Kimble Bent. Now I am Tu-nui-a-moa."

In three days and nights they built the stockades, trenches, bunkers, parapets and rifle pits. The fighting force grew with more Ngā Rauru from Perekama. They welcomed the warriors onto the marae with pōwhiri and hākari. Their children mingled with those of the pā. Three of the younger boys, not yet warriors, Ihaka Takarangi, Kīngi Takatua and Akuhata Herewini led new boys around the pā and out to hunt for pigs and geese at an abandoned farm. While the men were still preparing the hāngi they heard shots in the distance and ran with their weapons to find the boys. It was at the remains of Handley's Farm where they saw the mounted soldiers, led by Bryce and Maxwell and they fled as the warriors approached. Then they found the boys: Akuhata, shot in the back, Ihaka shot in the thigh and wounded with a sabre slash, but still alive; Kingi with his head split by a sabre from the top to his neck.

The warriors burned for utu to avenge the slaughter of their children but Tītokowaru would not be drawn into attacking in the open away from the pā. The Tekau mā rua rode out raiding, killing, looting and burning settler farms on their confiscated land. Whitmore's soldiers, likewise attacked undefended Māori villages.

Tītokowaru wrote a letter to Whitmore:

> *Salutations to you. This is to ask you whom does England belong to, and to whom belongs the land or country you are now standing upon?*

> *I will tell you; the heavens and the earth were made at one time. In one day was man created, and all productions of any kind that are in the world; and if you think or are aware that God created all, it is well, we are equal thereon. You were formed a European and England was named as your country; we are Māoris, in New Zealand. Bethink you—there has been placed between you and me a great barrier—an ocean. Why did you not consider, or take thought, before you crossed over here? I did not come from here over to you. Stand away from my place to your own country in the middle of the ocean; go away from the town to some other place. Arise and be baptised, and let your sins be washed away, calling upon the name of the Lord.*
>
> *Sufficient, from Tītokowaru*

The two warriors he sent to deliver the letter were seized and imprisoned.

Hāmana agreed with Tītokowaru. "The missionaries came with their Bible and their god. They told us to look to the heavens while the Pākehā stole the land from under our feet. Āwhina says the missionaries are men of God and men of peace. She has embraced the Pākehā God and turned her back on our gods, our atua. She married a Pākehā soldier and had his baby, a half-blood, neither Maori nor Pākehā."

Tītokowaru grew ever stronger with support of many chiefs and many warriors within his fortress. But in one stroke he lost his mana and lost his allies, by taking the wife of another chief to his bed. Hāmana saw her himself leaving his tent at night. It was Tītokowaru's cousin, Puaraurangi. There was much kōrero from Puaraurangi's husband and his men that Tītokowaru was a fornicator and betrayer, no longer a prophet, no longer their military leader. They said they would execute him, but after more kōrero, they abandoned Tītokowaru and the pā. Too much korero and too much raruraru for Hāmana's liking. *Men fight wars over land and lose them over women.*

Whitmore was building an army with the Whanganui warriors of that ruthless bastard Te Keepa to attack the pā and Tītokowaru knew the balance of power and fortune had shifted against him. They that were left followed Tītokowaru's orders to abandon the pā when the shelling began at dawn. In two groups, they fled into the bush at the back of the pā. In the first group, women and children and Tu-nui-a-moa, with his Māori wife, Rihi. Rihi's sister, Ngahuia, fled carrying her newborn baby.

Hāmana stayed close by Tītokowaru with Big Kereopa in the second group to ambush the soldiers Whitmore sent after them—Whitmore shouting, "Five pounds per head of Hauhau warriors and ten pounds for the head of a chief."

The fugitives made their way through the bush to the Waitōtara River and set an ambush in a peach grove. Hāmana shot a soldier reaching for a ripe peach and tomahawked another. They gorged themselves on peaches and relieved their hunger, then retreated further into the bush, with kete full of peaches. Tītokowaru retreated further into himself. They were tired. Even Big was exhausted. They hacked their way through the undergrowth, through tangles of supplejack and clinging vines of barbed bush lawyer. Some lost their way in the trackless bush and probably some deserted. The group of survivors were cold and wet in heavy rain, hiding in a makeshift camp near the Pātea River.

Hāmana went off on his own in the morning to the river and crept along the bank till he spotted an eel slithering languidly in the dark water shaded by overhanging trees. Wading stealthily and groping under the bank, he managed to grab two eels and toss them up onto the bank, where he decapitated them with his patītī. He followed the river upstream to a wider, shallower run, where he spotted a Pākehā crouching over the water. The Pākehā could not hear him approach above the sound of the running water. He raised his patītī ready to strike, when he saw the scars on his back. It was Tu-nui-a-moa snatching at freshwater crayfish. He slipped his patītī back into his belt and said, "Not much of a feed in those little kōura."

"I hope to eat Maine lobsters again one day," Tu-nui-a-moa said.

"Where are the others?"

"Somewhere in the bush. We've become scattered. Only Rihi and Ngahuia and her baby are still with me," he said, and they appeared at his side. They consumed the eels back at the camp, along with fern roots they'd foraged in the bush. Tu-Nui used the eel bladders for cartridge cases, in place of the usual newspaper wrappings. He was still Tītokowaru's manufacturer of ammunition.

Whitmore and his soldiers passed close by the camp and the fugitives cowered in silence. Ngahuia's baby cried and she put it to her breast but she had no more milk to give, so she smothered her baby to stifle its crying, and sobbed silently herself. Whitmore drove his soldiers on relentlessly. Hāmana thought Whitmore had a demon driving him. He felt the presence of Whiro, darkness and death, and in his weakness, prayed to Tūmātauenga for strength and Haumia-tikitiki for sustenance. He feared his body would return to Papatūānuku, to the earth, and his spirit to Te Reinga Wairua. The soldiers passed by and Big declared, "Ka ora. Ka ora. We will live." The survivors rested in the camp for the day and overnight, huddled together on beds of ferns on the cold, damp ground.

Shots were fired into the camp at dawn and those who were not killed fled again into the bush. It was Te Keepa, tracking them like a dog, and the Whanganui kūpapa bounty hunters. The dead were decapitated, not only by Te Keepa's men but also by the Pākehā Armed Constabulary, eager for trophy heads and bounties.

Tītokowaru addressed his band of survivors: "Do not despair. We will find sanctuary at Otautu and continue to Te Ngaere."

They were given food and shelter for the night in Otautu. Tītokowaru sat in a whare chanting, calling on Hinepukohurangi to come and spread her mist blanket over them to conceal them from their enemies. Hāmana woke with the light of dawn, an eerie half-light of heavy mist that had come down from the hills. Tītokowaru crawled through the low doorway of the whare and stood outside sniffing the air. "Death lurks in the mist."

Whitmore and Te Keepa descended on the village with their troops, still hunting their prey. The fugitives ran from the village through the mist to the edge of the cliff face above the Pātea River. Big pulled Hāmana down below a ledge. "Stay low. The soldiers shoot into the mist and their bullets pass over our heads. We shoot back and hold them in the village."

The standoff went on for over two hours, while the women took exhausted children and wounded down the cliff to the river. Ngahuia still carried her dead baby. Those who could not swim across were ferried in a single waka. As the fog lifted, the rearguard, made their escape. The trek to Te Ngaere was beyond the endurance of some and their numbers grew fewer. At Te Ngaere they came to a vast swamp and only Tītokowaru knew the safe route to the three villages on solid ground in the heart of the wetlands.

Whitmore and Te Keepa finally left off the chase, but returned when they learned of Tītokowaru's whereabouts. They were confounded by the impenetrable swamp and Whitmore ordered his men to construct fascines to lay a path to traverse the boggy ground. While the soldiers slugged their way to the village, the last hundred or so of Tītokowaru's followers, made their way back to Taranaki with replenished ammunition.

But they had no need of bullets now. Whitmore was gone, ordered to New Plymouth, where the Pākehā feared an invasion from Ngāti Maniapoto. Tītokowaru had finally had enough of war and returned to the way of Pai Mārire. He answered the call of the pacifist prophets, Te Whiti-o-Rongomai and Tohu Kākahi, who were building a citadel, as the new Jerusalem, a refuge for the dispossessed. The remnant, the lost tribe, followed Tītokowaru to Parihaka, where all who wished to live in peace were welcome. Hāmana went back to Te Kuiti.

# 14

Kelly's travelling companion back to Auckland was not the callow youth of former Auckland days. Rāwiri had grown in stature and maturity and had developed much of the regal bearing of his mother. Āwhina had devoted herself to supporting the Kīngitanga's efforts to protect what was left of their land and also to the education of her son. Rāwiri had become quite proficiently literate in English as well as te reo Māori and well-schooled in biblical studies. He had acquired practical knowledge of farming from working the land and some understanding of politics from being immersed in the highly charged Kīngitanga environment.

Kelly found Rāwiri thoughtful and, at times, challenging. He had many questions about the business, about Auckland, about the war, politics and religion, and about his Aunt Pania. Kelly had questions for him, about his beliefs and about Āwhina.

"I believe in God, the God of the Bible," Rāwiri said, "just as Māmā does. I respect her faith, but I will not make the same mistake that Tāmihana made by believing that the colonial government and all Pākehā are Christian and therefore honourable people."

Rāwiri stayed with Kelly at first and later moved into a cottage that Dilworth had got for him on the Great South Road, near his own home. There were plenty of vacant houses with tenants returning to farms after the war and rents were cheap. Auckland was going through a time of depression since the seat of the government had gone to Wellington and the Imperial troops had been recalled. There was a general downturn in commerce and less commissariat business. However, Dilworth's farms continued to do good business and he had diversified and invested in a number of other businesses, including New Zealand railway companies. The railway in Auckland cut through his estate, for which he received generous compensation from the government.

Dilworth was an astute investor but it was from the buying of land that he derived most of his wealth. He purchased properties throughout the Auckland province and some further afield, including 225,000 acres in the Waihou, Upper Thames Valley, in partnership with another Ulsterman, Joseph Ward. As a businessman, Dilworth was scrupulously honest and he was a generous philanthropist and supporter of movements such as the YMCA. But always at the back of Kelly's mind was the knowledge that the land Dilworth bought had first been acquired from its Māori owners, much of it by dubious means, if not outright seizure and theft. And many of the original owners were suffering from the loss of land that had been their home and their economic base.

Rāwiri worked with Kelly at first and then took over the management of cropping and grazing on the Dilworth estate. The stables and care of the horses continued to be the responsibility of young Bert Grabham, who had been the groom and wrangler since before Kelly started working for Dilworth.

Kelly continued to manage the warehouse, shipping and distribution of imports and produce. He managed the business well, as usual, but his particular interest in shipping at this time was the arrival of the Shaw Saville chartered Mary Shepherd, which was sailing from Gravesend under the command of Captain Croot with a cargo of one hundred and seven passengers, including one young Irish woman, Annie Gallagher. The ship would call first at the Bay of Islands, then at Auckland.

It was a cloudy autumn morning on the fifth of March, 1867, when Kelly and the Dilworths joined a crowd gathering expectantly at Queen's Wharf to await the arrival of the ship. The wharf was familiar territory to Kelly, with its storage sheds, cranes and winches, where coastal steamers were loaded and unloaded. Familiar also were the smells of tar, wet rope, horse dung and salt air. Harbour boats, barges and square-rigged ships were docked at the wharf. Masts and spars swayed with the rocking of boats at anchor, rigging humming and slapping in the breeze. A customs skiff and lighters stood by to meet the Mary Shepherd.

People milled about on the wharf, chatting and keeping an eye out for the appearance of the ship out at sea.

"There she is," a boy shouted. "I see her."

The chattering of the crowd ceased momentarily as they gazed as one, out to sea. Kelly scanned the horizon. The dark shape of the ship and the light sails appeared in the distance and gradually grew larger. As she approached the harbour, the crew shortened the sails. The three tall masts were almost bare, with topsails furled, fore and mainstay sails only, drawing enough wind to ease her into the Waitematā harbour. She anchored in the deeper water of the stream in the outer harbour and the crew brought the longboat and cutters alongside to ferry the passengers to the wharf.

Kelly watched from the wharf as passengers gathered on the deck—men, women and children, and descended the companion ladder, one at a time, into the waiting longboat. The sailors rowed the open boat to the wharf and Kelly searched the faces of the women passengers as it approached. Each young woman was Annie, for a moment—and then wasn't. The first-class passengers disembarked first and their luggage: sea chests and trunks followed in a lighter. A gentleman in a waistcoat and rolled up shirt sleeves was assisting another up the companion ladder and onto the wharf. The man who had struggled up the ladder sat on the wharf to catch his breath. He was clearly unwell.

As the last of the passengers left the longboat, Kelly asked the crewman at the bow, "Are you going back for the rest of the first-class passengers now?"

"No Sir," the sailor replied. "That's the last of them. There's only the steerage passengers now."

"There must be some mistake," Kelly said. "I'm waiting for a passenger who travelled first-class—a young woman named Annie Gallagher."

"Perhaps she's in one of the cutters."

Two cutters docked, crowded with steerage passengers: mostly young single men, some couples, babes in arms, and a few unaccompanied young women. None of them was Annie. Some looked a little worse for wear, dazed and bedraggled and unsteady on their feet, after one hundred and fifteen days at sea. Kelly watched as they climbed onto the wharf. All looked relieved and hopeful. He fretted and exchanged nervous glances with the Dilworths. A young woman squealed with delight as she ran to the waiting arms of a man on the wharf.

The gentleman who had helped the ailing passenger onto the wharf approached Kelly and asked, "Are you Finbar Kelly, fiancé of Annie

Gallagher?" He introduced himself as Doctor Clarance Chapman, Ship's Surgeon.

The fear that had lain dormant within Kelly rose suddenly again into his chest.

"Annie has been suffering quite badly from dysentery and seasickness," said the doctor, "and she's rather dehydrated and too weak to walk unaided. We'll bring her over on a stretcher."

Kelly looked desperately into the doctor's vapid face. "Will she be all right?

"Yes, yes, she should make a full recovery," the doctor assured Kelly.

"Take me to her, please."

Kelly and the doctor got into the longboat and were rowed to the ship.

The doctor told Kelly, "Some of the passengers contracted dysentery during our brief stopover at Saint Helena. Annie and a couple who had befriended her on the voyage became quite ill. The other couple went ashore at the Bay of Islands."

The breeze was blowing fresher and Kelly gripped the gunwale to steady himself against the pitching of the boat in the chop.

"I'm sure Annie will be all right once she's ashore and rested, and regains her appetite," the doctor continued. "She'll need a bit of building up. She looks frail but she has an inner strength. I can attest to that. I treated one of our steerage passengers for a head wound, a drunken troublemaker, who accosted Annie on the deck. He claimed she assaulted him. I'm inclined to believe Annie's account that he had groped her and she had pushed him away. He fell on the slippery deck and struck his head on the railing. Mr Cowell, the third mate put him in irons and we put him ashore at Kororāreka to join the other reprobates there."

The longboat pulled up to the ship's ladder, the boat rising and falling in the swell. The doctor mounted the ladder on the rise and Kelly followed in like manner. They went below decks, aft, past the saloon, down a dimly lit companion way. The doctor stopped outside a cabin, with its door ajar. "Here we are."

Kelly followed him into the small room, where a matron in an apron, with a basin and a washcloth, attended to the patient. A shaft of light from the porthole illumined a bottle of cloudy barley water and a smaller, darker bottle of laudanum, on a side table. There in the midst of the reek of vomit and faeces, the anguish of what Kelly had stoically endured in war and the uncertainty of waiting broke forth suddenly in heart wrenching weeping. He knelt down and embraced the wan, waiflike Annie, prostrate on a cot, clutching a string of rosary beads.

"Oh Annie, my darling, finally you're here with me." Kelly clutched her hand. "We'll be together now, always."

"Finbar." Her voice was faint, as though still far away. "I'm so happy to see you." "But I'm so unwell, I'm sorry, I can't get up."

"You'll soon be well again, now you're here."

The doctor stood by, now quiet and impassive.

"We've had a lot of sickness on the voyage," said the matron, "and two births— fortunately no deaths."

They carried Annie on a canvas stretcher up onto the deck. The doctor strapped the patient securely into the stretcher and a crewman rigged it to the yard arm with rope and tackle. The crew in the longboat kept it steady against the hull of the ship. One stood in the boat and shouted, "Lower it." Then, "Stop! Hold." He held the trailing guide rope and struggled to control the swaying and turning of the load while it was out of reach. Kelly clenched his jaw as the stretcher swung and thudded against the ship's hull. The crewman standing in the boat timed the rise of the swell to receive the stretcher. "Lower now!" he shouted, then grappled the stretcher into position on the boat. The crew secured it midship across the thwarts, for the trip to the wharf. Kelly crouched over Annie to shield her from the spray and held her as steady as he could as the crew pulled at the oars and the boat pitched into the waves.

At the wharf, the stretcher was hoisted from the boat by a loading crane. Kelly had received many goods from that crane, but none so precious as the cargo now brought onto the wharf. They carried the stretcher to a waiting carriage. Dilworth had already fetched her luggage, a single case, which had been unloaded from the lighter onto the dock. The carriage departed, not to the hospital, but to the Dilworths' residence, where Annie would receive the best of professional nursing care in an environment free of contagion.

Kelly visited Annie daily at the Dilworths. Day by day the invalid regained her strength. Colour returned to her pallid face and vitality again shone in her eyes. She walked about outdoors in the fresh air as soon as she was able and helped Isabella tend the rose garden. Isabella always wore a bonnet out of doors and ensured that Annie did likewise to protect her fair skin from the harsh New Zealand sun. Isabella was her constant companion.

Dilworth was glad of the opportunity to get first hand news of what was happening in Ireland, since his usual source, the newspaper *The Irish People,* had been closed down. Like most of the Irish, he was an ardent supporter of the Irish Republican Brotherhood. Annie's news was that the Fenians were demanding autonomy from British rule to be self-governing and hundreds of Fenian 'rebels' had been arrested and were being held indefinitely without trial.

"A familiar story," Dilworth reflected as they all strolled about the grounds together. "As in Ireland and India, so in New Zealand—Britain's taking the Empire to the antipodes."

"Do the Māoris want independence?" Annie asked.

"They were promised self-governing autonomy when they signed the Treaty."

"Well, there's hope, for Home Rule in Ireland I mean, with Parnell and Davitt and the Irish Land League."

"Good luck to them," said Dilworth, "but you know the Brits will fight to keep control."

# 15

Kelly brought Annie from the Dilworths to his home, to proudly show her around what would soon be their new home and he served tea to his guest at the dining room table.

"Not as grand as the Dilworths', but I think it'll do." Having toyed with Kelly for a moment, Annie laughed and hugged him. "I love it. I can't wait."

"We don't need to wait. We could get married tomorrow in the registry office."

"Now, you know we're not going to do that, Finbar. It'll be a proper church wedding at Saint Mark's Anglican Church in Remuera. Isabella's already busy making the arrangements. I'd always thought I'd be married in the Catholic Church but it doesn't seem to matter so much now we're away from Ireland."

"It's a compromise for the both of us then."

"I'm happy to get married in the Dilworths' church. They've been so kind and supportive. Isabella's even got a seamstress to sew a gown for me."

"Well, she'll never have the pleasure of seeing a child of her own get married."

"She also asked if we'd like to have a prenuptial meeting with Reverend Heywood."

"I've no objection to that."

"You know you'll be expected to make a declaration of faith."

"I can declare my faith in God. You know I've always believed in God, the creator of the universe, and all that. I just wonder why He's become so remote from His creation, and why there's so much injustice and suffering in the world."

"Why have you not been attending church here, Finbar?"

"I suppose I doubted that God was to be found in the Church. But I will happily repeat the vows in the church and obtain the blessing of the Church and hopefully the blessing of God Himself, *having put the affair with Pania behind me,* he thought to himself, but made no mention of her.

It was a small but formal ceremony. Kelly had invited a few parishioners in his own neighbourhood that he had got to know: the Taits, the Osbornes, the Bucklands, and Secombe, the brewer, all well-known to the Dilworths too. And Rāwiri.

James Dilworth, as a stand-in father of the bride, led Annie into the church on his arm. She looked quite angelic in her white gown, with its flowing train and gauzy veil. Kelly wore a suit on the day for the first time in his life, complete with a long frock coat and a top hat. It was either a suit or the uniform of the Imperial Army, which he swore he would never wear again.

Reverend Heywood welcomed the wedding party with a benediction, which Kelly had heard before, the same words that Āwhina had spoken when he left her at Te Kuiti:

> *May the grace of the Lord Jesus Christ and the Love of God and the fellowship of the Holy Spirit be with you all.*

The Reverend then began the ceremony with the words:

> *In the presence of God, Father, Son and Holy Spirit,*
> *we have come together*
> *to witness the marriage of Anne Marie Gallagher and Finbar Tomas Kelly,*
> *to pray for God's blessing on them,*
> *and to celebrate their love.*

He spoke of the Holy Spirit as though he were a real person and actually present with them and spoke of grace and blessings as though they were supernatural powers to bring protection and good things into the lives of believers. Kelly had never considered that the words of the Bible had a real life outside of the Bible, but something in the way the Reverend spoke of 'the spirit of the living God' touched his own spirit.

Of the various scriptures that the Reverend read during the ceremony, one in particular, from Ecclesiastes, also struck a chord with Kelly:

> *Two are better than one; because they have a good reward for their labour. For if they fall, the one will lift up his fellow: but woe to him that is alone when he falleth; for he hath not another to help him up. Again, if two lie together, then they have heat: but how can one be warm alone?*

Kelly could not help thinking of the many nights Pania had warmed his bed. He struggled now to put her out of his thoughts—thoughts that conflicted and convicted. He tugged at his shirt collar as heat was rising now in his body.

Before leading the bridal couple in their exchange of vows Reverend Heywood made the customary announcement: *If there is anyone present who can show just cause why these two persons may not be joined in matrimony, speak now or forever hold your peace.*

He completed the formality and was about to move on to the exchange of vows and rings, when a voice boomed from the back of the church. "I will speak."

A Māori couple made their way to the front, the man gripping the arm of the young woman, leading her, almost dragging her, he with a tattooed face and she with eyes downcast. "I am Hāmana Waharoa," he said, "and this is my sister Pania. She is carrying Kelly's child."

Gasps and murmuring reverberated around the church.

"Is this true?" the Reverend asked Kelly.

"I… I don't know," Kelly stammered.

"Is it possible?" the Reverend asked.

Kelly wiped his brow. "It may be."

The Reverend addressed the congregation: "This is very unexpected. I… we must adjourn for a moment, if you will excuse us." He then led Kelly, Annie and the two unexpected guests into the adjoining vestry.

Hāmana pulled Pania's dress tightly against her bulging belly and said, "You see?"

"Yes, it's true," Kelly said disconsolately. "I have committed this sin. I have confessed it before God."

"You should have made a clean breast of it, Finbar," said the Reverend. "You should also have confessed to Annie, and to me. You have sinned against her, against Pania, against your own body. I don't think you fully realise…" He broke off and quoted from Proverbs: "He that covereth his sins shall not prosper: but whoso confesseth and forsaketh them shall have mercy."

Annie was sobbing. "I saved myself for marriage, for you. I thought you would have done the same. I left everything to come here to the end of the earth. I've even become a Protestant, for God's sake! What will become of me now?"

Kelly fidgeted uncomfortably in his suit. "I'm so sorry Annie. I've prayed to God for forgiveness. Now I hope you can forgive me."

Annie removed her veil, which now seemed ridiculous, and wiped the tears from her eyes. "Maybe in time, but I can't forgive you today, and I can't go through with the wedding, not when I've been betrayed and humiliated like this. Why did it have to happen like this?"

She turned to Hāmana, who stood by smug and contemptuous. "Why have you done this?" she said. "Why did you wait till the wedding to bring this shame on us?"

Annie had stopped crying and had regained the steel that Kelly had admired in her back when they were first courting.

"The shame is his," said Hāmana.

"Why did it have to happen like this?"

"Because Hāmana still hates me," Kelly said.

"Why? What have you done to him?"

"I fought against him in a war that stole his people's land."

"That is the truth," said Hāmana.

Annie looked to Pania, who sat, sullen and downcast all the while, then to Kelly and said, "The honourable thing would be for you to marry her."

"That's not what I want," Kelly said.

"He will not marry her," Hāmana said, "and he will have nothing to do with the child."

"What will become of the child?" Annie asked.

"The Māori way is for the whānau to bring up the child."

"The far-now?"

"The extended family. They're a good family," Kelly assured her. "Their elder sister is Āwhina, who I told you about. She's the matriarch. Hāmana is the black sheep of the family."

Hāmana bristled, but restrained himself. He helped Pania to her feet and pulled her by the arm out the side door.

Pania turned as they left and said, "Aroha mai. I'm sorry, Finbar."

"I must get back to the congregation," said Reverend Heywood. "They'll be getting restless."

"Please bring the Dilworths in," Annie said.

The assembled guests ceased their murmuring and looked expectantly to the Reverend when he alone reappeared. "I regret to say the wedding is off," he said, "at least for now," he added as a hopeful afterthought.

Then he went to speak to the Dilworths and returned with them to the vestry. Isabella was wiping her eyes.

James was saying, "Yes, I knew of it, but I didn't know she was pregnant."

"Why didn't you say anything?" Isabella said.

"It was between Finbar and his conscience."

Isabella rushed to Annie and gave her a hug. "Oh my dear, what a shame. I mean, he's brought shame on himself."

"It's a shame the way things have turned out. I had such romantic notions. What will become of me?" Annie said again.

"I'm so sorry Annie," Kelly said again and reached for her hand, but she pulled away. "I can't be with you now. I'm leaving."

"Where will you go?"

"You must come home with us," Isabella said.

"Well, Finbar, I won't be going home to my parents—that's for certain. I believe I have a home with the Dilworths for now. You can support me till I can make my own way here. As you said, it's a land of opportunity." She left with the Dilworths in their carriage.

Only Kelly and the Reverend remained in the vestry.

Kelly slumped in a chair and moaned. "I've made such a mess of things."

"You have indeed," agreed the Reverend.

"So what do I do now? There's still hope for forgiveness and reconciliation, surely?"

"Well, yes, but don't presume on easy grace. You say you've asked God for forgiveness, but have you truly repented? Are you sorry for what you've done or are you just sorry for what you've lost?" The Reverend flipped through his Bible to the Psalms and read: 'The sacrifices of God are a broken spirit. A broken and a contrite heart, O God, thou wilt not despise'. Think on it, Finbar. Pray about it. Give it time. Feel free to come back and see me and come to church."

The Reverend went out to talk with a few parishioners who lingered in the courtyard of the church.

Rāwiri came by and peered in the vestry door. "Matua Kelly? Are you all right?

"No."

"Sorry."

"We're all sorry. Rāwiri, are they staying at your place?"

"Yes. They're going back to Te Kuiti tomorrow."

"Why didn't you tell me they were here?"

"Matua Hāmana told me not to. I thought he just wanted it to be a surprise."

"It was a surprise all right."

Kelly turned up for work on the Monday morning, as per usual. Dilworth commiserated with him over the unfortunate, but 'avoidable' events on Saturday, the aborted wedding ceremony.

"What's she saying?" Kelly asked. "Is there any message for me?"

"She says, 'Don't come calling. She doesn't wish to see you.'"

"Ever?"

"Probably not forever. Just give her time to get over her grief. It takes time to rebuild trust."

"I'll make it up to her, if she'll give me a chance—if she'll find it in her heart to forgive my…indiscretion…my dishonesty."

Dilworth nodded but made no comment.

"Yes, all right—my sin. Reverend Heywood called it for what it is. He takes a hard line."

"He does, but he's not wrong. Just give Annie time." Dilworth repeated. His tone suggested it was time to end the conversation.

"I've waited this long," Kelly said. "I can wait longer if I must, but the uncertainty weighs heavy on me."

"Now I'll leave you to get on with the day. Deliveries are waiting."

On the Sunday morning, Kelly woke from a dream, in which he had married Pania. He struggled to rouse himself to think lucidly. *Maybe I should marry Pania if Annie will not have me now. No, that's not how it's meant to be. I will not give up hope. I will attend church every Sunday. I will see Annie there. I will show good faith. I will show contrition. Well, I am contrite and I have the faith. Surely, they will see that. God will see it anyway. God sees the heart of man, the deceitful heart, the heart of faith and the broken heart.*

He washed and dressed in a clean white shirt, befitting church attendance. *It would have been easy to accompany Āwhina to church or to have gone with the Dilworths. But now I'm the pariah of the parish. Maybe it's too soon to show my face.* He sat on the edge of his bed and continued brooding till past nine o'clock, past the start time of the church service. When he finally roused himself from his despondency, he went out to the stable, saddled his horse and rode out along the coast to Hobson Bay, where he and Pania used to ride together.

Kelly kept himself busy at work and lonely and contemplative at home. He read his Bible every evening and became familiar with its contents. He went to the church, not on Sunday, but during the week, as per Reverend Heywood's invitation, for counselling. The Reverend was sympathetic to Kelly's desire for reconciliation with Annie, but he also advised him that there was much more at stake.

Kelly had not been particularly susceptible to taking advice in the past but was now following the exhortations of Reverend Heywood and the encouragement that Āwhina had given him to read the Bible.

John 3:16, they both said—the message of salvation through faith in Christ. 'For God so loved the world, that he gave his only begotten Son, that whosoever believeth in him should not perish, but have everlasting life.' *Am I saved? Certainly not by my own righteousness. By the righteousness of Christ.*

Other passages in the Bible began to speak to him:

> In the Gospel of Mark, a desperate man cried out to Jesus, 'Lord, I believe; help thou mine unbelief.' *Lord, I believe; help thou mine unbelief.*
>
> '…men ought always to pray, and not give up.' *I will keep praying.*
>
> 'Forgive us our sins, for we also forgive everyone who sins against us.' *Must I forgive others before I can be forgiven? Who do I need to forgive? Hāmana? Very well, I forgive him. Pania? My temptress? Yes, her too. What of myself? My failings. My betrayal. The lives I've taken. My sins. Can I forgive myself? That's a tough one. If God can forgive me I can forgive myself. Lord, help me to forgive myself.*
>
> 'Not forsaking the assembling of ourselves together, as the manner of some is.' *I will no longer forsake assembling at church.*

Dilworth told Kelly that Annie had found employment and had moved out of their home. It was at the end of the working week and they were relaxing together in the office, sampling the coffee Dilworth had brewed.

"Yes, Isabella arranged it. Annie's the nanny for the Bucklands' children and she's moved into their home. Alfred says the children adore her."

*Who wouldn't?* Kelly thought. He knew Alfred Buckland through the business—a wealthy landowner and businessman. He had nine children by his first marriage and another seven young children by his second.

"She had always wanted to be a nanny," Kelly recalled.

"How's your coffee?" Dilworth asked. "Auckland Coffee and Spice Merchants imported and roasted the green beans from Ceylon."

"Better than the coffee I had in the army. A little bitter, but I like the taste, and the smell," Kelly said, holding the bag of Arabica up to his nose.

"Most of our customers still prefer tea."

Kelly drained his bitter coffee and said, "I'll be going to church tomorrow."

"Good man. Isabella and I will meet you there before the service."

Both were as good as their word. They met outside the church and Kelly was relieved to not be entering on his own. He received a cordial greeting from a few friends and acquaintances and there were also those who shunned him. He resolved not to be deterred by any 'holier-than-thou' members of the congregation. *We're all sinners here.* He joined in the singing of the hymns and found that being a part of the corporate worship was uplifting to his spirit. It was briefly a transporting experience. When he became aware again of the people around him, he saw Annie with the Buckland family, with all their children, but she didn't notice him.

Reverend Heywood preached from the book of John, about Jesus, 'the light of the world'. He read the account of the scribes and Pharisees who brought a woman to Jesus. "'She was caught in the very act of adultery,' they said. 'Now Moses, in the law commanded us, that such should be stoned: but what sayest thou? And Jesus answered them, saying, 'He that is without sin among you, let him first cast a stone at her.'"

Kelly had read it recently himself and had the same thoughts now. *Why only the woman? Where was the man? Both were guilty. Jesus responded to the hypocrites with compassion for the woman. But he did tell her to stop sinning. I'm not quite an adulterer, just a fornicator and a liar, by concealing the truth. A timely message for the congregation. Let him who is without sin cast the first stone.*

Kelly attended church again the following Sunday and after the service he was talking with Dilworth when Isabella and Annie joined them. James and Isabella broke off into their own conversation and Kelly spoke to Annie for the first time since the aborted wedding. It was awkward and polite, as though they were distant acquaintances.

"Hello, Annie. You're looking well."

"Hello Finbar. How is Pania?"

"I don't know. She's gone back to Te Kuiti and I don't have any contact." Kelly drew nearer and said, "Annie, we've got to get past this. Come for a walk now and we can have a proper talk."

"I can't, not today. The Bucklands are going out and I have to supervise the children."

"Next Sunday then. Make the arrangements... please."

"I don't know. I'll pray about it."

"So will I," Kelly said. And with that he went home to his empty house. The following Sunday he started courting all over again.

# 17

Dilworth took Rāwiri under his wing, as he had with Kelly and the young man quickly became another asset to Dilworth's agricultural enterprises. Rāwiri also adapted well enough to life in Auckland, but because of the difficulties of travel and communications between Auckland and the King Country he felt cut off from his whānau. He particularly missed his mother. Dilworth was very aware of their close bond and was perfectly agreeable to Rāwiri making the journey back to Te Kuiti.

Kelly was also quietly keen for any news, especially as the time had come, by his reckoning, for Pania to give birth. Dilworth gave Rāwiri a letter to show anyone who sought to detain him that he was on official company business. He wished him Godspeed, and added, "but don't tarry too long."

Rāwiri was gone for about four weeks and returned looking downcast with the news he had to deliver. "Whaea Pania died in childbirth. There was something wrong with the whenua. She had seizures; she went into a coma and died."

This news struck Kelly like a punch in the guts and yet he thought, *how curious that the same word, whenua, means both placenta and land.*

"My grandmother died of the same sickness, giving birth to Pania," Rāwiri continued. "Maybe a curse in our family, the line of the women."

"It may be a case of eclampsia," Dilworth suggested.

"And what of the baby?" Kelly said.

"Māmā prayed to God to remove the curse, to spare Pania, but He took her and spared the baby. There's a wet nurse in the whānau caring for him. Māmā said she would raise him as her own."

*Him. So, a baby boy.*

Kelly and Dilworth both expressed their condolences.

"There have been many deaths," Rāwiri said.

"How is Āwhina?" Kelly asked.

"Saddened of course, but bearing up. Continuing with the struggle."

*The political struggle or the struggle that is life? Both*, Kelly supposed.

Kelly had begun to see Annie more than just on Sundays after church and things were getting back to the way they had been. They had not mentioned Pania again, not until the news of her death.

"Well, I suppose you're free of her now," Annie said.

"I didn't need to be free of her. I wasn't... *What was the right word?...* attached."

"Did you love her?"

"Not in the way I think you mean. Not in the way I love you. It was not a romance. If you think it's a kind of closure then we are free after all to get married."

"And what of the child?"

"He will be a whāngai, adopted by the family, by Āwhina and the whole whānau."

Kelly and Annie agreed they would first go to Reverend Heywood again for godly counselling. The good Reverend was happy for the wedding to proceed but Kelly said he first wished to be baptised.

"Were you not baptised as an infant?" The Reverend asked.

"Yes, I was but that was just a christening. It was not the baptism of repentance and new life in Christ."

"Quite so," the Reverend agreed, "but we believe infant baptism is sufficient, providing you adhere to the faith. However, I am willing to baptise you in the church if you will recite the creed."

"Actually I'd like to be baptised in the sea, not just a sprinkling of water, but a proper dunking, as John the Baptiser and the apostles baptised the first believers. To signify the death of the old nature and the birth of the new."

"It's not the way we normally do things here but I have no objection to following the precedent set by the Lord himself," the Reverend said, and he added, "I commend you for your study of the Bible and for your commitment, Finbar."

The following Sunday afternoon Reverend Heywood baptised Finbar Kelly by full immersion in the sea at Saint Mary's Bay in the presence of a small group of witnesses from among the church family. The Sunday after that the Reverend delivered a sermon on the themes of love and forgiveness. He read from First Corinthians 13:

*Love suffereth long, and is kind; love envieth not; love vaunteth not itself, is not puffed up, doth not behave itself unseemly, seeketh not her own, is not easily provoked, thinketh no evil; rejoiceth not in iniquity, but rejoiceth in the truth; beareth all things, believeth all things, hopeth all things, endureth all things.*

"Love rejoiceth not in iniquity," the Reverand repeated, and elucidated with, "Love keeps no record of wrongs." He finished by repeating, "Love endureth all things," and paraphrased, "Love never fails."

At the end of the sermon Reverend Heywood announced the upcoming wedding of Kelly and Annie. A murmur of general approval and perhaps of relief emanated from the congregation. Before leaving the church the couple were congratulated by various friends and acquaintances, with a few making comments such as: 'Finally' and 'This time, eh.'

The ceremony was a rerun of the previous, months before, beginning with

> *"In the presence of God, Father, Son and Holy Spirit, we have come together again..."*

All went smoothly, with a moment of tension at the point of, *"If there is anyone present who can show just cause..."* and an audible sigh of relief as the bridal couple completed their vows and Reverend Heywood proceeded to, "I now pronounce you husband and wife."

# 18

Kelly settled peacefully into married life and the following year Annie gave birth to a baby girl. They were devoted parents and together they contemplated their future as a family with more children. "But not so many as the Bucklands," Annie asserted. Kelly feigned disappointment, then laughed off the prospect of raising a whole rugby team.

Their baby girl was christened by Reverend Heywood, Eliza Mary Kelly. Annie was pleased to have the child baptised soon after its birth, though Kelly insisted the christening was their dedication of their child to God and not a baptism.

"She can get baptised," he said, "when she's old enough to make the decision for herself."

Two years later, the second Kelly child was christened Imogen Catriona, and their third, three years after that, Charles Michael. The Kelly home grew as their family grew, with Kelly enlisting the services of Jackson the carpenter again to add a room to the house after the birth of the second child. Annie had continued nannying for the Bucklands until she became a mother herself. She was no longer the waif-like girl of those early days in New Zealand. If she were a cattle beast, Kelly would have said she'd put on condition. He noted, with some pride, that when they were out and about, her pretty face still attracted admiring glances from other men.

It was a time of prosperity for the country, that is for the European population, who had taken possession of most of the land, and developed the best of the land for pastoral farming. The indigenous population declined in number, owing to the loss of their economic base and consequent poverty and sickness. Kelly and Rāwiri continued to contribute to, and benefit from, the Dilworth enterprises.

Rāwiri was still single and became something of a man of the world, of two worlds in fact: Māori and Pākehā. He was respected by most in the business community, despite some lingering prejudice against his Māori blood. But he identified primarily as Māori and kept in contact with his mother and other whānau in the Rohe Pōtae, with occasional trips to their home. Kelly continued to be a benefactor, making contributions to the whānau, particularly in support of the child he had fathered to Pania. Wiremu, Kelly's 'other son' was well aware that he had a Pākehā father in Auckland but had no interest in meeting him.

As Rāwiri explained to Kelly, "It's important to 'us Māori' to know our whakapapa, our genealogy, to know our identity. It would be wrong to withhold such information. Wiremu is named after our kaumātua, Wiremu Tāmihana, but actually he looks more like you." Rāwiri chuckled. "A darker version of Finbar Kelly."

"We named our boy Charles after our kaumātua Charles Stuart Parnell," Kelly said. "And his middle name Michael, after Michael Davitt."

Rāwiri was a regular visitor to the Kelly home and the children came to regard him affectionately as their 'Māori uncle'. They were unaware that they were in fact part of his whānau, by virtue of their father's liaison with Rāwiri's aunt, that they were almost cousins. It was never spoken of in the Kelly home, not until circumstances necessitated a decision regarding the delicate matter. The occasion was Tāwhiao's royal tour of the Waikato and Auckland. Āwhina was part of the King's retinue, and she would be bringing Wiremu with her to Auckland.

"Whaea Āwhina is eager to see you again," Rāwiri told Kelly. "And there is also a matter she wants to discuss with you, concerning Wiremu's education. He's been attending a native school in Te Kuiti, but Āwhina wants him to have a higher education too, to help him to get on in the Pākehā world."

"I'll support that," Kelly said. "What school does she have in mind?"

"Saint Stephen's Boarding School for Māori Boys."

"Right here in Parnell."

"What do you think?"

"I think it's a good choice," Kelly agreed. "You should have a word with Dilworth about it. He knows the headmaster there, a Mr. Davis, or Davies."

The Kelly children were twelve, ten and seven when their parents sat them down for a serious talk, old enough to understand and hopefully to accept, the truth they were about to hear.

"King Tāwhiao is coming to Auckland soon," Kelly began, "and Rāwiri's mother, Whaea Āwhina will be with him… and her nephew, Wiremu. Wiremu's mother, Whaea Pania died when Wiremu was born."

Kelly paused and glanced at Annie. "Before your mother and I were married, when I was here in New Zealand by myself and I was injured,

Whaea Āwhina and Whaea Pania helped to look after me, and Whaea Pania stayed with me for a time…"

Kelly had told many stories about the old days, about the fighting and about Rāwiri's mother, who was so dear to him, but the children had never heard of this Pania. Eliza looked at her father, then at Charlie and Imogen. There was something different about this story, about the telling of it.

"Well," Kelly continued, "Pania and I had a baby together. I am Wiremu's father. He is a half-brother to you."

The children responded to this revelation with stunned silence and looked to each other with expressions of *Did he really just say that?* Eliza looked from her father to her mother. Annie sat calmy with her eyes downcast.

"Will he be coming to live with us?" Imogen asked.

"No, his whānau in the King Country adopted him. But he may be coming to stay in Auckland, to go to boarding school."

The *New Zealand Herald* published a front page story about Tāwhiao, 'the King of the Māoris' and 'a man of peace' and reported on his grand tour of the Waikato and his much anticipated arrival in Auckland by steamer, from Ōrakei. Civic dignitaries and thousands of other Aucklanders gathered on the Queen's Wharf to welcome the King. Among the crowd were Rāwiri and the Dilworths, and Kelly and Annie, with their three children, excited at the prospect of a ship arriving with a king onboard, and uncertainly anticipating meeting their half-Māori half-brother.

Buildings near the waterfront and ships in the harbour were festooned with brightly coloured flags for the festive occasion. There were no Māori vessels in the harbour or at Mechanics Bay as in days past. Sailors on the deck of a German warship, the *SMS Habicht,* in the outer harbour, saluted the king as the steamer passed. The steamer docked at the wharf and Tāwhiao appeared on the deck, wearing a korowai, a cloak of fine flax fibre with an ornamental border, and a white top hat adorned with huia and peacock feathers. As he raised a whale bone mere in his right hand, a cheer rose from the crowd and a band struck up *Auld Lang Syne.* Tāwhiao strode barefoot onto the wharf and was welcomed by Mayor Clarke.

The King's secretary, Hōri Kerei, responded with a speech, in which he remembered the dead of the land and greeted the land itself, Auckland, Tāmaki-makau-rau, Tāmaki-of-a-hundred-lovers, and finally greeted the people congregated there. Tāwhiao was taken by coach to the Governor Browne Hotel and he saluted people on the way who had climbed onto the shop balconies to watch the procession.

More of Tāwhiao's party followed: some of his whānau and his closest associates: Major Mair, Wahanui and Manuhiri. And there, finally, were Āwhina and Wiremu, who was about the age that Rāwiri was when Kelly first made his home with Quinn and Āwhina. Rāwiri rushed to his mother and hugged her. When free of her son's embrace, she hugged Kelly.

"Kia ora Āwhina," Kelly said. "So good to see you again. You're looking well."

"Kia ora ki a koe hoki."

"I was so saddened to hear that Pania died," he said. "My condolences again to you and all the family."

"My condolences also to you," Āwhina said, quietly. "Now, finally you meet your—my nephew Wiremu."

Kelly wanted to embrace Wiremu but the boy hung back diffidently and Kelly instead extended his hand. Wiremu shook his hand with a formal Māori greeting: "Tēnā koe, Matua."

It was a poignant but awkwardly intimate moment in the presence of the others who had not yet been properly greeted.

"Aren't you going to introduce me to your family?" Āwhina said.

"Of course. This is Annie. Annie, Āwhina."

"Delighted to finally meet you," she said, shaking Annie's hand.

"And this is Eliza, Charles and Imogen."

After also warmly greeting the Dilworths, Āwhina gazed about at her surroundings and marvelled at how Auckland had grown and changed. "So many brick buildings and I didn't even recognise it from the sea. Fort Britomart and all the Britomart headland is gone."

Āwhina and Wiremu stayed with Rāwiri for the duration of Tāwhiao's Auckland tour and Āwhina was also a guest in Kelly's home for an evening. He drove a trap to Rāwiri's home to fetch his guests. Wiremu did not want to go with his mother to the Kelly home, and Āwhina took the opportunity, in the trap, to have the private conversations she'd been wanting to have with Kelly.

"When we all met at the dock, I was going to introduce Wiremu as your son, but I wasn't sure if you had acknowledged him."

"I've told the children. There's no secrecy now."

"Good. Then we can move on to talking about Wiremu going to Saint Stephen's School."

"I think it's a good idea and I'm happy to take care of the fees. And Annie and I are happy to have him staying nearby. I hope to have some contact with him and get to know him."

"He doesn't seem to be ready for that now. But hopefully, in time."

Āwhina found the Kelly home to be so like the one where she had lived with Quinn that she was assailed by memories of her former life, a life of joys and sorrows and loss. There was, of course, the extra room and the extra children. The children quickly warmed to Whaea Āwhina as she fondly recounted stories of the old days when Kelly came into her home and into her life.

Kelly pointed out, with obvious pride, the bits of furniture he'd built himself, including a rimu bookcase standing in the same place as the original. Āwhina noted on the shelves a collection of children's books and English novels by Jane Austen, Charlotte and Emily Brontë, and George Eliot, Butler's Erewhon, volumes of poetry by Keats, Shelley, Coleridge and Wordsworth, and a well-worn Bible. Annie had become a proficient reader, with Kelly's help, and progressed to become an avid reader of newspapers and books and *the* book. In the Catholic church back in Ireland, even those who could read did not read the Bible. That was only for the priests, and the common people received the word of God from the preaching of the priests. The Bible on the shelf was a wedding present from the Dilworths. It accompanied the Kellys to church every Sunday and the congregation were encouraged, even exhorted, to study the scriptures.

Annie called the family and their guest to the table and Kelly gave a prayer of thanksgiving before they started on the meal. Āwhina commended Annie on the roast lamb, which was a treat she seldom enjoyed these days, and the home-grown potatoes, kūmara and pumpkin. During the meal she asked about life in the city and directed questions especially to the children.

Conversations about life in the King Country would wait till after dinner when Annie and the children read bedtime stories and the children went to bed.

Kelly told Āwhina, "I've been following the news of the ongoing disputes over confiscated land, as best I can. But I'd like to hear from you about what's happening in the Waikato and King Country."

Āwhina did not long dwell on the past, with Kelly turning the conversation to more recent events. "I've read that Tāwhiao and his followers have surrendered all their weapons to Major Mair in Alexandra."

"That's how the newspapers reported it," Āwhina said, "but it was not surrender or submission. They laid their weapons down at Mair's feet as a gesture of peace. We are still fighting the government, but with words, not guns. We petition the government to challenge the legality of the raupatu in the Supreme Court but the government commissioners refuse to hear our arguments."

"The raupatu. That's the land confiscations?"

"Yes, the confiscation of over three million acres of the Waikato. Since the colonial government won't hear our case, we have decided to appeal directly to the Queen, our Sovereign and Treaty partner. Tāwhiao's tour of the Waikato and Auckland is to gain support and contributions of money for a trip to London."

"So, will you go as Tāwhiao's interpreter?"

"No, that honour will go to George Skidmore or Te Wheoro."

"Te Wheoro, who is now a Member of Parliament."

"Yes. Premier Grey and Native Minister McLean have been trying to get Tāwhiao to accept deals for himself. There was a meeting at Kawhia—actually at nearby Hikurangi, where they offered him five hundred acres of land at Ngāruawahia, a house at Kawhia and a pension of five hundred pounds per year. And he would be the 'administrator' within his own district."

"Nothing for the people?" Kelly said.

"Just some reserves: all the unsold land west of the Waipā and Waikato Rivers. Inferior lands. Crumbs from the Europeans' table. It's their best offer and there are some who are advising Tāwhiao to take it, but that would condone acceptance of the raupatu."

"So Tāwhiao still demands the return of all the confiscated lands of the Waikato?"

"Yes, just as Tāmihana did."

Annie had returned from putting the children to bed and made a pot of tea. Āwhina accepted a cup and said, "I'm afraid you'll find all this political talk rather boring, Annie."

"No, I'm keenly interested," Annie said and added, "And I thought it was bad in Ireland."

"What is happening in Ireland now?" Āwhina asked, bringing Annie into the conversation.

"We have our Irish Land League, and the Fenians are rebelling against British rule in Ireland and fighting for Home Rule to run our own affairs. I say fighting, but our man, Parnell is the President of the Land League now and he's anti-violence. They're trying to get justice by peaceful political means."

"This all sounds very familiar," Āwhina said. "Actually we had some Fenians out from Ireland with us in the King Country a few years ago. Their leader, Michael O'Connor, wanted to form a Fenian colony to fight the British and create a Kīngitanga-Irish uprising in the Waikato, but nothing much came of it.

"We are advocating for Home Rule just as the Irish are," Āwhina continued. "One of our members of Parliament, Hōne Tāwhai, told the House we are being deprived of our land in the same way the Irish were. He even went so far as to say, 'I am an Irishman.'"

Kelly wanted to bring the conversation back to Āwhina and with some hesitation asked about what had been happening in the King Country.

Āwhina sighed and said, "Life has been hard in the Rohe Pōtae. We've been living in the wind, but we have moved on from survival to protecting what remains of our land."

"The King Country is The Rohe Pōtae?"

"Yes, the District of the Hat. The King's Hat. The King Country."

"I've heard the government are wanting to get access to the King Country to put the railway through all the way to Wellington." Kelly hesitated and added, "and open it up for European settlement."

"Yes, open it up." Āwhina sighed again. She was not bitter, but sad and burdened. "The battle is to keep the Land Court out of the Rohe Pōtae. McLean is trying to get access for surveyors to mark out the boundaries of the Rohe and get land for the railway. His strategy is divide and conquer. He's dealing with Rewi Maniapoto as the paramount chief and setting him against Tāwhiao and creating more divisions by dealing with individual hapū to buy land.

"Many of our people are going to the Land Court in Cambridge to get deeds of title to retain ownership of our land. But we can't get title for communal land, so the land is divided into blocks with a few individual owners. Some of our people are selling pieces of land to settlers to get money to buy stock and grass seed and fences. One of our hapū sold his land to avoid prosecution for debts, for money he owed for the surveying costs and legal costs and also for food and alcohol. Now he has no land and nothing to show for selling it. They're stealing from our grandchildren." Āwhina fell silent for a moment and then added, "The land jobbers come in, the wealthy speculators, offering money as deposits on land even before the titles are issued."

"Isn't that illegal? said Kelly.

"Yes, of course, but it's happening and it's drawing us into the Land Court and there are disputes over who owns which bits of land. Our land is being divided and our people are being divided. The Pākehā, they build trig stations on the high points of the land to spread their mana over the land, to survey the land, to divide it, to slice it up like a piece of meat to buy and sell. The Pākehā buys the land and owns it forever, for evermore." Āwhina was tired and drifting into a reverie. "Mine, not yours. Gone for evermore. Evermore. Ever more." She shuddered herself back to wakefulness. "The rich Pākehā, the speculator, he buys much land and divides the land and sells it for more money and gets richer without working."

"That's capitalism," said Kelly. "It's the Pākehā way."

"It is not the Māori way," said Āwhina. "The Māori, we live on the land. The land, the whenua, is our mother. It is the mother of our tīpuna, our ancestors. Does the land belong to us? Do we belong to the land? Belong. Belong. Be long." Drifting again. "The land belongs to the hapū, not to any one person. We can live without courts, roads, railways, but not without land."

"And what's become of Hāmana?" Kelly asked, after a long pause. Rāwiri told me he's gone to Parihaka."

"Aye, you know he fell in with Tītokowaru. Waru went to Taranaki and he's joined Te Whiti and Tohu at Parihaka. Tāwhiao has told me that Hāmana will be there too if he is still alive. I'm sure I would know if he had been killed. So that's where he will be, at Parihaka. Tāwhiao is committed to peace and supporting Te Whiti and Tohu and he's encouraging his people in the Rohe Pōtae to go to Parihaka, those who are willing to go, especially the Waikato refugees, so as also to relieve the burden of survival in the Rohe Pōtae. But there is trouble brewing in Taranaki."

"What kind of trouble?"

"More land confiscation. Te Whiti and Tohu are prophets and leaders of peaceful resistance against the creeping confiscation. More and more of our people are joining them at Parihaka. The Minister Bryce won't stop until he has driven the people off the land."

"I see John Bryce is now also the Minister of Defence," said Kelly. "Are you sure it will be peaceful?"

"Yes, on the Māori side anyway."

"And will you go there yourself?"

"Yes, I wish to see Te Whiti and Tohu and I hope to see Hāmana too."

Āwhina was fading with weariness and Kelly returned her to Rāwiri's home.

"She's lovely," Annie said, when Kelly returned. "I can see why you have such a soft spot for her. And she's had such a hard life."

"She's a survivor and a battler."

"This is all very strange for the children. It was a strange experience for them to meet their half-brother at the dock. He's a boy from 'the other side' and yet he looks familiar."

# 19

King Tāwhiao was much fêted in Auckland, as he had been in his tour of the Waikato. He was taken on tours of modern industries and entertainments and treated to civic receptions, banquets and fireworks. At the end of his two-week sojourn in Auckland he met with Premier Hall, but was given little opportunity to discuss matters of real concern to the Kīngitanga. Negotiations regarding the King Country were left to Minister Bryce and Rewi Maniapoto.

Āwhina and Wiremu returned with Tāwhiao to the Rohe Pōtae and later joined a rōpū travelling to Parihaka, where they were welcomed with a pōwhiri. Te Whiti himself greeted them and Āwhina, especially, received a warm welcome: a hongi and kiss from Te Whiti. "Nau mai. Haere mai, Whaea." And to Wiremu: "Tēnā koe, e tama."

"Tēnā koe, Matua," Āwhina replied. "Ngā mihi nui ki a koe hoki nō Kīngi Tāwhiao." Greetings from King Tāwhiao.

Te Whiti gave his guests a guided tour around the village and the gardens: fields of potatoes, kūmara, cabbage and pens of pigs and bullocks. It was all so well ordered, and unprotected—no fortifications. So many dwellings, Āwhina observed, but not that many people, and those she did see were mostly women and children.

"Yes, we have many tātarakihi here," Te Whiti said.

"Tātarakihi? Cicadas?"

"Orphans. Many orphans."

"Where are all the men?" Āwhina asked.

"Many have been arrested and taken away to jail."

"Has Hāmana been taken?"

"Yes. And Tītokowaru and many others of his rōpū."

"Where? They can't all be in New Plymouth. The jail would be overflowing."

"Indeed it was," Te Whiti said. "And then the men were taken to Wellington and then to the South Island, to Lyttleton and Dunedin."

"Arrested for what offences?"

"The surveyors came," Te Whiti said, "and put their pegs in the ground to divide our land for their settlements and roads. We removed the pegs each day and escorted the surveyors off our land. We continued farming our land, building fences and ploughing the fields. The Pākehā labourers and the Armed Constabulary tore down our fences and we rebuilt them and this went on for some time. But the arrests started when we ploughed the fields on land they had claimed for their farms. Hundreds of ploughmen have been arrested."

"What are they charged with?"

"No charges. No trials, just two years imprisonment with hard labour."

"No trials?"

"They say the trials are postponed indefinitely."

"The Treaty says we have the rights and privileges of British subjects," Āwhina said.

"The colonial government enacts 'special legislation for the peace and safety of the colony'," Te Whiti said, with mock solemnity. "They have been very quick to pass laws that deprive us of the rights we were guaranteed under the Treaty."

"Do they intend to take all of Parihaka?"

"The surveyors showed us the plans of Parihaka partitioned, sliced up, with a reserve for Māori, for Taranaki iwi, a strip of land, with no access to the sea or the mountain. This, after we were promised large reserves, grants for fencing, our urupā, cultivations and fishing grounds, undisturbed."

"The government also promised us parcels of land as reserves," Āwhina said, "but they seem to forget their promises when it comes to selling the land to the settlers."

Te Whiti was a man of unremarkable appearance, of medium height and a quiet demeanour. But he was a commanding figure as he stood, barefoot, dressed in a grey woollen shirt, well-worn dark trousers and a blanket draped over his broad shoulders, to address the assembly. He exhorted his followers to non-violent resistance. His speech was lively and quick-witted, while Tohu's, by comparison, was a dull monotone, though he spoke in different voices when he communed with spirits.

Te Whiti was much admired, even by Pākehā for his ardent nonviolence, his eloquence as an orator, and his agreeably fine European-like features. Even Robert Parris, the Government Land Purchasing Agent, paid him grudging respect for his intelligence and incorruptibility. Te Whiti cared nothing for money and, like Wiremu Tāmihana, could not be bought with offers of land for his own possession. John Bryce claimed Te Whiti was insane.

The fame, or the infamy, of Parihaka spread throughout the land. Many dispossessed and homeless Māori continued to flock to Parihaka, from Taranaki, Whanganui and throughout the North Island, some just to attend the monthly hui, and some seeking a place of refuge and some for healing. One of the refugees, Wiremu Hīroki Te Mahuki, had arrived with a gunshot wound. He had fled from Waverly, after shooting the cook in a party of surveyors on his land, who were making sport of killing his pigs. He evaded his pursuers with the help of South Taranaki farmer, guide and former fugitive deserter from the British Army, Kimble Bent, who gave them wrong directions.

The people of Parihaka continued to trouble the surveyors, and the hordes of prisoners continued to trouble the government. Most of the prisoners survived the harsh conditions of their incarceration and were eventually released and reunited with their families. Hāmana marched with twenty-seven others, in chiefly procession back into Parihaka, all wearing the raukura, the white albatross feathers, in their hair, which signified their allegiance to Te Whiti. There was much consternation at the sight of so many emaciated and broken men, but Te Whiti, identifying as always with the patriarchs of the Old Testament, honoured them as heroes returning to Israel from the land of Pharaoh. Among the women welcoming their returning husbands, brothers and sons, was Āwhina, who rushed forward to embrace her brother. Her neck became wet with the tears of the battle-hardened warrior of Tītokowaru's wars. Hāmana had nothing to say to Wiremu.

When Āwhina had opportunity to speak to Hāmana privately she said, "Why will you not accept Wiremu? He is mixed blood like Rāwiri and he chooses his Māori side. He has chosen to be here at Parihaka."

"When I see him I see the Pākehā soldier who raped Pania," Hāmana said.

"It was not rape," Āwhina said. "Kelly is a decent man."

"He didn't marry her. Not like your husband. You say Kelly is a good man just because he is a Christian, like you. You believe in the Pākehā God."

"The Christian God is not a Pākehā God. He is the God of all people and He is above race and countries. You can believe what you want but Wiremu is innocent in all of this. It's not his fault."

Hāmana could find no reply to Āwhina's final comment. Brother and sister sat in silent impasse on a kauri bench in the shade of a totara. Then in more sympathetic demeanour, Āwhina asked Hāmana about his imprisonment. She waited out his brooding silence till he quietly recounted his ordeal.

"They treated us like animals—twenty-eight of us in a cramped cell, with nothing but bread and water, and a single bucket for a toilet. The worst of it was solitary confinement. One of the older men in the cell, Tipene Te Rua, was weak with sickness and beaten for not working hard enough. I refused to work, in protest, and the guards kicked and rifle butted me into another cell for solitary confinement. That's where I stayed for four weeks." He cradled his head in his hands. "I got very depressed. I had never been shut away completely alone before. Some of the others spent as much as seven weeks in solitary."

The New Zealand press did not unanimously support the colonial government's continuing confiscation of land in Taranaki and some Pākehā were highly critical of their determination to seize the last bastion of peaceful Māori resistance at Parihaka. James Dilworth was one such Pākehā sympathetic to the plight of Taranaki Māori. Finbar Kelly was another. At a company meeting, Dilworth agreed to grant his employee, Rāwiri Quinn, leave to join those of his whānau who were present at Parihaka.

"I hear they need more ploughs," Kelly said. "We'll load these four onto the dray to ship them with you from Ōnehunga to New Plymouth on the coastal steamer. Yes, I've checked with Dilworth. He said to take four single furrow ploughs and we'll cover the cost."

On his arrival at Parihaka, Rāwiri was greeted with some curiosity and suspicion, as a mixed blood Māori-Pākehā. To allay any doubts concerning his allegiance, he recited his pepeha in fluent te reo Māori. With his whakapapa established, he was directed to the whare occupied by his mother, uncle and cousin. Āwhina hugged her son. Wiremu greeted his cousin with a hongi. Hāmana shook Rāwiri's hand with an affected 'How do you do Sir,' in mock deference to his success in the Pākehā world.

Rāwiri replied with, "So you're still alive, you wild rebel."

Then the hongi—the greeting that mattered—hand on shoulder, forehead to forehead, nose to nose, and the sharing of breath.

The returned prisoners gradually recuperated and went to work when they were able, building more whare and working in the gardens. Those that worked at repairing fences and planting in the road that now extended to the village, were arrested again.

Native Minister John Bryce, now also Minister for Defence, grew increasingly impatient with the impasse at Parihaka and resolved to remove the 'squatters', by force if necessary. He assembled a militia of 1,600 conscripts and volunteers with heavy artillery to apply the necessary force. He then issued Te Whiti with an ultimatum to accept the 'dismemberment' of their land within fourteen days or it would 'pass away from them forever.'

At dawn on 5 November 1881, after the expiry of Bryce's ultimatum, at least 2,000 Māori assembled peacefully on the Parihaka Marae to await the invasion.

Te Whiti addressed the people: "We have our ark, as Noah of old. Let us abide calmly upon the land. Do not flee from the guns or you will fall by them."

He then sat calmly next to Tohu and their interpreter, the law clerk, Wiremu Pokiha Omahuru, who had been orphaned at the invasion of Tītokowaru's pā and adopted by former Premier, William Fox. Behind Te Whiti sat Tītokowaru, with Hāmana at his side and Āwhina, Wiremu and Rāwiri next to him.

Rāwiri got up and scouted around the perimeter and noticed two Pākehā men climbing over a fence and dashing into the pā and hiding behind a whare. *Unarmed. Not soldiers. Spies, perhaps.* He went to investigate and found one of the men inside the whare.

"Who are you?" Rāwiri said, and "What are you doing here?"

"Samuel Croumbie-Brown of the Christchurch Lyttleton Times, at your service." The reporter's manner was business-like, as though he were keeping an appointment. He showed his credentials and extended his hand in greeting.

Rāwiri hesitated, uncertain of the man's intentions, but returned the courtesy and shook his hand. "Rāwiri Quinn." and he said, "So you're here to report on what's happening at Parihaka?"

"Yes, on what's about to happen, more to the point."

"What do you think is going to happen?"

"Minister Bryce will lead a raid on the village."

"And then?"

"Hopefully, Te Whiti and Tohu and everyone here will maintain their passive resistance. If not it could be a massacre. So, let us hope no shots are fired. If there is any shooting, Bryce should be the first target. This is an outrage—an unprovoked attack on a peaceful community on their own land."

"At least now I know where you stand," Rāwiri said. "How did you get involved in this?"

"The government asked me to prepare a report on how the settlement can be taken. But the more I investigated the matter the more I saw the injustice of their intentions. I refused to provide what they wanted and so they refused to allow me to come here. I'll be arrested if they find me here."

"Why you? Why did the government ask you to give them a report?"

"I suppose because of my work as a war correspondent and my experience in civil war."

"The wars here in New Zealand?"

"No, I served in the Union Army in the American Civil War."

"So, you're an American?"

"Russian, actually, originally. And what about you, Rāwiri? Are you a resident of this community?"

"No, I've come here from Auckland. I'm a supporter of Te Whiti and Tohu and the Kīngitanga."

"Ah, I've been following the Kīngitanga with some interest as well."

"What about the other man who was with you? Where is he now?"

"My associate, Mr Humphries, of the Press Association, will be hiding out here somewhere, hoping to get a close look at the proceedings."

Rāwiri went out and looked back to where his whānau were still sitting. "I'm here with family," he said. "I'll get back to them now."

"Before you go, may I have your address?" Croumbie-Brown got out his notepad and pencil. "I'd like to keep in touch and keep up with what's happening with the Kīngitanga. In exchange I can keep you informed on what our devious government is getting up to." He wrote the address in his notepad and gave Rāwiri his card.

"Thank you and good luck to you."

"And to you."

As the sun rose, in a clear sky, clear even of birds, over the perfect cone of Mount Taranaki, the troops arrived at Parihaka and surrounded the village, running furtively from cover to cover. There were no defence works in sight and the officers suspected a trap. As the first unit advanced on the main entrance their way was blocked by two hundred children, the tātarakihi, dressed in ceremonial shoulder cloaks, singing and playing. Older girls, skipping together, followed by women, offering gifts of freshly baked bread, formed the second and third lines of defence. The cavalry tried to force a way through, waving swords and threatening to cut the heads off 'the bloody black niggers' but the women and children held their ground. The tātarakihi clapped their hands and took off their cloaks and waved them at the horses. Horses shied and reared and some threw their riders to the ground.

The belligerent, black-bearded Bryce, resplendent in his lieutenant's uniform and mounted on his white steed, had the look of a man trying his best to cut a dashing figure. He had a reputation as a straight talking, no nonsense politician. The Europeans called him Honest John Bryce. Māori had another name for him: Kōhuru Bryce—Bryce the murderer, in remembrance of the slaughter of the children at Handley's Farm.

He advanced on his white charger and read the riot act, commanding, "persons unlawfully, riotously and tumultuously assembled to disperse or receive a possible jail sentence of hard labour for life." The people sat in silence and continued to sit for the duration of the one hour they were given to leave. Bugles then signalled for the troops to advance.

"Let the man Bryce, who raised the war, finish his work today," Tohu growled. "Let none be absent. Stay where you are, even if the bayonet be put to your breast, do not resist."

Bryce told Mr Hursthouse, the surveyor-interpreter, to order Te Whiti to come forward.

"If Bryce and Rolleston want to see me, let them come to me," Te Whiti replied. "I will remain with my people. I have nothing to do with the trouble this day. It is not my trouble, but the Pākehās'. If you have anything to say I will listen."

The standoff continued with Bryce demanding a clear passage for his horse and Te Whiti insisting he come on foot lest some of his children get hurt. Finally Bryce ordered the constables to arrest both chiefs on charges of "wickedly, maliciously, and seditiously contriving and intending to disturb the peace". Te Whiti and Tohu made a dignified exit, under armed escort, wearing korowai cloaks, and encouraged the people to remain steadfast in peaceful works and not to be fearful or dismayed. The chiefs' wives and Te Whiti's niece followed and all were taken by gig to Pungarehu blockhouse. One other resident of Parihaka, Wiremu Hīroki, was arrested at the same time, for the murder of a surveyor three years before. The rest of the village remained quietly on the marae till the evening, while the troops set about putting the village under siege. They pitched their army tents around it and built a compound for prisoners.

Rāwiri, Wiremu and Hāmana stuck close by Āwhina as the ill-disciplined soldiers went about the village searching for weapons, looting whare and raping women, with impunity. A number of guns and swords were found but not the sought after sword of Major von Tempsky.

Bryce had other leaders of the village arrested, those that he could identify. He sought out Tītokowaru especially and arrested him for 'wilful, unlawful obstruction'. Bryce tried to force all who were not of the Parihaka tribe back to their place of origin but his attempts at drafting the people into their different iwi met with no response, despite the threatening show of bayonets and Armstrong guns. He was eventually able to identify north Taranaki iwi with the aid of the collaborator, Utiku Potaka.

In the days that followed there were mass arrests and whare were demolished. Hāmana and Rāwiri were handcuffed together as they refused to give their names when arrested. They were force-marched with about two hundred other men, women and children from South Taranaki, spending the night in the open; in pouring rain on the way to the New Plymouth railway station and on to Waitara.

The 'ringleaders of the rebellion' were remanded in custody for trial. Most of the others detained in the mass arrests at Parihaka were released soon after their arrest. Hāmana returned to Te Kuiti with Āwhina. Rāwiri returned to Auckland and resumed his employment on the Dilworth estate, but not before taking Wiremu to his new home in Auckland at Saint Stephen's Boarding School for Māori Boys.

Croumbie-Brown escaped arrest, and he wrote to Rāwiri, as promised, with news of the aftermath of the invasion. He had returned to Parihaka and reported on the devastation. The village lay in ruins and a road was being surveyed through it. In a little under three weeks the 'squatters' of Parihaka were evicted and scattered throughout Taranaki. The rampaging troops had left a legacy of syphilis in Parihaka, which had hitherto not had any venereal disease. Homeless and hungry families in Taranaki sought refuge in the Waimate Plains. The Armed Constabulary had slaughtered pigs on the Parihaka farmland and destroyed crops there and further afield into North Taranaki to hasten the starvation of the natives.

Croumbie-Brown also followed the ensuing trials. Tītokowaru was jailed along with Te Whiti and Tohu in the Pungarehu Stockade. Wiremu Hīroki was convicted of murder and hanged. Tītokowaru went on a hunger strike to protest his treatment until he was threatened with force feeding. After six months of imprisonment, during which his poor health further deteriorated, he was brought to trial, acquitted and released.

Te Whiti and Tohu appeared in the New Plymouth court for a trial that failed to bring a conviction and were held on remand for six months and then also acquitted, much to Bryce's chagrin. At the end of the trial Te Whiti simply said, "We wish to continue to cultivate our land and live on our land peacefully, without quarrel. We do not wish any evil to come to Māori or Pākehā."

Much of this news was also reported in the newspaper The Star, but Croumbie-Brown had also written a poem to commemorate the invasion of Parihaka. A couple of stanzas memorably expressed the writer's feelings:

*There was bustle in the tented field, there was marching*
*to and fro,*
*For Bryce had said, "The time has come to strike the*
*fatal blow;*
*Call it conquest, call it murder, bring it credit or*
*disgrace,*
*I care not, I have spoken, I will crush a hated race."*

*O shame upon the nation that could stoop to such a deed,*
*To send an armed battalion where no foe had dared to*
*lead!*
*O curse upon the coward blow that struck at men*
*unarmed—*

*The blow that left a people crushed, betrayed, and deeply harmed.*

Rāwiri and Croumbie-Brown continued to correspond. Rāwiri shared information about the Kīngitanga and the reporter kept him informed of the government's egregious treatment of Te Whiti and Tohu.

It was another two years before the two prophets returned to Parihaka, as they were exiled to the South Island by means of a hastily drafted piece of legislation called the West Coast Peace Preservation Bill, whereby 'the two aboriginal natives named Te Whiti o Rongomai and Tohu Kākahi are not to be tried, but jailed indefinitely, and if released they can be rearrested without charge at any time'. It also provided for a fine of £500 for anyone attempting to defeat the effect of said law. When they did finally return to Parihaka it was not to the peace they had hoped for. The village lay in ruins and the people dispersed. With the remnant that remained they again resisted the continuing confiscation of their land, again ploughed and quarrelled with the government and continued to be arrested. Peace and justice were still far off.

# 20

James Dilworth expanded his business and civic interests. He served on the Auckland Provincial Council and on the boards of various companies, including the Auckland Fibre Manufacturing Company, the Thames Valley and Rotorua Railway Company and the New Zealand Frozen Meat and Storage Company. He had prudently or, perhaps fortunately, diversified his business enterprises at a time when the thriving economy slumped into a period of depression, with low commodity prices for agricultural exports. He was fortunate to have able managers to run the day-to-day business of his agricultural enterprises. Kelly assumed the main managerial responsibility and Rāwiri served more of a lieutenant role.

Rāwiri was occasionally absent from work, however, to attend Kīngitanga Parliament meetings in Te Kuiti, and later, thankfully, closer to Auckland, when Tāwhiao moved to Pukekawa on an area of Waikato land the government returned to Ngāti Maniapoto, and he set up a Māori Parliament based at Māungakawa. Rāwiri took leave without pay to attend the political hui, often at short notice. Dilworth was not unsympathetic to the Kīngitanga and their political objectives but he was unhappy about Rāwiri's divided loyalty. However, in the short term, there was less business activity in the agricultural sector, and less revenue, so in that regard it could be seen as a convenient arrangement.

During one of Rāwiri's absences, Dilworth asked Kelly to pick up some sacks of seed potatoes and maize seed, at Rāwiri's home, as it was time for planting a fodder crop for the cattle.

"They're in the shed at the back," Dilworth said, handing Kelly a ring of keys. "And there's a bill of sale you can pick up from in the house as well."

Kelly drove the cart to Rāwiri's place and as he walked down the path to the shed with keys in hand, he noticed the door was already open and a window at the back of the house was broken open. He went to take a closer look and heard movement within the house. He returned to the cart and fetched a heavy wrench from out of the toolbox and quietly entered the house through the front door. Seeing Kelly come through the door with the wrench upraised, the intruder dashed to the kitchen and seized a knife, to even the odds for a confrontation. In the brief standoff Kelly recognised the boy. It was Wiremu.

Kelly put the wrench down and said, "I thought you were a burglar." A tense moment passed and he said, "Are you going to put the knife down?"

Wiremu held Kelly's gaze and put the knife on the kitchen table, still within reach.

"What are you doing here?" Kelly said. "Why aren't you at school?"

"I'm not going back there," Wiremu said.

"Why? What's happened?"

"They beat me. They beat me with sticks and kicked me."

"Who? Who beat you?"

"The older boys. They call me names. They call me half-caste and bastard. I am a half-caste bastard, because of you."

"I'm sorry." There were scrapes and bruises on Wiremu's legs. "Do they beat other boys?"

"They make the younger boys do jobs for them and beat them too."

"Have you told the masters?"

"No, they'll beat us more if we tell. Anyway the masters don't care."

I'll go and see the headmaster. I'll go with my boss Mr Dilworth. He's a friend of Mr Davies."

"I'm not going back there. I want to go back to Te Kuiti."

Kelly was resisting an impulse welling up within him to put his arm around the boy, but he kept a careful distance, physically, and emotionally.

His eyes swept the room. "You can't eat that," he said, looking at the bowl of maize on the table. "It's cattle food. Help me load the sacks onto the cart and I'll take you to my home for a proper meal."

Kelly was dignifying the offer as payment for labour. He manoeuvred the cart to the shed while Wiremu dragged the sacks outside, where he grappled them and heaved them up to Kelly to stack on the cart. With the cart loaded they sat side by side on the wooden seat.

"Tell me about the school," Kelly prompted Wiremu, on the way to the warehouse.

"The masters are strict, but I enjoyed the lessons. I like Mathematics. I got good marks, at the beginning. And I enjoyed the games. I played rugby."

"What about the hostel?"

"Bad things happen in the dormitory."

Kelly didn't press for details. "Did you make friends?"

"Yes, some boys in my class. But the older boys pick on us."

Wiremu was becoming more sullen and reluctant to speak and Kelly let it rest. Wiremu unloaded the cargo at the warehouse and Kelly spoke to Dilworth, who was still in the office.

"I'm sorry to hear the lad has been mistreated at the school," Dilworth said. "I'll have a word to Davies about it."

"You and I both," Kelly said.

"I'll make the arrangements," Dilworth said.

Kelly hitched up the gig for the return home. Wiremu followed him diffidently into the house when they arrived and Kelly announced, "Wiremu will be joining us for dinner."

"You're welcome here, Wiremu," Annie said, and she raised a brow at Finbar with unspoken questions.

"There was a problem at school," Kelly said. "And Rāwiri is away, out of town."

To Wiremu he said, "You remember meeting… Whaea Annie at the dock, don't you. He decided on the Māori honorific Whaea, which could mean mother or aunt. "And Eliza."

Eliza said a shy hello and continued stirring the pot on the stove. Annie called Charlie and Imogen in for dinner. They'd been playing boisterously at the back of the house but were suddenly quiet on entering the kitchen and exchanged greetings with Wiremu. Eliza set the places for dinner while Annie brought the pot of stew and the potatoes to the table. Wiremu waited to be told where to sit, which was at the end next to Kelly. He was also accustomed to waiting for grace to be said before eating. Kelly thanked the Lord for the food and pronounced a blessing on it in Jesus' name.

"How's your appetite, Wiremu?" Annie asked.

"I'm hungry," he replied, and ate with gusto.

"Wiremu's been helping me shift the sacks of maize and seed potatoes," Kelly said. "The fields are ready for planting."

He asked the children about their day at school but avoided talking about Wiremu's school. "What about homework?"

"Did it after school." Charlie and Imogen both said.

"I still have to do some Maths," Eliza said. "We've started doing algebra. Equations with Xs and Ys. Can you help me, Da?"

"Wiremu's good at Maths. Perhaps he can help."

Which he did, with ease, after dinner, while Charlie and Imogen did the dishes. After that they played a game of draughts, and while they played, Kelly heard, for the first time, Wiremu laughing.

"There's a bed for you in Charlie's room," Kelly told Wiremu. "You can stay here till we sort something out. Matua Rāwiri will be back within the week." Kelly referred to him as 'Matua or Uncle Rāwiri' just as Wiremu did, though he was actually his cousin.

"Well, that broke the ice," Annie said, after all the children were in bed. "He seems to have taken a shine to Eliza."

"Yes. Good to see him coming out of his shell," Kelly said. "I hope he'll be friends with our children,"

"He's a good-looking boy," Annie said. "Takes after his father."

Kelly took Wiremu to work with him in the morning and intended to take him to the school with Dilworth, but Wiremu refused to go.

"What do you want to do?" Kelly asked him.

"I'll stay at the warehouse."

"And after that?"

"I want to go back to Te Kuiti and stay with Whaea Āwhina."

"You know she wants you to stay here and continue with your schooling."

"What school does Eliza go to?"

"Parnell District School. It only goes to Form Two. You're past that."

"What school will she go to next year?"

"Auckland Grammar School."

"Could I go there?"

"Possibly, but you might feel more out of place there."

"Because it's a Pākehā school?" Wiremu said. "Out of place either way."

"Let's see if we can fix things at Saint Stephen's," Kelly said.

It was a short jaunt up Parnell Rise to Saint Stephen's School. Kelly and Dilworth were shown into a wood panelled office, where Mr Davies came out from behind his desk to greet them, and exchanged pleasantries with 'James'. The headmaster was an imposing figure in his black academic gown and his stylish mutton chops. He resumed his seat behind his desk, on which he had Wiremu's enrolment form. "I see Wiremu's guardian is Mr Rāwiri Quinn, the boy's cousin," he said.

"He's out of town on parliamentary business," Kelly said.

"He's an MP then?"

"Of the Kīngitanga Parliament," Kelly said.

Davies scanned the enrolment form and said, "I see Wiremu's mother is deceased," and looking sidelong at Kelly, "and you are the boy's biological father, Mr Kelly."

"Yes," said Kelly. "He was adopted by his whānau in the King Country, principally by his mother's sister, who is administrative assistant to King Tāwhiao." Kelly was at pains to intimate Wiremu was well connected, but Dilworth was probably the most influential connection as far as Davies was concerned.

"I understand you're concerned about some rough treatment Wiremu received at the hands of some senior boys," Davies said.

"He said he was punched and kicked," Kelly said.

"Well, boys will be boys, you know," Davies said, airily.

"He's got bruises all over his body. It was a serious assault, and from what he's told me, it was not an isolated incident."

"The older boys do sometimes take advantage of their seniority," Davies said.

Dilworth showed some support. "But surely you don't condone that sort of behaviour, John."

"We try not to let it get out of hand. If you want the boys responsible punished you will have to give me names."

"Wiremu won't give names."

"Well then," Davies said, as though that were the end of the matter.

"If I may make a suggestion," Dilworth said, "you could talk to the senior students as a group, and talk to the other staff so they can be more vigilant."

"Of course, I'll do that," Davies agreed.

"There's also a matter of misconduct in the dormitory at night," Kelly said.

"What sort of misconduct?"

"Wiremu wouldn't say, but I would assume something of a homosexual nature."

"This is a serious allegation, Mr Kelly."

"It's not an allegation, Mr Davies, it's a suspicion that needs investigating. You'll need to talk to the House Master as well."

Davies nodded and frowned.

"The Inspectorate will need to be informed too," Kelly added.

"I'll log your complaint, Mr Kelly, and it will be on record when the inspectors visit." Davies took his watch from his fob pocket and said, "Will that satisfy you, gentlemen?"

"For now," Kelly said.

"And when can we expect Wiremu back at school?" Davies asked.

"He's refusing to go at the moment," Kelly said, "but if we can assure him this matter is dealt with… Let's wait and see."

"Very well." Davies rose from behind his desk to see his visitors out. "Leave it with me."

Rāwiri duly returned from Maungakawa and Wiremu returned to his home. A week or so later Wiremu turned up at work with Rāwiri.

"He's been expelled from school," Rāwiri said.

"Why? What happened?"

"He took another beating from those boys. He came home in a bloody mess."

"They said it was payback," Wiremu said. He still bore the bruises on his face and a cut over his left eye.

"Then he gave the boys a thrashing with a taiaha."

"A taiaha!" Kelly said. "Where did you get a taiaha?"

"Not a real taiaha," Wiremu said. "It was a broom handle."

"He was given weapons training on the marae," Rāwiri said. "No boxing, but taiaha and mere."

"So what now?"

"He can go back to Te Kuiti."

"Is that what *you* want?" Kelly asked Wiremu.

"I could stay in Te Kuiti for a while. It's not long till the end of the year. Maybe next year I could go to the other school, the one Eliza will go to."

"Auckland Grammar."

"Yes."

And so Wiremu returned from Te Kuiti in the new year to stay with Rāwiri and attend Auckland Grammar School in Symonds Street. If he thought he would see Eliza at school, he was sorely mistaken. The school was co-educational but strictly segregated, with separate entrances for boys and girls and in the playground a fourteen-foot wall separated the sexes. Rāwiri continued to make occasional trips to the King Country and Wiremu stayed at the Kelly home while he was away. On the first such occasion Kelly asked him how he was finding the school.

"I'm coping all right with my studies," he said. "I'm enjoying English, Maths and Science. But History… It's all about Britain and the Empire. And languages… why so many languages: Latin, Greek, French? Why not te reo Māori? You know they punished me for speaking te reo at the Native School."

"Auckland Grammar School wants to turn you into a scholar and a gentleman."

"I think they want to turn me into a Pākehā," said Wiremu, sourly.

"You can have the best of both worlds. What do you want to do when you finish school?"

"Matua Rāwiri wants me to be a lawyer."

"But what do you want?"

"I don't know."

"You still have time to figure it out." After some hesitation, Kelly asked, "How are you getting on with your classmates?"

"All right. Some are a bit rude, but most are all right and I've made a few friends."

It seemed to Kelly that the boy had put on a growth spurt and filled out and would probably be able to handle himself in a fight if it came to it.

Eliza was thriving at the school and was sure that she wanted to become a teacher. She was also maturing and still enjoyed a sibling friendship with Wiremu.

Young Charles also appreciated having an older brother staying with them. Wiremu was clever at playing games and making things. He flew kites he'd made from toetoe stems and he had wooden tops he whipped with strips of flax to make them spin and hum. He had a shanghai he'd made from a forked branch and a bag of pebbles for shooting birds, and he used the pebbles also for games of knucklebones. The children sat on the ground or on the floor and tossed and scooped and caught the smooth, round stones. Wiremu had a pocketknife, which he used for carving bits of wood and there was plenty of wood in Kelly's workshop, next to the stable. Together the boys made pairs of stilts and went striding out like giants.

One of the games Wiremu liked to play with Eliza was cat's cradle. He had a length of flax string which he wove with his fingers into various patterns that he'd learnt on his home marae. He then dextrously wove the string in and out of Eliza's fingers to create the same configurations, and they laughed together as their fingers became intertwined. Eliza soon mastered cat's cradling but the game was too difficult for Imogen, who felt put out, at times, when Wiremu got all of Eliza's attention and there was no time for hopscotch in the yard or playing with dolls. But all that Imogen required to keep herself occupied was pencil and paper. She went back to her desk, where she'd spent many self-absorbed hours drawing scenes from story books she'd read and other scenes and images from dream worlds of her own imaginings.

After another of Wiremu's visits, Kelly reflected contentedly on how well the children got on together.

"Yes. Wiremu and Eliza especially," Annie said. "Did you see that he kissed her when he was leaving?"

Annie seemed to think this was a matter of concern, a romantic attraction, but Kelly said, "It was just a peck on the cheek. A brother farewelling his sister. Nothing more." And yet, and yet, Kelly knew Annie to have some intuition regarding relationships and feelings and he could not dismiss it entirely, so he resolved to be more vigilant in future. In subsequent visits, Kelly more often took Wiremu and Charles to the beach or the wharf for a boys' day out fishing.

Wiremu was a diligent student at Auckland Grammar School, excelling in Mathematics, and with much encouragement from Rāwiri, he focussed on the goal of going on to university to study Law. There were no incidents such as those that occurred at Saint Stephen's School. Wiremu's reputation as a boy with a wild Māori side had followed him from St Stephen's and the other boys were wary of him as someone not to be trifled with. He continued to move between his two homes and became part of the Kelly family.

Annie's suspicions regarding the friendship between Wiremu and Eliza proved to have some justification. Kelly came upon them unexpectedly in the garden at the back of the house in an embrace that was beyond mere sibling affection and they abruptly separated when Kelly appeared.

"This cannot be!" Kelly commanded. "Remember who you are."

Wiremu left, shamefaced; he'd been preparing to depart anyway, and Eliza went into the house in tears.

Wiremu duly graduated from school and was admitted to Otago University College. The family saw him off on that journey at the wharf, with mixed feelings. Kelly was proud of Wiremu's achievements, as was Rāwiri, but while Rāwiri regretted that Wiremu had to go all the way to Dunedin to study Law, Kelly was actually relieved that he was moving so far from Auckland. Eliza was tearful again and their parting was sad and awkward.

Wiremu boarded the coastal steamer and, as it sailed out of the harbour, he stood stoically on the deck and waved to all the family, though his gaze was fixed on Eliza.

For her part, Eliza discovered a love of language and European languages, at Auckland Grammar School and, though at times she became distracted from her studies, she never wavered from her goal of becoming a teacher. Actually, Eliza's love of words had begun with story time on her mother's knee. At home, she was often in her room, engrossed in a book.

"I'm pleased to see you have a love of reading Literature," Annie said. "I came to reading only later in life. And I can only read in English."

In Eliza's senior year at school, there was discussion at home concerning her future prospects. "Mr Reid recommends I become a teacher," she told her parents. He says now that education is free and compulsory there's a lot of demand for more teachers. And he thinks I would be a fine teacher."

"What do you think?" her father asked.

"It's what I want to do."

Eliza, in due course, graduated from school and entered Auckland Teachers' Training College, in Wellesley Street East. At the College, she developed new friendships with likeminded young women and even among the few young men who were also training to be teachers. It was quite a novelty to have male classmates. A novelty also for the fortunate men to find themselves in the company of so many young women. The male trainees fancied they had entered hunting grounds with plentiful game and joked among themselves that there were more than enough women to go round. Eliza found their ribald humour off-putting but didn't mind the attention she received from Oliver Steadman, a classmate whom she considered stood out from his peers as more urbane and more respectful of the women, especially of her.

Eliza's parents were also approving and perhaps even relieved when Oliver came courting their daughter. Wiremu had faded into the background.

"Oliver seems a very personable young man," Kelly remarked, "but I'd like to know more about his character and his prospects, as he's a possible candidate for our daughter's hand in marriage."

"Eliza's told me he's a church-going Christian," Annie said. "He goes to a Baptist church."

"And what of his family?"

"He was born in Australia. His father's an industrialist, in the iron and steel business. So probably quite well off, not that that matters, particularly. He has a secure job as a teacher. And he likes children."

"You seem well-informed."

"A girl will sometimes confide in her mother in matters of the heart."

Charles and Imogen continued the family tradition of going to Auckland Grammar School, though neither stayed there long. Charles disliked academic study and instead got apprenticed to a builder. His love of carpentry had begun in his father's workshop, where they worked with wood together. A good honest trade, as Kelly said, when he made the arrangement with Ernest Samuel, the builder in question, whom Kelly knew to be a man of good character with a reputable construction company. Charles wasn't completely done with schooling, though, as he attended evening classes at a technical school to properly learn the trade.

Imogen had a precocious talent for art and applied herself to the study of Art at Auckland Grammar School but showed little interest in any other subject. She left the school toward the end of the first year because of her failing grades and failing health. She had a congenital heart condition, for which the doctors had no remedy and she had consequently always been a bit sickly and prone to fainting. So Imogen worked on her art quite happily at home, with the occasional supervision of Mrs Paddock, her art teacher, who had been so impressed with her work at school and continued to take an interest. Mrs Paddock made sure her protégée was well supplied with materials, especially water colours, with which Imogen painted landscapes and still lifes, many of which adorned the walls of the Kelly home.

Āwhina continued to work with the Kīngitanga, petitioning Parliament in their quest for justice. She corresponded frequently with Rāwiri now and they kept each other informed about Kīngitanga business. After a meeting between Tāwhiao and Native Minister Bryce, Āwhina wrote to say:

"Bryce tried to bully Tāwhiao into accepting deals offering less than what Grey and McLean had laid on the table. We get less and less from the government. We think it is time to seek legal redress from the British government. With the help of our Māori MPs, we have written a letter to the Aboriginals Protection Society to take to Parliament to plead our case."

Some months later Āwhina sent an update:

"The British government referred our request back to the New Zealand government and Bryce just dismissed it. He tells the Colonial Office 'the Māoris are being treated fairly.'

Disappointing but no great surprise. Now Tāwhiao is preparing to go to London and call on the Queen himself. We reminded him that a deputation of northern iwi had already taken a petition to London and were denied an audience with the Queen, thanks to the lobbying of New Zealand Government officials. They saw only the Secretary of State for the Colonies and he also ruled it was a matter for the colonial government. Tāwhiao says, 'They were chiefs but I am a King.' He is confident of success. I hope he is right."

Tāwhiao led a deputation to London with the MP, Te Wheoro, who had been a loyalist in the wars with the British, Taingākawa Te Waharoa, three other chiefs: Topia Turoa, Patara te Tuhi, Hori Ropiha, and the loyalist half Māori–half European, George Skidmore, as interpreter. All the New Zealand newspapers regularly reported on the activities of the delegation.

They were comfortably accommodated at Demeter House, Montague Place, in Russell Square, which became the Māori High Commission for the four-month duration of their visit. The party had a busy itinerary of sightseeing, civic receptions and theatres, although Tāwhiao was confined at home by sickness for a time. He was troubled by rheumatism and a cold, for which he chewed lozenges, and smoked cigars. The tattooed 'King of the Māoris', with his long pounamu ear pendants, was an object of great interest in high society and much fêted in London and in the British press. He was fêted also by British temperance leagues for his support of their cause. When Tāwhiao and his entourage had visited Grey to obtain letters of introduction in preparation for the trip to London, Grey, being mindful of Tāwhiao's weakness for alcohol, had them all sign a pledge to abstain for twelve months and Grey's niece sewed the blue ribbon temperance insignia on their tweed jackets. They were true to their word and drank only ginger ale and none of the champagne proffered on many civic occasions. At a temperance fête at the National League at the Crystal Palace at Sydenham, Tāwhiao spoke of the damage alcohol had done to his people and announced his intention to banish drink from his country, for which he was enthusiastically cheered.

It took a full six weeks before Tāwhiao's petition, or 'memorial', was fully prepared and he was able to get an audience with Secretary of State for the Colonies, Lord Derby. The deputation did not succeed in getting an audience with the Queen, as they had hoped.

Tāwhiao's delegation was met by civil servants at the Government Office complex at Whitehall, signed in and ushered into the Colonial Office. After a brief wait in the reception area, Tāwhiao, Te Wheoro and Skidmore were invited into the ministerial room. Tall windows admitted a thin London light into the large chamber. The ceiling was so high there was room enough for another floor. Lord Derby rose from his leather upholstered chair and came out from behind his large mahogany desk to greet his guests. He introduced himself and John Gorst, Tory MP, formerly Waikato Civil Commissioner. Behind Lord Derby was a wall of shelves of books. On the wall to the right were maps of the British Empire, with New Zealand and other colonial territories marked in red.

Tāwhiao introduced himself and his retinue with handshakes all round. He carried himself with confidence and dignity and shook hands with everyone, as he did at all formal occasions, including the footmen, which, according to the Pall Mall Gazette, his hosts considered an amusing gaffe.

Lord Derby resumed his seat behind his desk and said, "King Tāwhiao, I am glad to receive you and those who accompany you. I am sorry that it will not be possible for you to meet with Her Majesty the Queen. The New Zealand government representative in England, Francis Dillon Bell, has been working behind the scenes to ensure that no such meeting will take place. I regret to say, Dillon Bell advised the Colonial Office that you have very limited authority among the Māori of New Zealand and are not of fit character to meet with the Queen."

"Dillon Bell was formerly our government's Native Minister," Tāwhiao said. "He never represented Māori fairly and he has not represented me fairly. He is a liar and a slanderer."

"That is all very unfortunate," Lord Derby said. "But let us try to make the most of our meeting." Assuming a more positive demeanour, he addressed the group. "So, gentlemen, how did you enjoy the Grand Military Tournament at the Agricultural Hall?"

Skidmore replied on behalf of the group. "We enjoyed the riding display, but we were not much interested in the military manoeuvres. We have seen more than enough of British soldiers in New Zealand."

"Quite so," Gorst agreed, as he had witnessed the invasion of the Waikato for himself and was sympathetic to the Kīngitanga. "But I hope you have been enjoying your stay in London."

"Yes, we have been treated well and seen many interesting things," said Skidmore, and Tāwhiao added, "I enjoyed the opera and the ballet."

"Good, good, and so to business," said Derby rising to receive the memorial.

Discussion of the petition ensued, with Tāwhiao stressing their allegiance to the Queen and the Treaty of Waitangi and the necessity of bringing their petition before the Queen. "The New Zealand government has trampled on our rights," he said, "and they ignore our petitions."

"But you are a member of the New Zealand Parliament, are you not, Mr Te Wheoro?" said Derby.

"I am," said Te Wheoro, "but the Māori members are ignored, and we are sorely under represented. There is provision for only four MPs to represent all of Māoridom."

"I see you have serious grievances particularly with regard to land," Derby observed.

"They were driven off their land in an unprovoked attack and their lands confiscated," said Gorst.

"Yes, the land seized by the government must be returned to us, to Māori ownership," said Tāwhiao. "And Māori judges should be appointed to the Native Land Court, not the European judges who use the court to take more land."

"Then there is the matter of political autonomy," said Derby.

"This was guaranteed by the Treaty. We want to be able to legislate for ourselves with our own government and for Her Majesty to appoint a native Chief as Commissioner."

"Perfectly reasonable and responsible," said Gorst. "I've been an advocate for Irish Home Rule, and I feel the same about Māori self-rule."

"And what of the cost of running your own administration?" said Derby.

Tāwhiao replied, "A large part of the taxes levied on us by central Government should be returned to us to cover the cost of our administration."

After some further discussion Lord Derby concluded, "Her Majesty's Government agrees that the Treaty obligations should be respected, but the authority and administration of the law have passed to the New Zealand authorities. We cannot dictate to the New Zealand Parliament.

"However," Derby continued, "I am confident that the New Zealand Government will not fail to protect and promote the welfare of the natives by a just administration of the law and by a generous consideration of all your reasonable representations. And that is what I shall communicate to The New Zealand Parliament."

Parliament was duly informed and the activities of King Tāwhiao's deputation in London were regularly reported in the New Zealand press. Tāwhiao took heart from Lord Derby's response, as their 'representations' were most certainly reasonable, and he expected that the New Zealand Government would now be forced to comply with the requests of their petition. The New Zealand Government, however, had no trouble with ignoring Lord Derby's 'advice'. New Zealand Governor Jervois reported to the Colonial Office that "the natives have been exceptionally well treated and have nothing to complain about."

Tāwhiao and the Kīngitanga continued their political activities and petitioned the Queen to approve their proposal for a separate Māori Parliament in New Zealand. All to no avail. Seventy tribal chiefs, who did not recognise Tāwhiao's authority and his claim to govern the entire country, took a different approach and formed a separate, independent Māori Parliament, the Paremata, or Te Kotahitanga, as it was also known. Together with the four Māori Members of Parliament of the constituted New Zealand Government, Te Kotahitanga organised and agitated for redress of injustices suffered by Māori and return of confiscated land. The New Zealand Parliament ignored most of the petitions presented by the Paremata, and any bills presented, such as the Native Rights Bill, were defeated and Māori land continued to be alienated.

The Kīngitanga did not join the Kotahitanga Parliament, nor did the followers of Te Whiti. Tāwhiao continued to claim sovereignty and issued an edict banishing Europeans from New Zealand. "The Governor, the

Government and all government officers must leave the island," he said. "The island is mine. The blacksmiths, the carpenters and storekeepers may remain. I will look after them all. All other Pākehā must leave this island and return to England."

# 22

On returning to work from one of his sojourns in the King Country, Rāwiri placed an envelope on Kelly's desk in the warehouse. Kelly expected it was an invoice for goods he had purchased, but he found, to his surprise, the envelope contained an invitation to the wedding of Rāwiri Quinn and Roimata Hērangi.

"Rāwiri, you dark horse," Kelly exclaimed. "So, you weren't just visiting your mother in Te Kuiti."

"Actually, we're already married. We had our wedding at Roimata's home marae at Mangatāwhiri. But I want to have an official wedding in the church here as well."

"So you are already married. Congratulations." Kelly rose from his office chair to shake Rāwiri's hand. "Two weddings, eh."

"You had two weddings."

"The first one didn't count," Kelly said, his smile faltering for a moment. "And I thought you were a bachelor for life. So where's your wife now? Have you brought her back with you?"

"Yes, she's here at home."

“Here, take a seat.” Kelly pulled up another chair and resumed his own seat. “Whaea Roimata. A new auntie in the home for Wiremu. Is he going to stay with you still?”

“Yes, for now anyway. He can stay as long as he likes. He’s whānau.”

“I haven’t seen Wiremu since he’s come back from Dunedin. He hasn’t even contacted me.”

“He’s been back in the King Country. They’re celebrating his success down there. You should make contact with him when he returns. He became very fond of your family and he was sad to leave.”

“He was especially fond of Eliza,” Kelly said.

“Do you think he was sweet on her?”

“Yes. I was getting concerned about it.”

“That might explain why he was getting so moody and miserable before he left.”

“Still, he’s done well for himself, hasn’t he,” Kelly said.

“Yes, he really threw himself into his studies. You know he graduated LLB with honours?

“What’s LLB stand for?”

“It’s Bachelor of Law.”

“Why isn’t it a BL then? A Bachelor of Arts is a BA.”

“I don’t know why it’s LLB. Anyway, it’s a Law degree.”

“He’s got a good brain, all right,” Kelly said.

“I wonder which side of the family that comes from.”

“Well, I’ll take some of the credit.”

“He was lucky to get a good job here,” Rāwiri said. “A lot of law firms are struggling with the downturn in business.”

“Who’s he working for?”

"Russell and Campbell. One of the best. But he's also doing some work for Te Kotahitanga, the Māori Parliament, helping with land issues and submissions to Government."

"He's a busy boy."

"Sure is. His work for Te Kotahitanga is pro bono publico."

"What's that?"

"Unpaid."

"I suppose he makes enough with Russell and Campbell," Kelly remarked.

"He's very clued up on land issues and how to deal with Government and Councils. He specialised in Land Law in his degree, as well as Constitutional and Public Law, Colonial Self-government, Crown Powers, and Parliamentary Sovereignty. Russell and Campbell thought he'd be useful to them, especially dealing with the Land Court and the Māori perspective and all that. You should come round and talk to him yourself. I'm sure he'd appreciate a visit, if you can catch him at home."

Which Kelly did, one fine Sunday afternoon when neither of them was working. Wiremu welcomed Kelly and poured them both a beer. Kelly didn't drink at home, but didn't hesitate to imbibe with Wiremu, for the sake of camaraderie. They sat on the veranda and chatted about his life in Dunedin. Kelly prompted him to talk about his work.

"Russell and Campbell are a very modern and progressive, all male firm," Wiremu said. "No women. They've got telephones and hansom cabs for visiting clients and they've just got those new typing machines. One of my jobs is I'm a typewriter."

Kelly smiled at the irony, the humour, the self-deprecation and he asked about Wiremu's clients, to turn the conversation to what he really did.

"Most of their business comes from their big clients: the Auckland Harbour Board, the Waitematā County Council, the Ōnehunga Borough Council, and the liquor industry," he said, raising his glass and taking a draught. "But a lot of the work I do is pretty mundane: drawing up agreements for leases, conveyancing, property taxation, litigation on debts, and the like. I'm just a law clerk. The work I do for the rūnanga is actually more interesting."

"The rūnanga?"

"The Māori Parliament. Te Kotahitanga."

Wiremu seemed to have grown in every dimension.

Of the Kelly children, Imogen was the only one still in the family home, and Annie was glad of her company. After graduating from Teachers' College, Eliza started work at Parnell District School, the very school she had attended as a child. And she stayed living at home until her marriage to Oliver Steadman. The wedding took place in Saint Mark's Church, in Remuera, the only church she had ever attended, where she and Charles and Imogen were christened, and where her parents were married.

Wiremu was invited to the wedding, along with Rāwiri and Roimata, and they sat in a pew near the back of the nave. At the front of the church, the bridal couple knelt at the altar, as the vicar recited the prayers. Then they stood together as he led them through their vows. Wiremu had heard the story from Rāwiri of how his Uncle Matua Hāmana had stopped Kelly and Annie's wedding with his shocking objection. Now, as the vicar looked up and addressed the assembled guests with:

> *If there is anyone present who can show just cause why these two persons may not be joined in matrimony, speak now or forever hold your peace.*

Wiremu pictured himself jumping to his feet and shouting, *It's me she loves! I am her first love!* But no, he would not scandalise the family. He would hold his peace, forever hold his peace. Instead, at the end of the ceremony, he congratulated the newlyweds, he kissed Eliza on the cheek, shook Oliver's hand, and wished them well.

Annie and Imogen went on outings together, where Imogen would sketch scenes of the Auckland environs, harbour and bays, from which she painted landscapes, at home. She did her painting in the studio she had set up in the bedroom which had become spare, since Charles had moved out. His employer, Ernest Samuel, had offered him a house in Ōnehunga, where there was a building boom, and a shortage of qualified tradesmen.

Annie recognised in Imogen's paintings the scenes they had admired together but the mystically dream-like landscapes also made her realise that Imogen had a different way of seeing the natural world. Imogen's old art teacher, Mrs Paddock, had retired from school teaching to work on her own art and had opened a studio and gallery in the town. She was a great encouragement to Imogen and a few other 'promising young artists'. Imogen's outings often included visits to the Paddock Gallery and she exhibited some of her own work there, at Mrs Paddock's invitation, first alongside other artists, and subsequently as sole exhibitor. Her exhibition was well received and several of her paintings sold.

Annie had sometimes to be caregiver and nurse to Imogen, but she had enough time of her own to pursue outside interests. She had garnered a circle of friends within the church and joined a group of women who were opposed to the sale and consumption of alcohol and were campaigning for prohibition. They became politically involved in the cause by forming a local chapter of the New Zealand Women's Christian Temperance Union. It seemed to Annie a worthy cause, as she had seen much harm caused by liquor back in Ireland, even in her own family, and also in New Zealand. With Isabella, she attended a meeting at church, convened by Isabella's friend, Amey Daldy, President of the Auckland branch of the Women's Franchise League. Kate Shepperd, the founder of the WCTU had informed Mrs Daldy that she would be coming to Auckland as part of her national speaking tour. Mrs Shepperd was Secretary of the Ladies' Association of the Trinity Congregational Church in Christchurch and Isabella had met her previously when she came to Auckland on church business concerning Bible classes and fund raising.

Annie was not long home from the church meeting when she told Kelly about Kate Shepperd coming to Auckland and that she wanted to go to hear her address at the Town Hall.

"Kate Shepperd, you say," Kelly said, looking up from his newspaper. "The Christian socialist."

"Yes, she's coming to speak about prohibition and political reform."

"To get women the right to vote. That'll be a hard battle."

"Some of the MPs are in favour."

"Really? Who?"

"Alfred Saunders, for one. And Sir John Hall." Annie was sure there were a few more but couldn't think of any others. "Most women would vote for prohibition in the referendums."

"I can see the point," Kelly said. "The country won't go dry if it's left to the men."

"The King Country's dry."

"True, and they're better off for it."

"The meeting's in two weeks' time, on the Sunday afternoon. Isabella's going and she's asked me to accompany her."

"Should be an interesting meeting," Kelly remarked, from behind his paper.

Annie waited for more of a response.

"Oh, well all right. I'll have my day of rest at home."

"Thank you Finbar. Not all the husbands are as supportive. Josiah Gooch said he won't have Eunice meddling in masculine concerns. Henry Sweetman says Nora needs to stay home and attend to what nature designed women for: cooking meals, emptying slops, and looking after children."

"Yes, that sounds like Henry all right."

Sitting in the auditorium of the Town Hall, Annie was anticipating a strident, rousing call to action. But she was a little surprised when the elegantly dressed Kate Shepperd walked out onto the stage and addressed the assembled women in a calm and pleasantly feminine voice, a cultured voice with a touch of the Liverpool accent. Mrs Shepperd began by commending the many women who had come out to get involved in much needed social and political reform.

"We are tired of having a 'sphere' doled out to us," she said, "and being told that anything outside that sphere is 'unwomanly.' Women should not be confined to the sphere of domesticity and we should be valued as more than just the property of men."

After these introductory remarks Mrs Shepperd addressed the issue of prohibition. "Alcohol is the cause of many social ills, the cause of poverty, immorality, social and economic instability, ill health and even death. The main causes of death in this country are: drink, drowning, and drowning while drunk.

"Prohibition can be achieved by proper democratic process. Liquor is already banned in some electorates, but our objective is prohibition for the whole country. Prohibition is decided by referendum. A sixty per cent majority vote is required. Yes, it is a high threshold, but it is achievable. If women are given the opportunity to vote I believe we will carry the day."

Annie and Isabella, nodded, agreeing with Mrs Shepperd and with each other.

"So, our first objective," Mrs Shepperd continued, "is to secure the right to vote, ahead of the next general election. Why should we women be excluded from voting, along with juveniles, lunatics, and criminals? We cannot wait for men to allow us to vote. We must fight for the right to vote and win it for ourselves. We will keep lobbying our politicians and petitioning Parliament. Our last petition procured almost 20,000 signatures. Support for the cause is increasing, even among some of the men in our government. We shall keep petitioning Parliament. They can't ignore us forever. I tell you the day will come when we shall even have women members of parliament."

Women in government? This last claim prompted some applause from the audience and some sporadic murmuring of approval, and disbelief from some for whom it seemed too idealistic, too revolutionary.

"The time has come for concerted action," Mrs Shepperd proclaimed. "We will take our petition the length and breadth of the country and give every woman the opportunity to sign it, and any men who so wish. We have pamphlets to distribute and petition forms." She indicated the stacks of papers on the stage. "We need many volunteers. We need you. Our committee will record the areas of the province you are willing to cover."

Most of the audience, including Annie and the women she'd come with, caught the vision and committed to volunteering for the campaign. When Annie got home, she gave Kelly an account of the meeting while the zeal for the cause was still upon her. Kelly agreed it was a worthy cause and supposed it would be all right for her to devote a bit of time to take the petition on the road with Isabella, as long as Imogen didn't need looking after at the time.

"Of course, Isabella doesn't have any children to worry about," he said. "What about Mrs Shepperd? Does she have a family?"

"She has one child. A boy."

"And what's her husband?"

"A grocer and merchant."

*Kate Shepperd's suffrage campaign resulted in a petition with an unprecedented 32,000 signatures, almost a quarter of the adult female European population. She glued the five hundred and forty-six sheets of the petition together and the resulting scroll, measuring over three hundred yards long, was ceremoniously unrolled across the chamber of the House of Representatives. Prime Minister Richard Seddon, who had implacably opposed bills to extend the vote to women, had to concede. The Legislative Council voted twenty votes to eighteen in favour of the Bill and, despite the opposition of the powerful liquor lobby, the Electoral Act 1893 was passed into law. The right to vote was extended to all women who were British subjects, including Māori women—but not Chinese.*

Thus was heralded in the newspapers an historic victory for women and for New Zealand leading the way for women's suffrage. As for prohibition, there was a 'no liquor licence' vote in some districts but not for national prohibition.

The Kellys paid occasional visits to Charles in Ōnehunga, where they enjoyed family picnics on the beach and fishing from the wharf. Wiremu joined the family on one such outing, at Kelly's invitation. It was just a short train trip south from Newmarket Station across the isthmus to Auckland's western port on the Manukau Harbour. They disembarked at the Ōnehunga Station next to the sprawling ironworks and from there back from the waterfront to Charles' home on Princes Street. Charles was the proud owner of a new, solid kauri house right in the town.

"Not that I actually own it yet," he explained. "It's rent to own at a fixed, below market price. A company perk."

With preparations for the day, the family made their way back to the waterfront. Annie and Imogen settled on a rug on the black sand of the beach. It was the miles of black iron sand along the west coast that fed the blast furnaces of the ironworks.

The men carried on to the wharf with their fishing gear. There was a ship berthed at the port, loading kauri timber, and the town was busy with industry: the Manukau Steam Sawmill, the Bycroft flour and biscuit factory, and the woollen mill. And the towering brick chimney of the New Zealand Iron and Steel Company, with its plume of black smoke, could be seen from anywhere in the town.

Kelly sat contentedly on the wharf, with rod in hand, gazing at the sea and Māngere Mountain in the distance. It was like a scene from the past, with Charles and Wiremu at his side. A couple of hours of patient fishing produced only a few small snapper.

"They say the fishing used to be much better here," Charles said. "I fish here with a friend from church sometimes. He's lived here for years and he says there's not so many fish in the harbour because the water's getting polluted from all the industry."

"I've heard that too," Wiremu said. "The local iwi used to get a lot of kaimoana from the harbour. The Māori who still live here have complained to the Borough Council about the pollution of their fishing grounds. They say most of it's coming from the ironworks. And it'll only get worse. They're planning to build ten new furnaces and a rolling mill."

"What does the Council say about it?" Kelly asked.

"They say their inspector monitors the factory and the water quality, and it's all within safe limits," Wiremu said.

"That's exactly right," Charles said. "My fishing mate, Henry, works for the Council, in the Rates Department, and the inspector, Mr Sowry, is one of his colleagues. Sowry is catching fish all right, going out of the harbour in his new boat. I'm pretty sure he's collecting bribes from the ironworks manager to doctor his reports."

"We suspected something of the sort," Wiremu said.

"Who's we?" Kelly and Charles both said.

"When the iwi were fobbed off by the Council, they contacted Te Kotahitanga to try to get legal action. It's a breach of the Treaty of Waitangi. The Treaty guarantees protection of customary fishing grounds."

"Right, and you work for Kotahitanga," Charles said.

"In an advisory capacity."

Kelly retrieved his fishing line. "Small fish stripping the bait," he observed and rebaited the hook. "I see a conflict of interests here. Ōnehunga Borough Council is one of your employer's main clients. Do you think Russell and Campbell will want to prosecute the Council? And Wesley Steadman is the Operations Manager of the ironworks. Do you want to prosecute Eliza's father-in-law?"

"Can you get proof of the false inspection reports?" Wiremu asked Charles.

"Maybe," Charles said, doubtfully.

"I just want to know if we have the option to prosecute," Wiremu said. "The threat may be sufficient."

"The Council needs a shake up from what I hear," Charles said. "And Henry would have the backing of the mayor. Mr Sowry is one of the councillors always obstructing the mayor."

"Elizabeth Yates," Kelly said. "Annie knows her. She's the only female mayor in the British Empire. Some of the councillors resigned in protest when she was elected."

"Ma knows her? Small world," Charles said.

"Small colony," said Wiremu.

# 23

The Kellys attended two funerals in one year, in the year of 1894. The first was in September on a fine spring day, though it was still cool enough to be wearing coats. Imogen especially needed wrapping up against the cold. The Kelly family, plus Eliza's husband, Oliver Steadman, boarded the special train at 8:00 am, along with a thousand others. The crowded train travelled south to Taupiri, for the tangihanga of King Tāwhiao, and arrived at 11:30.

The passengers disembarked at Taupiri Station and made their way to the site between the Waikato River and the sacred mountain, where Tāwhiao was to be buried next to his father Pōtatau Te Wherowhero, the first Māori King. There they joined the throngs of mourners from throughout the country, including many dignitaries, among the tents and whare of nīkau and raupō, and enormous quantities of food, cooked in at least fifty hāngī pits.

Hundreds of Māori men gathered together, near naked, as warriors, and broke out into a thunderous haka. The warriors chanted, and slapped their thighs and their chests, raked their chests with their fingernails, drawing blood. The ground reverberated under their feet as they stamped in unison.

And then the pūkana: the bulging eyes, the protruding tongue. A ferocious display to terrify an enemy. Kelly had seen it before on the battlefield and he had indeed been terrified. The protruding, lapping, flicking tongue of cannibal blood lust, that said *I want to drink your blood.* Or was it a show of *Your head will look like this when I cut it off? Your tongue will hang out. Your eyes will roll back.* The chanting, slapping, stamping. It was all a pulsating, mesmerising rhythm.

"Are you all right Finbar?" Annie said, threading her arm through his. "What hath thee in thrall?"

"What?" Kelly gave her a blank look.

"It's a line from a poem, *La Belle Dame Sans Merci.* I've been reading John Keats' poetry and the words have been running round in my head. That one just came to mind.

*O what can ail thee, knight-at-arms,*

*So haggard and so woe-begone?*

"It's a lovely poem. I'll read it to you when we're home."

Another band of warriors formed an honour guard and performed a haka, brandishing weapons of the recent wars: mere, taiaha, a few swords and many muskets, and fired volleys of blanks into the air.

"It's a pity they got their hands on muskets in the first place," Oliver remarked. "They would have all killed each other off, tribe against tribe, if the British hadn't come and brought peace."

Kelly shook his head. "We brought them more war."

"How could a bunch of primitive savages hope to defeat a modern European army?"

"We only defeated the so-called savages in the end because we had an unlimited supply of soldiers and weapons and treachery."

A brass band played *The Dead March*, while kuia, wearing wreaths of greenery about their heads, wailed a lament for their dead King. A press photographer recording the spectacle was ordered off the site, as his camera on a tripod, apparently bore a sinister resemblance to the theodolite of a surveyor's equipment.

Kelly had only a brief reunion with Āwhina, as she was an integral part of the Kīngitanga retinue at the tangi. She accompanied Tana Taingākawa, the son of Wiremu Tāmihana. As successor to Tāmihana, the Kingmaker, he had performed the same function, at Taupiri, by anointing Tāwhiao's son Mahuta as the new Māori King.

Āwhina seemed more distant. Pākehā were kept at a distance from the ceremony anyway, behind a cordon. Rāwiri, Roimata and Wiremu were there but had come with a different rōpū. Rāwiri had become increasingly involved in Māori politics and was greatly influenced by Hamiora Mangakahia, who became the Premier of the Great Council of Te Kotahitanga, the new Māori Parliament, based in Waitangi. Rāwiri consequently shifted his allegiance from the Kīngitanga to Te Kotahitanga, which was a disappointment to his mother, who remained loyal to the Kīngitanga.

The aroma of cooked meat and vegetables wafted into the air as the food was uncovered from the many umu, the earth ovens, in which they had been steaming during the day. The iwi commissariat brought the hāngi food to tables and fed three thousand hungry mouths at the end of the day. Hunger satiated, the throngs of mourners from Auckland and all points north boarded the train again at 5:15 pm. They arrived at Auckland station at 8:30 pm, where carriages and omnibuses waited at the gas-lit cab stand. It had been a long and tiring day and the Kellys were relieved to return to the comfort of their home.

"What a marvellous meal that was," Annie remarked, from her favourite armchair. "So succulent, and I love the earthy taste of hāngi food. I especially liked the pork and kūmaras."

"We were well-fed, all right," said Kelly, patting his stomach. "And they catered as efficiently as any army commissariat." He yawned and said he was ready for bed.

"So am I," said Annie, but first there's the matter of the poem I said I would read when we got home."

Kelly had forgotten about it but was prepared to humour her enthusiasm for poetry.

She took the book from the shelf, flicked through the pages to the poem in question and began to read.

*O what can ail thee, knight-at-arms,*
*So haggard and so woe-begone?*
*I saw pale kings and princes too,*
*Pale warriors, death-pale were they all;*
*They cried – 'La belle dame sans merci*
*Thee hath in thrall!'*
*I met a lady in the meads,*
*Full beautiful—a faery's child,*
*Her hair was long, her foot was light,*
*And her eyes were wild.*
*She looked at me as she did love,*
*And made sweet moan.*
*I set her on my prancing steed,*
*And nothing else saw all day long…*
*She found me roots of relish sweet,*
*And honey wild, and manna-dew'*
*And sure in language strange she said -*
*'I love thee true'.*

Yes, it was a charming poem, but somehow also unnerving. Kelly suspected something personal, a barbed message.

But Annie more than put his mind at ease. She closed the book and, with a coy smile, said, “I’m well-acquainted with your ‘prancing steed’, Finbar, and I love thee true.”

“Ah, time for bed then.”

The second funeral, on Christmas Day, was that of James Dilworth. In the last few years of his life, Dilworth had suffered from a debilitating palsy that caused his hands to shake and his legs to walk with difficulty, but it was an attack of peritonitis that caused his sudden death. The funeral at St Mark’s Church in Remuera was attended by a good many mourners, including many civic dignitaries, though not on the scale of the thousands at Tāwhiao’s tangi. Nor did it have the lively spectacle of the tangi, but rather a solemn dignity. Many of Isabella’s friends from the Christian Temperance Union also attended.

The Kellys sat in the front pew of the church, with Isabella, the grieving widow, her usually benign countenance, drawn and sombre. Dilworth left a very substantial estate and Isabella was well provided for. Ownership of his lands and buildings and shares in companies passed to Isabella, and it was Dilworth’s wish that Kelly would pay a nominal lease on the farmlands and manage the farms for as long as he wished and receive the income from them. Having no heirs of his own, Dilworth became a benefactor to many other children. The eulogy for Dilworth was lavish in its praise for his philanthropy and his support for the Kindergarten Movement, the YMCA and Auckland University. It included also the announcement that he had set up the Dilworth Ulster Institute to establish a school ‘to take in, and provide a first-class academic and religious education for orphans and sons of widows and persons of good character, of any race, and in straitened circumstances'.

J. B. Russell, the senior partner of the law firm which employed Wiremu, died in February of the same year and Wiremu would have attended his funeral as well, except that it was held in London. J B, as he was known in the legal fraternity, had gone to London in search of a cure for the actinomycosis, which had afflicted him and ultimately caused his death. In the ensuing restructuring of the firm, Wiremu advanced to a higher position, probably in consequence of proving his worth in the Ironworks Affair, as it became known. That is to say, it was referred to as the Ironworks Affair within the firm, but was not publicly known at all, as it never went to court.

What transpired after the day's fishing on the Ōnehunga Wharf was that Te Kotahitanga contracted an independent scientist to investigate the pollution of the harbour in the vicinity of the Ironworks and began proceedings to prosecute the Ōnehunga Borough Council for failing in their duty of care for the environment under their jurisdiction. The Borough Council sought the advice of their solicitors, Russell and Campbell and, as Mr Campbell was aware of Wiremu's connection to Te Kotahitanga, he brought him into the case. Wiremu advised his bosses that the Ōnehunga Borough Council had no defence, but they had a scapegoat, and Mr Sowry was dismissed from his position on the Council. Wiremu was also able to provide information on the source of the pollution.

Russell and Campbell informed the solicitors acting for the New Zealand Iron and Steel Company of their intention to prosecute for breach of bylaws with regard to discharging toxic waste into the Manukau Harbour, and more serious charges in respect of bribery and corruption. After much negotiating, and with the assistance of Elizabeth Yates, in her capacity as Mayor and Justice of the Peace, Te Kotahitanga agreed on an out of court settlement, with the assurance of immediate remediation of the toxic waste issue and the payment of a considerable sum of money, including compensation to the local iwi. It was a minor victory for Te Kotahitanga and for the harbour, at least in the short term. The tide of industrialisation around the Manukau Harbour and its impact on the environment could not be held back in the longer term.

Mrs Yates was defeated in the mayoralty election the following year, even though it was acknowledged she had been an able administrator and accomplished many improvements in the borough's infrastructure, amenities and finances. She returned as a councillor in subsequent elections.

Wiremu and Rāwiri met on a number of occasions to discuss the legal proceedings and later, when all was settled, there was a more celebratory meeting at the Grand Hotel in Princes Street. They strode up to the bar and waited to be served. When other customers had been attended to, including one who arrived after them, Rāwiri leaned across the polished wooden counter and ordered two pints of draught beer.

"Wait a moment please," the bartender said, "while I get the manager."

"Fine," said Rāwiri, nonchalantly. "We'll be at that table in the corner."

Wiremu looked around the bar at the all-white patrons, who were looking askance at him. He sat at the table and leaned toward Rāwiri. "They're not going to serve us."

"Sure they will," said Rāwiri. "Relax. I know the owner. Anyway, congratulations Cuz. I hear you got a promotion."

"Yes, they moved me up a notch with the restructuring after JB died."

"They must have thought you earned it with your work with the Ironworks Affair."

"Yes, I got some kudos from that."

An impeccably groomed gentleman approached their table and gave a cheery greeting. "Hello Rāwiri. Nice to see you."

"Nice to see you too, Moss," said Rāwiri, rising to shake hands and introduce his cousin Wiremu, now also on his feet.

"What can I get you, gentleman?" said Moss.

"Two pints of draught, please. The barman didn't seem to understand my order."

"I'm sorry. I'll have a word with him," said Moss and he went to the bar.

"How do you know him?" Wiremu asked.

"Moss Davis. He's a friend of Matua Kelly's. I met him through the business. He's a big client. He's a Jew, so he's no stranger to prejudice himself."

The waiter arrived promptly with the two glasses.

"Cheers and congratulations," said Rāwiri, clinking Wiremu's glass.

When both had taken a decent draught and set their glasses down, Rāwiri said, "Now Wiremu, you sly dog, who's the young blonde lady I've seen you in town with? New girlfriend?"

Wiremu gave a coy smile. "Her name's Caroline Fairburn. She's recently joined the firm—the first female employee in the history of the company."

"Changing times, eh."

"The boss hired her as a secretary and typewriter. Women are being trained to use the machines now."

"Now that typewriting is too boring and menial for the men."

Wiremu nodded. "She caused quite a stir among the men in the office. But I got the job of showing her the ropes."

"Why you? Because you're the best looking?"

Wiremu's smile widened to a grin. "Sure, and the most charming. The other young men are mostly just legal clerks, so I've got seniority over them. The other barristers and solicitors are all older men."

"And you're the rising young star, all set for a successful career as a barrister and solicitor."

"I'll drink to that," Wiremu said and drained his glass.

"So, what's she like, this Caroline Fairburn?"

"She's nice."

"Come on."

"She's outgoing and sporty. She plays tennis and cycles to work. And she's a lover of nature."

Rāwiri waited expectantly for more information.

"She's modern and fashionable," Wiremu continued. "She comes to work wearing a shirtwaist and cloak and a straw boater. At break times we go to Leydon's Coffee Palace in Pitt Street."

"You know what I think?" Rāwiri set his glass down and leaned toward Wiremu again. "I think she looks a lot like Eliza Kelly."

Wiremu nodded but made no comment.

Wiremu and Caroline were soon seeing each other out of work, at weekends. They would meet at the office, even when it was closed, as male visitors were prohibited at the Girls' Friendly Society Hostel where she was boarding. Wiremu indulged Caroline's love of the theatre by taking her to Abbott's Opera House to see a performance of *Humanity,* by the Mostyn-Dalziel Dramatic Company. But before the show they went to the Grand Hotel for dinner. Soon after they entered the dining room, Wiremu spotted Moss Davis and greeted him as an old acquaintance.

"I've never been to the Grand before," Caroline said, "but I can see you have. It is really quite grand. But Wiremu, have you noticed that people are staring at us?"

"It's just because we're such a handsome couple," he assured her.

The maître d' showed them to their table by a large window with a view of the city. Wiremu ordered a sirloin of beef with Yorkshire pudding for them both. And glasses of champagne—well, sparkling wine. They chatted and laughed about gossip at work till dinner arrived, then ate and drank, with an eye on the clock, mindful of the start time of the show. They left promptly after dinner and walked hand in hand through Albert Park. Gravel crunched beneath their feet as they walked along the path, Caroline a little unsteadily, as she was not accustomed to drinking champagne. The early evening air was redolent of roses, jasmine, and pohutukawa blossom. The winding path through the trees and gardens took them past the fountain and statue of Queen Victoria, out to Victoria Street and on to the Opera House.

They returned along the same path after the show, now by the light of a gibbous moon and gas lamps in the park. And back to the Grand Hotel, to the lounge bar for a night cap. They sat at the same table that Wiremu and Rāwiri had recently occupied. The atmosphere in the gas lit lounge was pleasant and romantic, despite the fug of cigar smoke and the sidelong glances again from other patrons.

"It's been such a lovely evening," Caroline enthused. "I so enjoyed the drama. Dora Mostyn was just marvellous as the young soubrette. And the dinner and the wine. The wine made me a bit tipsy though… Yes, I'm fine now. A glass of port? Yes, it's just a little glass."

And so Wiremu and Caroline got to know each other more, chatting, while supping Old Crusted Port. "Tell me about yourself," Wiremu prompted.

"Well, I'm a second generation New Zealander," she said, with some pride. "My grandparents came out to New Zealand from Ireland. I came to Auckland from a Waikato dairy farm, for training and employment and the attractions of the big city. I studied shorthand, typewriting, and book-keeping at Hannah's Commercial College and had the good fortune to land a job at Russell and Campbell."

"And here you are."

"Now you," said Caroline. "Is Auckland your hometown?"

"No, I was born in Te Kuiti. My mother died in childbirth and I was raised by my aunt, in a Māori community there. I have Irish blood too. My father is Irish and he lives here in Auckland. He had an illicit relationship with my mother before he married his Irish fiancée, before she came out to New Zealand."

Caroline's blue eyes were all rapt attention. "Did you come to Auckland because your father was here?"

"No. I didn't want anything to do with him back then. We get on all right now though. I came to Auckland to go to Saint Stephen's School and stay with my cousin who lives here. I was bullied and beaten at Saint Stephen's so I left and went to Auckland Grammar School. After that I went to Otago University to study Law and I became a lawyer."

"You've had an interesting life, I must say… But my goodness—is that the time?" said Caroline, suddenly alarmed. "I'm afraid I've missed the night curfew at the hostel. I won't be able to get in now."

"You'll have to stay the night at my place, then," said Wiremu. "There's nothing else for it."

Wiremu and Caroline married after a short engagement. The wedding ceremony was held in Saint Mary's Catholic Church in Hamilton, Caroline's home church. The train brought Wiremu's whānau from Auckland to

Hamilton for the event and some from the King Country, from the terminus of the railway at Te Kuiti.

The reason for the brevity of the engagement was soon apparent as Caroline had got pregnant quite early on. Her first pregnancy, unfortunately ended in a miscarriage, the result of a cycling accident. She took more care with the next pregnancy and was rewarded with a healthy baby girl the following year. The baby was christened Mere—Mary to Caroline's family and Mere to Wiremu's whānau.

# 24

Rāwiri continued to divide his time between managing the cropping and pastoral farming that Dilworth had initiated, and his work for Te Kotahitanga, as an elected member of the lower house of its Parliament, and now also as a family man with a wife and a child at home. Wiremu had moved into his own home in Parnell just before his marriage, when Rāwiri and Roimata had their first child.

Kelly kept an eye on the business in his absence and stepped in and supervised whenever it was necessary. Rāwiri returned from a Kotahitanga meeting in Rotorua and met Kelly at the warehouse.

Kelly sat on a sack of grass seed and said, "So, how was the meeting?"

Rāwiri took a seat on a sack and considered his response. He decided on: "Frustrating."

"What exactly is it you're trying to achieve? Kelly asked. "Are you going to contest a general election as a political party?"

"No, we'd never get elected. We're trying to work with the government to achieve some of the political objectives that the Kīngitanga failed to accomplish."

"Not Home Rule then?"

"No, we know that's never going to happen. We're stuck with British sovereignty, and a Prime Minister who tells us that 'Māori are incapable of self-government and that there can be only one parliament in New Zealand.'"

"What then? Are you trying to get confiscated land returned?"

"We know that confiscated land that's passed into private ownership won't ever be returned. It's more a matter of protecting what's left. We have to set realistic objectives and work with the Māori members in Government."

A sparrow flew into the warehouse and pecked up stray seeds on the floor.

"You're sounding like a politician," Kelly remarked. "I'll give you that. You still haven't said what your real objectives are."

"The most we can hope for at this stage is a limited form of autonomy to improve the position of Māori in the colony. We want better laws. We want the rights that are guaranteed under the Treaty of Waitangi. But we're constantly working against the precedent set by the Chief Justice of the Supreme Court, Judge Prendergast, some years ago, when Wī Parata took Octavius Hadfield, the Bishop of Wellington, to court over a land dispute. It was a landmark case. It was a breach of contract and breach of the Treaty. Parata lost the case because Prendergast ruled the Treaty was—quote, 'a simple nullity'."

"Really? When was that?"

Rāwiri thought for a moment and watched the sparrow hopping about on the floor. "Late seventies."

"How could he just sweep the Treaty aside?"

"He said that Māori are—quote, 'primitive barbarians, who are incapable of performing the duties, and therefore assuming the rights, of a civilised community.'"

Kelly shook his head. "What can you do against such injustice? How can you get laws changed?"

"Well, we've drafted the Native Rights Bill and the MP for Northern Māori, Hone Heke, introduced it in the House."

"What's that about?"

"It's about land rights, property rights, and civil rights."

"So is that going to become law?"

"No, the Bill was defeated. But at least it was voted on. The same Bill was debated last year but there wasn't even a quorum to vote on it because a lot of MPs walked out during the debate. We had a similar Bill before the House the year before and it wasn't even debated. It was just ignored."

"The Liberals, eh," Kelly said.

"They're not very liberal with us," Rāwiri said.

"I have to admire your perseverance in trying to work with the government."

"Some good came out of it. We worked together for a time with the Kīngitanga and presented a united political front. You know Kotahitanga means Unity? Āwhina, especially was pleased to see us working together. She says now the baton of political activism will be handed on to Wiremu."

"So, what's the way forward?"

"We're agreed we need to establish a Māori Council to replace the pernicious Land Court. We must have full authority over Māori land. We must take control over tenure, sale and lease."

# 25

Eliza and Oliver were both prospering in their work at Parnell District School. Oliver was the only male on the staff, so he was the natural choice for promotion to the position of headmaster, and while he had the respect of pupils and staff, Eliza also enjoyed the genuine affection of her pupils and colleagues. As an experienced teacher, Eliza had the confidence to occasionally depart from the curriculum and introduce ideas of her own. One day, a particular day, the sixth of February, she introduced a new topic into the Social Studies syllabus.

"Does anyone know what day this is?" she asked her class.

There was no response beyond, "It's Monday, Miss."

"On this day in 1840, the Treaty of Waitangi was signed," Mrs Steadman announced, "the founding document of this country, and partnership between the Queen of England and the Māori people."

"Why did the Māoris go to war against the British?" a pupil asked.

Mrs Steadman gave a potted history of New Zealand that was quite unlike anything the children had heard before. The Treaty was broken by the British. Māori were forced from their land by invasion, conquest and confiscation. A war in which her own father had fought for the British, "and some of your grandfathers," she told the class. More questions ensued, which Eliza answered as candidly as she could in simple terms that ten-year-old children could comprehend.

The upshot of the New Zealand history lesson was that some of the children asked more questions at home and parents subsequently asked questions of the headmaster concerning what sort of lessons Mrs Steadman was teaching. Oliver reprimanded Eliza for her inappropriate interpretation of New Zealand history and the controversy she'd caused, and told her to stick to the curriculum. It was his opinion that she had been unduly influenced by the unconventional views of her unpatriotic father.

"Unpatriotic? He may not be a patriot for Britain," Eliza said, "but there's no one more patriotic for this country."

In the discussion that ensued, Oliver referred to Eliza's father as 'a Māori lover'.

"A Māori lover?" Eliza exclaimed. "Only a Māori hater would say that. You know we have Māori in our family. Really, Oliver, this is inexcusable."

Oliver regretted the phrase he'd used in the heat of the argument, but there it was; he couldn't unsay it and he feared he'd caused irreparable offence.

It was around this time that Eliza became pregnant and other disagreements arose. She and Oliver had agreed from the start on having a family together, but when the prospect of starting a family suddenly became a reality, they discovered they had differing assumptions about their future. Oliver was delighted that he would soon be a father, but less than delighted that Eliza hoped to return to work after having the baby, not straight away of course, but after a decent period of leave and after the baby was weaned and could be minded by its grandparents. Oliver had envisioned a family of more children with a proper stay at home mother, not a career woman. There was really no need for Eliza to return to work. It was Oliver's opinion that a mother's place was in the home, and that Eliza had been overly influenced by her mother's involvement with the likes of Amey Daldy and Kate Sheppard and 'the women's movement'.

"Besides," he pointed out, "you'll have more time at home to write those children's books, you've been working on."

For her part, Eliza had been feeling the burden, especially when she was pregnant, of working full-time and taking care of everything at home. She felt Oliver could be more helpful and suggested he take a turn at cooking meals.

"But you're such a marvellous cook, my darling," he said. "I could never do it as well as you."

"You could learn to cook if you had a mind to, instead of making excuses."

"Cooking is a wife's role," he insisted, "and there's an end to it."

"You may be the boss at work, but we are equals at home."

"Of equal value, of course, but we have different roles."

Eliza responded with, "Your thinking is so last century..."

But before she could say more, Oliver shouted, "Enough!"

"Well, I never took you for a tyrant who would forbid me to speak," Eliza said, and left the room to avoid Oliver's rancour. She knew the dramatic effect of a well-timed exit.

Eliza was obliged to resign when she was four months pregnant, when her condition became obvious. It was a full year after she had given birth that Oliver agreed to allow her to resume a portion of her former duties at the school. He would have her at home part of the time rather than returning to her parents' all of the time.

On the occasion of the turn of the century, Annie organised a family dinner on New Year's Eve to celebrate the event. All the family attended, except Wiremu and Caroline and their children, who had gone to Hamilton for a Fairburn family celebration. It was a happy family gathering with all the children at the Kelly home. Everyone was doting on the first grandchild, Eliza's baby boy, none more so than the proud mother. But it seemed to Annie that Eliza and Oliver were not so much at ease with each other as they had been. Perhaps it was the strain of having a new baby in the home.

Kelly prayed a blessing over the meal when the family were all seated around the table, as always before an evening meal. He was not normally given to making long prayers or speeches but on this occasion he was moved to give thanks to the God, who spared his life in battle, who brought his wife safely from the other side of the world and, while they had got off to a shaky start, the Lord had blessed them with a happy marriage and three beautiful children and a grandchild, the first of many, he hoped.

Likewise, the country had got off to a shaky start, Kelly said, but at the dawn of the twentieth century, he looked forward to a future of peace and prosperity. He went on to speak of the accomplishments of his clever children: Imogen, the talented artist, with an exhibition in the Auckland Art Gallery, and the illustrator of children's books, written by Eliza Kelly; Eliza the talented teacher and author, and mother of the first of the next generation of the family; Charles, the skilled craftsman, builder of houses and now also draughtsman/designer of houses.

Charles had an announcement of his own. He was engaged to be married. The wedding would be in the Ōnehunga Saint Peter's Anglican Church, where he'd met his fiancée, Miriam Cooper. He'd been courting Miriam for months before finally asking her father for his daughter's hand in marriage. Her father, like Kelly, had fought for the British in the New

Zealand wars, and he later joined the merchant navy. All the family were happy for Charles and full of warm congratulations.

Kelly chatted with his son-in-law, over dinner, about his work—a safe topic. Oliver was successful in his career as a school teacher and principal. *That was the way of it,* Kelly thought to himself. *Male teachers first in line for promotion. Clever enough at his job, but too opinionated and he has a very one-sided view of things.*

Oliver was all for progress and it became evident that he felt his father-in-law didn't understand the times he was living in. It was Kelly's opinion that Oliver didn't understand the times. He kept these thoughts to himself, though, just as he'd made no mention of Wiremu, when enumerating the accomplishments of his children. But he was certainly proud of his other son, the successful lawyer.

# 26

The New Zealand Herald and other dailies were trumpeting a new era of prosperity at the beginning of the new century. There was a mood of optimism with the recovery of commodity prices for primary produce on the international market. The Seddon government embarked on a grand programme of public works, begun by the Vogel administration: road construction, and the long-held ambition of building a railway line from Auckland to Wellington was finally realised. The government managed to purchase 700,000 acres of land from Ngāti Maniapoto and open up the King Country for the main trunk railway line. The Public Works Land Act empowered the government to take Māori land as required for roads and railways, with payment of compensation—payment which often never materialised. Land values in the interior of the North Island soared, industry flourished, and more settlers poured in.

The first passengers to make the 423-mile journey from Wellington to Auckland were a party of politicians. The Parliament Special arrived in Auckland to greet six battleships docked in the Waitematā harbour, part of the US Navy 'Great White Fleet'. The American visitors were fêted with a civic welcome by the New Zealand government, who disregarded the rumour that the US Navy was on a reconnaissance mission in preparation for an invasion of New Zealand and Australia to establish strategic Pacific naval bases.

The main trunk railway was a great convenience for those wishing to travel north and south on the North Island. Rāwiri made the journey to the King Country with Roimata and their children more often. Wiremu travelled to Hamilton and occasionally to Te Kuiti with Caroline and their children. Āwhina visited her whānau in Auckland by just getting on the train at Te Kuiti. She would not make the journey otherwise, at her age. She still tended her garden and split firewood but she had no desire to be tossed about in a coach over rough roads.

Āwhina sat on a bench at the Te Kuiti station, a kuia, wearing a black headscarf, holding an ornately carved walking stick, a kete at her side and a bag at her feet, waiting for the northbound train. The chuffing, hissing, great beast of the locomotive arrived and she made her way to a seat in the third carriage. She sat gazing out the window at the so-called 'waste land' as the train passed through the Rohe Pōtae and on into the Waikato, through Kihikihi, Te Awamutu and Hamilton, past back yards of houses and shops. The train slowed to a stop at Frankton Junction, alongside the cast iron posts holding up the veranda of the wooden station building, where passengers disembarked and boarded, and went for refreshments. Āwhina decided to treat herself to a cup of tea and a scone but she was jostled in the crush of the crowd, clamouring for their food and drink, and she decided to wait until she got to Auckland. So many people. So many white faces.

From the platform where she waited, Āwhina watched as workers with steel hooks grappled bales of wool off a dray and stacked the huge hessian cubes into a wagon. When a bell summoned passengers to board, she settled back into her seat and continued the journey out of Hamilton, over the Waikato River. As the train approached Taupiri maunga, she bowed her head in silent prayer. It rattled the bones of the dead buried within the sacred mountain as it rumbled past. Through Ngāruawahia, over the rail bridge, on to Huntly, and the towns that brought to mind the battles of the invasion of Waikato: Rangiriri and Meremere.

Alongside the tracks at the Auckland Railway Station, at the bottom of Queen Street, were long buildings housing station facilities, various shops and rows of advertising billboards: Sunlight Soap, Pearson's Carbolic Sandsoap, Standard Tea, South British Insurance, Kemps Merchant Tailor, Burberry Coats, Dexter and Crozier Motor Engineers, Royal Enfield Bicycles, Dunlop Tyres, Motor Cars. Motor cars? Yes, there were motor cars on the street, and trams, not horse-drawn trams but electric trams with overhead wires.

From out of the throngs of travellers and loiterers at the station, a voice called out, "Tēnā koe Māmā!" Rāwiri waiting to pick up his mother. He gave her a hug and relieved her of her bag. "How was your trip, Māmā?"

"Fine. The railway is an impressive feat of engineering, but for me, it's also a sad journey through the raupatu."

"I can understand," Rāwiri commiserated. "As for the engineering, you must take the train south to Wellington some time, over the viaducts, spanning the gorges, and through the tunnels. It's really quite a marvel."

"A journey for another time, perhaps. Right now I'm tired and hungry."

"Of course. Roimata's got dinner ready."

So it was dinner, family time and an early night for Āwhina.

"She seems to have aged just since we last saw her," Roimata said.

"She's tired from the journey," Rāwiri said, "but yes, she is getting on in years."

"And lost weight, don't you think?"

At breakfast in the morning, Āwhina appeared rested and refreshed.

Rāwiri was solicitous. "Did you sleep all right, Māmā? Feeling all right? Feel like going on a little tour?"

He took his mother around the Dilworth estates: the nearby gardens, the stables and the new Dilworth School for Boys in the grounds of the old homestead. He knew that gardening, horses and education were all dear to her heart. And the tractor. A new Ivel tractor had just been imported and brought to the farm. Anyone would be interested in that. It was the way of the future for farming.

Āwhina kept up a good pace walking around, but stopped in the school grounds with a coughing fit.

"Are you all right Māmā?" Rāwiri said. "Are you looking after yourself?"

"Yes, all right. Just got a cold."

"Are you taking anything for the cough?"

"Some kumārahou tea for the sore throat and the hūpē."

"Don't you think it's time you came to live with us here in Tāmaki-makau-rau? With your mokopuna. Wiremu's whānau live nearby, so you can visit them too. We've got a room for you."

But no, she was still reluctant to leave Te Kuiti. The Rohe Pōtae had become her home and she had become a kuia, a matriarch of her adopted whānau. "Who would be the kaikaranga on the marae?"

"I'm sure they've got other kuia. My tamariki want to see their Nannie."

"I can come and visit on the train and you can put them on the train and send them to me."

"Please think about it," Rāwiri insisted. "We're concerned about you."

"I'm all right. Now when am I going to see Wiremu? I want to see Wiremu and his Pākehā wife and my nearly Pākehā mokopuna."

"They're all coming here for dinner. And I'll take you to the Kellys tomorrow."

"Kei te pai."

Āwhina was happily surrounded by her mokopuna later that day, though the cousins took their noisy conversations and laughter outside, much of the time, away from the adults. Rāwiri's children especially were quite boisterous. They played some backyard cricket with a tennis ball while there was still daylight.

The adults got into discussions about the government and land issues, which were never far from Āwhina's mind—all except Caroline, who had little interest in political matters, but could hold her own on sports. She and Wiremu had been following the All Blacks tour of Great Britain and Australia.

"The All Blacks won the test match series in both countries." Wiremu informed the others. "They played the Northern Union rules of rugby league for the first time and won most of those games as well."

However, sport didn't rate much as current affairs with the other adults. They talked about the King Country and the newly opened main trunk railway line, which was much in the news.

"So, Whaea, you're keen to take a train trip to Wellington?" Wiremu said.

"Rāwiri's idea, not mine," Āwhina said.

"Good idea, though, Whaea. I have to go to Wellington on business next week. Why don't you come along for the ride? There's an express train now with a dining car and a sleeping carriage. Leaves Auckland 8:30 pm. Travel overnight in comfort. I'll get us first-class tickets with company travel vouchers."

"If I go I want to see the maunga. I don't want to pass them in the night."

Wiremu thought for a moment to recall the timetable. "We should pass them around dawn on the way to Wellington and late in the day on the way back. They'll look beautiful in the sunrise and the sunset."

"All right then. And you and your whānau can get on the train and come and visit me too. If it leaves Auckland at 8:30, what time does it stop in Te Kuiti?"

Wiremu shut his eyes for a moment to picture the timetable. "About 2:00 am."

"2:00 am?" Āwhina frowned. "The middle of the night."

"Just stay on here a bit longer, Māmā," Rāwiri said. "More family time."

"All right then. I still want to visit the Kellys too."

It was a happy reunion with the Kelly family—the children, now grown, and the grandchildren, Eliza's boys. And Āwhina met Eliza's husband.

"From the King Country, eh," Oliver said. "You must be relieved they've finally opened up the King Country, what with the railway, the roads, the telegraph, the shops."

*Opened up the King Country.* How Āwhina loathed that phrase. "Oh yes," she said. "We've joined the civilised world."

Only Oliver was unaware of Āwhina's sardonic tone.

# 27

Āwhina boarded the southbound train of the North Island Main Trunk Railway with her nephew and her son, travelling to Wellington, the Empire City. Roimata and Caroline stayed behind and assured their children there would be other opportunities for train trips. By way of consolation, it was a chance for the cousins to get together again. The sisters-in-law organised a day at the beach with loads of picnic food and an afternoon at Caroline's tennis club. But the young people mostly created their own entertainment without the help of doting adults.

The travellers were not long seated in their first-class carriage when Rāwiri asked Wiremu about his meeting: "So you're going to meet with James Carroll, our Minister of Native Affairs?"

"Yes, our first Māori Minister of Native Affairs."

Rāwiri repeated the name: "James Carroll. That's not a Māori name."

"His father's Irish. His mother's Ngāti Kahungunu. He's got a Māori name too: Timi Kara."

"So he's half-Māori, half-Irish, That's a good pedigree."

"It works for us."

Āwhina smiled at Wiremu's last remark, closed her eyes and dozed on and off in her recliner seat.

"So, any chance of Māori self-government with a Māori minister?" Rāwiri asked.

"No, the last attempt was when Seddon was Minister of Native Affairs and he rejected the Māori Constitution Bill. Carroll was on the Executive Council, but he had no real influence. He's abandoned constitutional autonomy as unattainable. The Crown will never give up control."

"What's this meeting you're going to then?" Rāwiri said. "Is it about the Native Land Act?"

"Yes, it's mainly about finalising the Native Land Act to safeguard Māori land rights, especially in the Rohe Pōtae. There'll be a delegation of Native Land Court judges and Carroll's invited presidents of the Māori Land Boards. Carroll's under a lot of pressure from all sides: from settlers, and from both sides of the House. They all want cheap, freehold Māori land. And settlers don't want Māori landlords."

Rāwiri frowned. "You know Carroll supports converting Māori land to individual titles so more land can be sold."

"Preferably leased," Wiremu said, "and only sold or leased by public tender, so Māori can get decent prices and get enough money to develop their own farms. No more government pre-emption and no more secret deals at cheap prices. And no Māori selling all of their land."

"That'll mean more Māori land alienated."

"But also more Māori land developed," Wiremu said.

"Time for bed, eh," Rāwiri said, when Āwhina began to doze in her seat.

They made their way to the sleeping carriage, along the narrow aisle with compartments on either side.

"Good night, Māmā," Rāwiri said and left Āwhina to settle into her compartment.

"Give us a wakeup call just before we get to Ohakune, please," Rāwiri said to the attendant.

He and Wiremu went into the compartment opposite and pulled down their fold up bunks—Wiremu in the top and Rāwiri in the bottom. Both settled into their berths and were lulled to sleep in the swaying carriage and the rhythmic *rakititak, rakititak* of the wheels below the floorboards. They travelled through the night on to the volcanic plateau. The train swept around the curving Hāpuawhenua Viaduct and, as it approached Ohakune, the attendant roused them with a gentle rapping on the door.

Rāwiri got up and called out to Āwhina, "The maunga, Māmā."

The train stopped at Ohakune Station just as dawn was breaking and the travellers went back to their day seats.

"Bring your blanket, Māmā," Rāwiri said.

At first they looked out the windows and then went outside, the better to get a view of the mountains. Āwhina wrapped her blanket close about her against the chill of the air and gazed at the majestic snow-capped volcanoes.

"Ruapehu, Tongariro, Ngauruhoe." She spoke the names as though they were an incantation. "I haven't seen the maunga since I was a child."

They boarded the train again after the ten-minute stop and went to the dining car for breakfast. Rāwiri led the way along the aisle and Wiremu followed close behind Āwhina in case she lost her balance in the lurching and swaying of the carriages. The train continued into the hill country, through tunnels and across rivers, over the dizzying viaducts of Mangaweka and Makōhine. The countryside slid past the window beyond the dazed reflection of Āwhina's face. Rāwiri and Wiremu were watching the scenery and also exchanging glances that acknowledged their observation of Āwhina.

"So what do you think, Māmā?" Rāwiri said.

"Beautiful countryside, and the engineering is impressive. And all the technology."

"It's the twentieth century, Whaea," Wiremu said.

"Yes, it had to come," Āwhina said. "The Pākehā had to come, but they didn't have to force us off our land. We could have had the civilisation without all the uncivilised behaviour."

Āwhina dozed on and off through the Manawatū farmlands and woke up coughing.

"Still got that nasty cough, eh Māmā," Rāwiri said.

"Nothing to worry about," she said. "All the coal smoke in the air is not helping."

"Let's go for a cup of tea and lunch in the dining car."

The train stopped briefly at Palmerston North and continued south, along the Kapiti Coast. It slowed as it reached Wellington and pulled into Thorndon Station, a conglomeration of industrial buildings, sheds and workshops. Wiremu had booked the new Hotel Windsor in Willis Street, a modern five-storey brick edifice with a large dome on top. The travellers were ushered into the foyer, from which a grand, double staircase ascended to the upper floors. But they took the lift to save Āwhina climbing stairs. After some hesitation about stepping into the cage, she found it to be a safe and convenient conveyance. They settled into their rooms and Āwhina, wearied from the journey, had an afternoon nap and went to bed soon after dinner.

Next morning, Rāwiri and Āwhina went on a tour by horse-drawn cab along Lambton Quay, after dropping Wiremu off at the Parliament—not the proper Parliament Buildings; they had been destroyed by fire, but Government House, which was serving as government offices, while the new, grand Parliament Building was under construction.

Their cab driver was a knowledgeable, but uncouth fellow, who liked to use coarse language. He pointed out sights of interest, like the enormous Government Buildings on Lambton Quay, "second biggest wooden building in the world", he informed his passengers, "full a bloody bureaucrats".

"It looks like concrete," Rāwiri remarked.

"No, mate", the driver said. "It's solid kauri. Concrete was too expensive. But they designed it to look like an Italian stone palace. There is a proper stone building in this street—the new Public Truss—that flash looking building there with the big dome on the top."

The driver then took his passengers to the cable car and declared, "You'll have to take a ride in the Red Rattler, up the hill here, through the tunnels, up to the Gardens. Get a view a the harbour."

A steam engine pulled the juddering car up the hill and it justified its Rattler name. The tourists were rewarded with a stroll in the Botanical Gardens and a view over the city. Wellington, they observed, was a compact city set between hills and sea, with many substantial houses perched on hillsides.

Their driver fetched them back to the hotel when their sightseeing was done and Wiremu joined them there for dinner when he returned. After they'd ordered their meal, Rāwiri asked Wiremu about his meeting.

"The land issues are a bit messy," he said. "The Crown still retains the right to purchase Māori land directly, but sales require Native Land Court confirmation."

"So the Crown still holds the power. What about the leasehold provisions?"

"We'll still retain the leasehold system but Māori landowners can't reject a lease or reclaim leased land for their own use. The Opposition are pushing for conversion of leasehold land to freehold, and compulsory acquisition of so-called surplus and idle land, converting unproductive land to European tenure and economic use. Settlers will get perpetual leases and tenants' right to purchase leased land."

"So, it'll be easier for Māori land to be leased and sold—and lost."

Āwhina had been listening to this discussion without comment, till finally she said, "It's a constant battle against the settlers' greed for land."

The white-coated waiter glided noiselessly along the carpet from the side-board to the table, with bowls of ox tail soup, followed by roast duckling with apple sauce.

"He reka te kai, nē, Māmā?" Rāwiri said.

"Ae." But Āwhina had little appetite.

Āwhina and Rāwiri chatted about their day's sightseeing, over dinner, and Āwhina said, "I never got to see Whanganui-a-Tara but now I've seen Wellington."

It had been a long day and Āwhina was a weary traveller. She went to bed early and Rāwiri and Wiremu went to the lounge bar for a time and had a nightcap of whisky. They settled into leather armchairs and Wiremu talked about his day at more length. They kept their voices low in the quiet atmosphere. The gas lamps hissed faintly and the wall clock ticked like a beating heart. A lone traveller rustled his newspaper at a nearby table.

"I met an old alumnus at Parliament," Wiremu said. "Our Minister of Justice and Attorney-General, John George Findlay KC. We were both at Otago University Law School at the same time, though he was a few years ahead of me. I remember he was regarded as such a brilliant student and became an outstanding lawyer from all accounts." Wiremu paused to sip his whisky. "He made a speech about law reform and said New Zealand should be a morally guided state."

"And what does Findlay, King's Counsel, reckon about the land issue?"

"He says individualisation of title is inevitable and Māori land will be integrated into the settler economy through law."

"I fear he may be right, Rāwiri said, "but certainly not morally right." He tossed back the whisky and said, "Time for bed. I'll check on Māmā, first. I'm concerned about her."

"Me too," Wiremu said. "She's looking frail and that cough doesn't sound good."

"I'm trying to persuade her to move in with us. She needs looking after. I'm telling her she should be with her real family. You could mention it too. Help convince her."

"Will do. See you in the morning."

Rāwiri heard Āwhina coughing before he knocked on the door to her room and he found her sitting up in bed coughing into a handkerchief, which came away spotted with blood. There was a moment of silent consternation as they both stared at the bloodied handkerchief, before Rāwiri said, "Oh Māmā, have you coughed up blood before?"

"Kaore." She was reverting to te reo.

"I'm taking you to the doctor tomorrow."

Āwhina sullenly acquiesced and got back under the covers.

At Wellington Hospital, Āwhina admitted to the examining doctor that she'd been having chest pains and night sweats. The doctor said he would admit her straight away and they would run some tests.

"No," she said. "I can't stay here."

"We're going back to Auckland tomorrow," Rāwiri said. "I'll take her to Auckland hospital."

"All right," the doctor agreed, "but get her admitted without delay. In the meantime, I'm prescribing laudanum and Chlorodyne, and bedrest today. Make sure the room is well ventilated with fresh air. I suspect she's suffering from tuberculosis."

"I was afraid that's what it was."

Rāwiri returned to the hotel with Āwhina, and Wiremu returned later in the day, having gone out early in the morning.

"How's Whaea today?" Wiremu asked.

"Not good. I'm pretty sure it's consumption. We've just come back from the hospital."

They commiserated together about their dear 'Māmā and Whaea' and Wiremu said, "Well, I guess she'll be coming back to Auckland now." He read the labels on the bottles of medicine and said, "Opium and cannabis."

They'd had to spend another day and night in Wellington in any case, to get the next train to Auckland, and they took a cab to the station in the morning. Rāwiri helped Āwhina board the train and she slumped drowsily into her seat.

"This laudanum is making me sleepy," she said. "If I'm asleep when we come to the maunga I want you to wake me up. I want to see them again."

Rāwiri and Wiremu gazed blankly out the window as the countryside passed in reverse, and they roused Āwhina when the mountains came into view at Taihape, just visible in the fading light.

"Ah, Ruapehu," she said, looking out the window, and she recited a whakataukī:

*Whāia te iti kahurangi; ki te tūohu koe, me maunga teitei.*

Rāwiri repeated it in English: "Seek the treasure that you value most dearly; do not be deterred by anything less than a lofty mountain."

Back on the train, the travellers went to the dining car for dinner and, at the Ohakune stop, they retired to the sleeper. Āwhina had a restless night, despite the medicines she took when she went to bed. Her coughing could be heard throughout the sleeping carriage.

When they arrived in Auckland in the morning, Āwhina was exhausted. Rāwiri took her directly to the hospital in Grafton. More Italian Palace architecture. He waited anxiously, with Āwhina coughing, and nurses coming and going all the while. Āwhina was finally attended to by a doctor. She was examined briefly, admitted and given a bed. Rāwiri stayed with her till she was settled and returned the next day with Roimata and the children. Āwhina especially wanted to see her mokopuna. The doctor had done the tests and he confirmed the diagnosis of tuberculosis. He recommended that Āwhina be transferred, either to Te Waikato Sanitorium in Cambridge or to the Costley Home in Greenlane.

"Let's have you in the Costley Home, Māmā," Rāwiri said, "so we can have you close to home."

"I can recommend it," the doctor agreed. "It has an open-air TB ward, where patients get excellent care: fresh air, sunshine, exercise and nourishing food."

"Why should I go to a costly home?" Āwhina said.

"Ah," said the doctor, "it's not a costly home. It's actually free. Mr Edward Costley is your benefactor."

# 28

Āwhina was well cared for at the Costley Home, but it became apparent that the disease would take its usual course and her care was palliative. She received regular visits from Rāwiri and Wiremu and their families. And occasionally some of the whānau from Te Kuiti. Kelly and Annie also visited—Kelly more often. He preferred to come with Rāwiri or Wiremu, as Āwhina often reverted to speaking te reo Māori. Kelly had acquired only a little of the reo and needed an interpreter.

Āwhina was not always fully conscious and lucid because of the medications she was taking, particularly the laudanum, which seemed to induce a dream-like state. On one occasion, when Kelly and Rāwiri came to visit, Āwhina was reclining on a lounger with a light blanket, in the open-air courtyard ward. It was a pleasantly rural outlook just beyond the city and Cornwall Park. Tūī were calling, fluting and clacking, in the kowhai trees beyond the lawns. Fantails flitted around the courtyard.

Āwhina was singing:

*Tiwha tiwha te pō.*
*Ko te Pakerewhā*

*Ko Arikirangi tēnei rā te haere nei.*

Rāwiri listened pensively and translated for Kelly:

*Dark, dark is the night.*
*There is the Pakerewhā*
*There is Arikirangi to come.*

Āwhina continued singing the same refrain.

"It's a prophecy about the coming of Arikirangi Te Tūruki," Rāwiri explained. "You would know him as Te Kooti. That was the name he took when he was baptised, from the Pākehā name Coates. The prophecy came from Te Kooti's grandfather."

"Who is the Pakerewhā?"

"The Pakerewhā are strangers with white skin or red skin."

"The Pākehā?"

"Yes, and this was before the coming of the Pākehā. The grandfather, Toiroa Ikariki, was a matakite, a visionary, a seer. He foresaw the coming of the Europeans three years before the arrival of Captain Cook. He drew images in sand and made models of what he saw: a wooden sailing boat, with a rudder and smoking funnel, wheeled carts, horses, hats, trousers, pipes—things never seen before in New Zealand."

"Really? I've never heard this before."

Kelly was more incredulous when Rāwiri added, "He said of the white men who would come, the name of their god will be Tama-i-rorokutia, the son who was killed, a good god; however, the people will still be oppressed."

"Their God will be the son who was killed," Kelly repeated, absorbing the gravity of the statement. "Te Kooti was a notorious outlaw, but who was he really? You say he was baptised. Was he a Christian? Did Āwhina know him?"

"Ae, Te Kooti Arikirangi. Te Kooti Tāwhaki," Āwhina said, and then lapsed back into a stupor.

"Yes, she knew him well," Rāwiri said. "I met him too. He lived in Te Kuiti for ten years. He was a Christian, an Anglican in fact, and a Bible scholar, but then he founded his own sect, the Ringatū. His followers called him Te Kooti Tāwhaki, Te Kooti the Twice-born, because he had tuberculosis and he recovered from it. It was when he was banished to the Chatham Islands. The prisoners on the Chathams suffered from the cold and the harsh conditions. Te Kooti got sick and, in a fever, he saw visions. They say he was visited by the Archangel Michael."

The quietude was interrupted by another patient nearby, with a rasping cough. Kelly and Rāwiri were both following the flight of a fantail, fluttering close around Āwhina.

"Te Kooti led the escape of the prisoners from the Chathams," Rāwiri continued. "He seized a government supply ship. There were about three hundred prisoners in all, men, women and children, and they became his followers. He wasn't a chief, but there were many chiefs among his followers. He became their prophet. He had many enemies, both Māori and Pākehā and he was on the run and causing a lot of trouble. He couldn't find refuge anywhere."

"Why did he go to Te Kuiti? Was he a Kingite?"

"No, in fact he was going to challenge Tāwhiao as the spiritual leader of Māori. Of course, Tāwhiao and Rewi Maniapoto rejected him, even when he became a pacifist, but he finally made peace with Tāwhiao, and Tāwhiao granted him refuge in Te Kuiti."

On another occasion when Kelly visited Āwhina with Wiremu, she was sitting up in the lounger, reading and she was quite lucid, except that she thought Wiremu was her mokopuna.

She greeted him with, "Tēnā koe taku moko."

The fantail returned and she greeted it too. "Tēnā koe pīwakawaka."

Then to Wiremu again: "Kei te pēhea tōu mahi?"

"Kia ora, Whaea. E pai ana te mahi. Still challenging the government in the courts."

Āwhina talked about the raupatu, the Māori land issues, protecting the Rohe Pōtae, and commended Wiremu for continuing the struggle for justice, for mastering the Pākehā Law, pursuing the way of the Law. She spoke of Te Kooti again: "Te Kooti ceased fighting, and at the end, he said, 'The canoe for you to paddle after me is the Law. Only the Law can be set against the Law.'"

To Kelly she said, "Kei te pēhea tou whānau, e Tama?"

Kelly knew enough to say, "Kei te pai, Whaea."

After a few minutes, Āwhina lay back and drifted off into a reverie and chanted:

*Kei muri i te awe kapara*
*He tangata kē*
*Mana i te ao*
*He mā.*

Kelly looked to Wiremu for a translation.

"It's an old pre-European prophecy".

*Shadowed behind the tattooed face*
*A Stranger stands*

*He who owns the world*
*And he is White.*

While Kelly, Annie and Rāwiri were visiting Āwhina, they spoke to her doctor about what they perceived to be her worsening condition. The doctor confirmed that indeed she was deteriorating and he had prescribed an increase in her medication, 'to keep her as comfortable as possible'. He reported also that she was experiencing episodes of what he called 'dissociation', and she was praying aloud and chanting in Māori.

"The chanting is mōteatea," Rāwiri said. "It's a lament, like a tribal song. And she's always been in the habit of praying."

The doctor went about his rounds and left Kelly, Annie and Rāwiri at her bedside. Āwhina was sitting up in her bed with her eyes closed, unaware of her visitors, and quietly chanting, just as the doctor had said, in te reo Māori, interspersed with some English, some unintelligible, but she quite clearly recited:

*And 'mid this tumult Kubla heard from far*
*Ancestral voices prophesying war!*

"Oh my goodness," Annie said. "She's quoting from *Kubla Khan*," It's a poem by Coleridge. They say he wrote it under the influence of opium."

Rāwiri called out to Āwhina as if to bring her back from some distant place and he spoke to her both in English and te reo Māori, but she made no response.

Āwhina uttered more mōteatea and then in English: "Ngātapa. Men shot like dogs and thrown down the cliff. Passchendaele. Men lie dead in the mud."

"Do you know what she's talking about?" Kelly asked Rāwiri.

"Ngātapa. It's a pā in Tairawhiti, Poverty Bay, on a steep hill. Many of Te Kooti's men were captured and executed there and their bodies thrown off the cliff."

"What about Passiondale?"

"Never heard of it. Maybe something she's dreamed up."

It was sad to see Whaea Āwhina in this state, apparently oppressed by memories of war and by 'the rulers of the darkness of this world, and against spiritual wickedness in high places,' as she said, when she was praying aloud and quoting from the Bible. But there was at least a glimmer of light and hope at the end, as she continued with, "… and behold the darkness shall cover the earth and gross darkness the people; but the Lord shall arise upon thee, and His glory shall be seen upon thee."

# 29

Āwhina was much in Kelly's thoughts since that last visit to the hospital. He'd come away with a sense of foreboding and it was no surprise when Rāwiri told him she had died. Rāwiri turned up late for work and found Kelly mucking out the stables.

"Māmā's passed away," he said.

"Oh, Rāwiri, my condolences. Your dear mother. Our dear Whaea Āwhina."

"They say she went peacefully in her sleep."

Kelly leaned on the handle of his pitchfork and said, "Well, that's a blessing," and added, "I guess it was her time."

"I think she knew it was her time." Rāwiri's bottom lip trembled as he spoke. "I've sent a telegraph to Te Kuiti to let the whānau know."

"She said she wanted to be buried in the Saint Mark's cemetery, next to Quinn," Kelly said, "—so, Saint Mark's Church."

"That can be her final resting place," Rāwiri agreed, "but first she needs to lie in state on a marae."

"Where? In Te Kuiti?"

"No, The Kīngitanga want to honour her by having the tangi at Waahi Pā, in Huntly."

"Well, it's closer to home at least, and on the railway. I'll send food for catering."

"All right."

There seemed to be nothing more to say and they stood quietly for a moment till Kelly said, "I'll get the clean hay."

And Rāwiri said, "I'll go and make the arrangements."

Rāwiri's and Wiremu's families and other whānau kept a vigil by the open casket in the Waahi Pā wharenui for three days. Wave after wave of mourners arrived at the marae each time the train stopped at Huntly Station. Each rōpū gathered at the entrance of the marae and waited for the karanga, to be called onto the marae. They were welcomed with harirū, hongi, kisses, hugs and often, tears. Many of Āwhina's Ngāti Hauā iwi and Te Kuiti whānau, gathered at the marae, many kuia dressed all in black, the Waharoa hapū, the Hērangi hapū, Te Puea, and other Waikato whānau. The mourners wept and wailed, made speeches and sang waiata. Meanwhile, in the wharekai, a small army of tangata whenua prepared food and kept the many manuhiri well fed. Altogether it was a send-off befitting a rangatira of Te Ao Māori.

But Āwhina also had an appointment to keep in the whare karakia of Te Ao Pākehā. The casket was taken to St Mark's Church for the Pākehā funeral. The Kelly family sat in their accustomed pew in the middle of the nave. Rāwiri and Wiremu sat at the front with their families and Hāmana. Also in the crowded church were some elderly parishioners and Christian Temperance Union members who remembered Āwhina and came to pay their respects.

The vicar stood before the casket and greeted all who had come from near and far, and the people stood as he began the liturgy:

*We have come together*
*to remember before God the life of Āwhina Te Waharoa*
*Quinn,*
*to commend her to God's keeping,*
*to commit her body to be buried,*
*and to comfort those who mourn*
*with our sympathy and with our love;*
*in the hope we share*
*through the death and resurrection*
*of Jesus Christ.*

Kelly's gaze fell on the lights of the four candlestands placed in a cross formation around the casket, then on the familiar illuminated saints of the stained-glass windows.

The vicar continued:

*Gracious God,*
*surround us and all who mourn this day*
*with your continuing compassion.*
*Do not let grief overwhelm your children,*
*or be unending,*
*or turn them against you.*
*May we journey more peacefully because of today,*
*and come at last, in the fellowship of all your people,*
*to the haven where we long to be;*
*through Jesus Christ our Lord.*

It fell to Rāwiri to deliver the eulogy. He stood on the podium and addressed the congregation. "I have been blessed to have had such a beautiful mother. I am her only child but she was also a mother to Wiremu and was like a mother to many. She was our Whaea. She was a woman of great learning and great faith and she put God first in all she did. Many credited her with the gift of prophecy and say she was a matakite. She was a rangatira of great mana but so humble all her life. She worked tirelessly and generously in the service of our people and the pursuit of justice for our people. The cause most dear to her heart was the whenua, the land, our ancestral land. She often quoted the whakataukī:"

> *Whatungarongaro te tangata, toitū te whenua.*
> *As man disappears from sight, the land remains.*

"Now I shall read from Psalm 103:"

> *As a father has compassion on his children,*
> *so the Lord has compassion on those who fear him;*
> *for he knows how we are formed,*
> *he remembers that we are dust.*
> *The life of mortals is like grass,*
> *they flourish like a flower of the field;*
> *the wind blows over it and it is gone,*
> *and its place remembers it no more.*

"We pass away. The land remains. Our Whaea will not be forgotten."

At the conclusion of Rāwiri's tribute to his mother, Roimata stood to sing a waiata and many joined in the singing.

Then Hāmana came forward to speak. "I have come to honour my tuāhine today."

Kelly felt suddenly uneasy as he recalled the last time he had seen Hāmana in the church.

"They say we Māori are a warrior race," Hāmana said. "It's true we fought against each other. But the British are also a war faring race. They brought us war and they have drawn us into more of their wars."

Kelly's heart sank. He dreaded what might follow, but was relieved when Hāmana continued, "My tuāhine, Āwhina, was a wāhine toa. She chose the path of peace and she accomplished more than we who chose the path of war. She chose the right path. Now may she forever rest in peace."

Another waiata followed Hāmana's speech. Hāmana sat down and the vicar asked if anyone else wished to speak.

Kelly walked up to the front of the nave and said, "It's true what everyone has said about Whaea Āwhina. She was a great woman of God and a champion of her people and a mother to many. She was like a mother to me. She was so gracious to me when I had been an enemy to her people. I became a better man because of her.

The vicar concluded the service with the benediction Āwhina had once prayed over Kelly:

*To God's gracious mercy and protection we commit you;*
*the Lord bless you and keep you;*
*the Lord make his face to shine upon you*
*and be gracious to you;*
*the Lord lift up the light of his countenance upon you*
*and give you peace:*
*and the blessing of God almighty,*
*the Father, the Son, and the Holy Spirit,*
*be with you, now and always.*

The pall bearers went forward: Rāwiri, his two sons, Wiremu, his son, and Hāmana.

They took up the casket and carried it out to the churchyard cemetery. All gathered at the graveside, next to Patrick Quinn's plot, and the vicar pronounced:

> *We therefore commit this body to the ground, earth to earth, ashes to ashes, dust to dust; in sure and certain hope of the resurrection to eternal life.*

The threat of war was in the air, in Europe, in Great Britain, on the other side of the world, but it was bound to affect New Zealand. It became a topic of serious conversation between Kelly and Rāwiri at work. What would become of New Zealand if Britain went to war against Germany and her powerful allies, if Britain were defeated, if the Royal Navy no longer ruled the seas? New Zealand a German territory? It was unthinkable. Then there was the trade with Britain, the guaranteed market and shipping routes for New Zealand's produce and prosperity.

But there were concerns closer to home than politics and business. "We're part of the British Empire." Kelly said. "We'd be expected to back Britain with manpower and send troops. There'd be plenty who would volunteer, but the government would likely bring in conscription as well. We've got sons eligible for conscription, you and I and Wiremu."

"My boys wouldn't volunteer and I don't think Wiremu's would either, because of their political views. They don't think they owe anything to Britain after all the land confiscation. And the government doesn't have the right to conscript Māori for a white man's war. Roimata's cousin Te Puea has become very influential in the Kīngitanga and she's strongly opposed to Māori fighting in a war on behalf of the British."

"Maybe the government won't conscript Māori, but what if your sons were conscripted?"

"I think they'd refuse."

"Would they be prepared to go to jail as conscientious objectors?"

"Let's hope it doesn't come to that," Rāwiri said. "What about your son Charles?"

"He wouldn't be a volunteer. They'd conscript single men first, then married men with no children, so hopefully he wouldn't be called up." *Charles' only child, Isaac—still just a boy. Miriam hadn't conceived for years and they had all but given up hope, when she became pregnant. It was a difficult birth and her doctor said she was unlikely ever to conceive again. Forever their only child.*

When Britain declared war on Germany, New Zealand followed Mother England into the Great War in Europe, as it had done in the South African War. The call went out to fight for King and country, and many young men in New Zealand rushed to volunteer. In the second year of the war, the New Zealand Expeditionary Force sailed from Wellington to France, via Australia. It was initially a white man's war, but when Indian troops joined the alliance, Māori were also included in the New Zealand contribution, and a Native contingent was sent to Malta and on to Gallipoli.

The war demanded ever more replacements for the killed and maimed. The flow of volunteers dwindled, leaving a pool of 'shirkers', fit young men who, as the recruiters said, were too cowardly or unpatriotic to enlist. The press agreed, the public agreed, the shirkers were unfairly leaving it to others to do the fighting. The government compiled a register of men eligible for military service. The government knew who they were. Those exempted from military service were given arm badges to wear. The public knew who the shirkers were. Charles was handed a white feather by a young woman in the street as a token of his cowardice for not volunteering. Recruiters went door to door, to get more volunteers. In the third year of the war, the government introduced conscription for single men who had not volunteered, but that pool would soon be exhausted and conscription would be extended to include married men up to the age of forty-five.

A recruiter came to Charles' door. "It's only a matter of time before you're called up," he said. "You may as well enlist now."

"I'm not refusing to serve," Charles said. "I'm not a conscientious objector. I've just been leaving it to the younger men, the single men."

"What's your occupation, Mister Kelly?"

"I'm in the construction business."

"Are you claiming to be an essential worker?"

"No, but I do have important contracts I'd like to see completed."

"You could volunteer to join the engineers' division," the recruiter suggested.

Miriam was loath to let Charles go into the army and her father agreed that he had a responsibility to his family, but also a responsibility to his country. Miriam's father was serving in the navy as an officer of a ship carrying troops and horses to France. Charles had resolved not to volunteer, but neither to resist if he was balloted for conscription. And so it was that in the third year of the war Charles Kelly was drafted into the New Zealand Expeditionary Force. He reported to the drill hall to fill out an attestation form and make the oath of allegiance. He then stripped off his clothes for a medical examination and was deemed medically fit for active service beyond the seas. At Trentham Camp, he was enlisted for General Service, not Engineers, as there was a shortage of men for the infantry. On completion of training, Charles' cohort was shipped to France to join the British Expeditionary Force at the Western Front.

Māori volunteered in good numbers at the beginning of the war and the Māori Battalion within the New Zealand Expeditionary Force gained a reputation as courageous and fierce warriors in battle. When conscription for military service was also extended to include Māori, in June 1917, at the behest of Māori members of Parliament, it was applied only to Tainui-Waikato and Maniopoto-King Country, as these sectors of the Māori population had contributed very few volunteers.

Among those called up in the first draft of Māori conscripts was Rāwiri's eldest son, Tāne. Tāne had moved to Mangātawhiri, in the Waikato, where he was working as a sharemilker on a dairy farm on land purchased back from the government by the Hērangi whānau. It was originally land of their hapū, near Mercer and Huntly, and it was in the heartland of the resistance to Māori conscription. Tāne refused to be conscripted for military service and in this decision, he had the full support of his parents and of the Waikato rangatira Te Puea Hērangi, who had risen to prominence as a leader of the resistance movement. Te Puea was the granddaughter of the second Māori King, Tāwhiao and niece of the third king, Mahuta. Rāwiri had married into the royal whānau of Hērangi, though Roimata was some distance from the throne.

A Native Contingent Committee, including the Minister of Defence James Allen and Māori MPs Māui Pōmare and Apirana Ngata met with Te Puea and those opposing conscription, at Waahi Pā in Huntly to try to persuade them to join other Māori throughout the country who had answered the call to fight for King and country. The tangata whenua assembled on the marae-ātea and the visiting dignitaries sat on the paepae.

Ngata stood and addressed the assembly. He appealed to the Māori tradition of utu and sense of shame and honour. "Māori blood has been spilled on the battlefields overseas and it is a matter of honour to avenge the deaths of Māori soldiers and restore the balance. I have received letters from Māori soldiers at the front crying out for reinforcements."

In Pōmare's whaikorero, he claimed, "Serving New Zealand in this war is a way to earn equal citizenship status with Pākehā. It will gain benefits for the advancement of Māori."

"Why should we fight for the British King," Te Puea replied. "We have our own King. My grandfather, King Tāwhiao, made peace with the Crown and swore not to take up arms again." Then she came to the crux of the matter. "Why should we fight for the British? It was the British who confiscated our land. Give us back our land and we might reconsider our position."

Minister Allen addressed the conscripted men: "You have been called up to serve in the army. If you ignore the ballot, you will all be arrested for sedition. By not supporting your country, you are traitors. You are supporting the enemy."

To Te Puea he said, "I warn you not to continue to support these objectors." He also suggested that she was in fact a German sympathiser. "Is it not true, Miss Hērangi, that your surname is a transliteration of the name Searancke and that your grandfather William Searancke is of German origin?"

"I do have a grandfather on my father's side by the name of William Searancke," Te Puea replied. "Searancke is not a German name. It is

British. And what of King George and the British royal family? Are they not German?"

Warrants were issued for the arrest of Tāne Quinn and the other men who had ignored the ballot that selected them for military service. Te Puea gathered the fugitives together in the meeting house of Te Paina Pā, at Mangatāwhiri. The police arrived at the pā with a list of men liable for arrest and were escorted into the meeting house. They read out the names on their list and waited for the men to come forward. There was no response and Te Puea refused to identify them. The police officers waded into the crowd and seized seven suspects. They trampled over the Kīngitanga flag, the personal flag of King Te Rata, to seize his sixteen-year-old brother, Te Rauangaanga. Another sixteen-year-old, Rāwiri Katipa was mistaken for his elder brother and arrested, and a sixty-year-old was also arrested. Tāne was one of the few correctly identified. Te Puea blessed the arrested men as the police carried them out of the meeting house.

The arrested men were taken to the army training camp at Narrow Neck in Auckland and forcibly inducted. Tāne refused to wear the army uniform he was given and, for his insubordination, he was punished with harsh conditions: a diet of bread and water and just a blanket for a bed. Rāwiri tried to visit Tāne at the camp but he was denied access.

Kelly sympathised with Rāwiri and the plight of his son. "I can understand why Waikato Māori are refusing to go to war for the British, after what the British have done here—after what the colonial government has done," he added, trying to distance himself from the injustice.

Rāwiri, for his part, commiserated with Kelly, for his son, in the battlefields of the Western Front. The dangers were in the news daily. Thankfully,

Charles had not been involved in the Gallipoli fiasco. But in France and Belgium, in bloody trench warfare, the New Zealand troops in the British Expeditionary Force were facing heavy artillery, tanks, gas, being sent 'over the top' into enemy fire, and suffering heavy losses, in the battles of the Somme, Longueval, Arras, Messines, and Ypres. And for what? The stalemate dragged on.

Tāne continued to refuse to put on the army uniform and comply with the demands of his jailers at Narrow Neck. With a group of other recalcitrants he was court-marshalled and given a two-year sentence with hard labour at Mount Eden Prison. The sentence was read out in a muster parade of all the recruits to shame them and frighten other resisters. The colonel said the convicted men were taurekareka—slaves, the lowest of the low, and their elders were seditious traitors.

In another ballot, Wiremu's son was selected for military service. He joined other resisters at Te Paina Marae. Subsequent police raids on the marae resulted in more arrests, and more resisters and absconders joined those already incarcerated in the prison.

Rāwiri and Wiremu tried to visit their sons and were again denied permission. All they could do was go to the prison and bring food and hope that it would actually reach them.

"They're cruel conditions," Rāwiri said. "Caged in cold dark cells. Hard labour on a diet of bread and water."

They met Te Puea and some of her whānau at the prison, as they were also bringing food and keeping a vigil outside the black, iron-studded door set in the heavy, arched gate. The whole building, constructed of black basalt blocks had the look of a foreboding medieval fortress.

"It seems we are enemies of the British again, Wiremu said, "first for fighting against them and now for refusing to fight with them."

"And for defending our own homes," said Rāwiri.

"And enemies of the colonial government for peacefully occupying our own land," said Te Puea.

"True," said Rāwiri. "We were there at Parihaka."

"I was just a child," said Te Puea, "but I remember it."

"They've arrested Pākehā objectors too," Wiremu said. "They've got two brothers, Archibald and Clement Baxter and they're shipping them off overseas with the army. They'll be forced to face the enemy with no weapons."

Te Puea returned to Te Paina Marae as more conscription resisters sought refuge there. Māui Pōmare visited the marae, with his ally Te Heu Heu, hoping to persuade Te Puea and the Kīngitanga to support conscription, for the war effort. It was midwinter, the Waikato River was in flood and most of the Mangatāwhiri flats were under water. Pōmare and Te Heu Heu sat on the one piece of dry land on the marae.

Te Puea addressed her guests: "It seems we are rebels again, but who is the traitor here?" She glared at Māui Pōmare. "Minister for Western Māori, Pōmare, elected to represent the Kīngitanga, why are you conscripting Waikato and Ngāti Maniapoto and not your own iwi Taranaki? You already have some volunteers from Maniapoto. Are you seeking utu for Maniapoto-Waikato for defeating Taranaki in the past?"

The men of the marae stood knee deep in the water, stripped to the waist and performed a haka, with a whakapohane, turning and baring their buttocks to insult their visitors.

A group of women performed a poi dance, and one of the women approached Pōmare and Te Heu Heu, lifted her piupiu and indecently exposed herself. "What use are my private parts," she said, "if you are going to take away my husband?"

The VIPs were mortified and Pōmare opened his umbrella to shield himself from the lewd spectacle.

And still the work at home went on, essential work producing and exporting food for the war effort. The war was actually good for business, except for the occasional loss of shipping. A load of sheep carcasses was sent to the bottom of the sea when the refrigerated cargo ship was torpedoed by a German submarine. Another ship carrying a cargo of grain was sunk when it struck a mine laid by a German merchant raider, all in New Zealand territorial waters.

There were few men left to work in the fields and Kelly put his hand to the plough, literally, albeit a mechanised tractor-drawn plough. Kelly and Rāwiri also tended to the horses in the stables, those that were left. Kelly had donated a few surplus draught horses to the army, to be sent to Egypt where they would pull guns and wagons. Bert Grabham had left the stables, having volunteered for service early on and gone with his riding horse to join the Auckland Mounted Rifles, also in the Middle East. New Zealand bred horses were in great demand for the war effort, especially in the sandy deserts of the Sinai Peninsula.

Kelly and Annie paid frequent visits to Ōnehunga to be with Miriam and young Isaac. It had been a painful and tearful parting for Miriam when Charles boarded the troopship that took him away to an uncertain fate in France. She worked at the woollen mill while Isaac was at school, and they were at home together outside of school hours. Her days were filled with the unspoken fear that her husband may never return. Her in-laws were welcome adult company and Isaac always looked forward to visits from Grandma and Grandpa. Miriam and Isaac would also get on the tram and visit them from time to time. Auntie Imogen painted pictures and Grandpa made wooden toys in his workshop. Isaac had a set of carved wooden soldiers at home, each with a different face. He set them up in a triangle, as ninepins, all standing to attention and rolled a ball at them to knock them down.

The letters Miriam received from Charles and shared with his parents were written with many loving endearments but also spoke of ghastly conditions at the Western Front: stuck in trenches, surrounded by death, deep in mud, wet, cold, dirty, sick, scared; but sustained by his faith and prayers and the hope that he would return home safely.

Kelly and Annie were there with Miriam the day the telegram was delivered to her door. She laid the buff envelope on the table and stared at it as though it would not be true if she didn't open it. In the eerie silence, Isaac looked into the frozen faces of his mother and his grandparents, looking for what had gone wrong. With trembling hands, Miriam opened the envelope and read the words that said Charles Michael Kelly had been killed in action at the Battle of Passchendaele, in the service of his country, for the cause of freedom.

*Passiondale?* That name sent a cold shiver through Kelly's body. *It's the word Āwhina had uttered. She prophesied this. He read the telegram. Passchendaele. Āwhina had seen it. She had seen the horror of war, past and future.*

"Dada's gone," Miriam said.

"Dada's gone to war," Isaac said.

"Now he's gone to heaven. Dada's not coming back."

Miriam was the first to weep and the others followed.

The death of one's own child is surely one of the heaviest blows life throws. It's not right for a child to die before his parents. At home Kelly and Annie prayed together and talked through their grief, their sadness, their anger. Kelly was angry, not at God, but at war, the futility and madness of war. He clung to his faith. He prayed as Job did, "Though He slay me, yet will I trust Him."

It did not seem right either to have a funeral without a body. Charles' body still lay blasted and buried somewhere in the battlefield of Passchendaele. Reverend Haselden, Vicar of Saint Peter's Anglican Church, Ōnehunga, conducted a memorial service for Charles and other local men who had not returned from the war. Their names were engraved on a plaque to commemorate all who had died in the Great War.

Among the returned soldiers, Kelly met up with a former workmate from the Dilworth days, who attended the service to pay his respects.

Bert Grabham greeted him with, "Finbar Kelly, good to see you again. I was sorry to hear Charles didn't make it home. My condolences."

"Hello Bert. Thank you. Good to see you've survived. Were you wounded? I see you walk with a limp."

"Yeah, I took a bullet in my left thigh at the battle of Ayun Kara."

"I don't suppose your horse came back with you."

"No sadly. I had to leave him there. Such a fine horse he was. The British Yeoman on their posh purebred mounts scoffed at us, but we easily outperformed them and the Aussie Walers from the outback. A good Kiwi horse. You couldn't beat him for strength and endurance. Yeah, sad to leave him. It was like losing a good mate. Anyway, I'll let you get back to your family."

The whānau gathered around the Kellys, offering heartfelt condolences to the bereaved widow and parents.

Eliza greeted Wiremu with a hug. She hadn't done that since that day, long ago. A fleeting frisson gave him pause. Then he kissed her on the cheek and said, "It's a sad day for all the family."

"I wish things could have been different," she said, and turned away to speak to Miriam.

Wiremu embraced his father and, choking back tears, he said, "He was my brother."

Wiremu's daughter Mary also embraced her dear old Koro.

"We grieve with you, for your loss," Rāwiri said to Miriam, his voice strained with emotion, and turning to Finbar and Annie, "and for the loss of your son. He was a good man."

Some of the bereaved spoke at the service. For his part, Kelly paid tribute to all the soldiers who had sacrificed their lives in the war, and he said, "I grieve with all of you here who have lost a loved one in the war. I grieve the loss of my son and I grieve with his family, with Miriam and their son, Isaac, but I serve a God who sacrificed His only son for our salvation, and I take comfort knowing Charles had a strong faith and an assurance of resurrection to eternal life, and I hope to see him again in heaven."

It was a moving proclamation of faith that also brought solace to other believers at the service. But there were some among the mourners who found no solace in their grief. Grief is the price of love and some who had lost loved ones suffered the anguish of grief unrelieved by any such hope.

After his experience of wars in New Zealand, Kelly had become anti-war and more anti-British. He had fought in an unjust war and more recently had been struggling with the concept of a just war and fighting for Britain.

Finally, he said, "I'm proud of Charles for having served his country, the country of his birth, and courageously facing an enemy who would ultimately have threatened our freedom. Charles' son will carry on the Kelly name, but in the end, it's only a name. I have other children and other grandchildren and I hope to have many descendants. Life goes on."

Ko te tāngata.

# GLOSSARY OF MĀORI TERMS

| | |
|---|---|
| ae | yes |
| aroha | love |
| aroha mai | I'm sorry |
| atua | deity |
| aukati | boundary marking a restricted area |
| E pai ana te mahi. | The work is going well. |
| haere mai | welcome |
| haere tonu | keep going |
| haka taua | war dance |
| hākari | feast |
| hāngī | earth oven, food cooked in earth oven |
| hapū | subtribe |
| harirū | handshake |
| He reka te kai, nē | The food is delicious, isn't it |
| hui | meeting(s), gathering(s) |
| hongi | a pressing of noses in greeting |
| hūpē | mucus |
| iwi | tribe |
| Ka whawhai ahau tonu ake | I will fight forever. |

| | |
|---|---|
| kaikaranga | the woman who makes the ceremonial call to visitors on the marae |
| kaimoana | seafood |
| kaore | no |
| karanga | ceremonial welcome call |
| kaumātua | an elder, a person of high status |
| kei te pai | good |
| Kei te pēhea tōu mahi? | How is your work? |
| Kei te pēhea tōu whānau? | How is your family? |
| kete | woven flax basket |
| kia ora | hello / good health to you |
| kia ora ki a koe hoki | hello to you too |
| kīngitanga | king movement |
| koro | grandfather |
| koura | crayfish |
| kuia | elderly woman |
| kumārahou | a native medicinal shrub |
| kōrero | talk, speak |
| korowai | ornamental cloak |
| Ko te tāngata | It is people (from the last lines of a whakataukī: If you ask me, 'What is the most important thing in this world?' my answer is, 'It is people.') |
| kūmara | sweet potato |
| kūpapa | collaborator |
| mana | authority, prestige |
| manuhiri | visitors |
| mānuka | a tree native to New Zealand |

| | |
|---|---|
| marae | buildings and courtyard that make up the meeting place |
| marae-ātea | courtyard, open area in front of the wharenui |
| matakite | prophet, seer |
| matua | father, uncle, or respectful way of addressing a man |
| maunga | mountain(s) |
| mere | a short, flat, hand-held weapon |
| mihi | greeting |
| mokopuna | grandchildren |
| nau mai | welcome |
| nīkau | a native palm tree |
| pā | fortified village |
| paepae | orators' bench |
| pai | good |
| Pākehā | European(s) |
| patītī | short-handled axe |
| pepeha | saying of ancestors, tribal identity |
| pīwakawaka | fantail, a New Zealand native bird. In Māori mythology, a messenger of death |
| piupiu | flax skirt |
| pounamu | greenstone, jade |
| pōwhiri | ceremonial welcome |
| pūkana | dilate eyes, stare wildly, when performing haka |
| rangatira | chief |
| raruraru | trouble |

| | |
|---|---|
| raupatu | confiscation |
| raupō | bulrush |
| Rohe Pōtae | King Country (literally District of the Hat) |
| rōpū | group of people |
| rūnanga | tribal council |
| tā moko | traditional Māori tattoo on face or body |
| taiaha | fighting staff |
| tama | son, boy, nephew |
| tamariki | children |
| tangata whenua | people of the marae |
| tangi | cry |
| tangihanga | funeral |
| tātarakihi (also Kihikihi) | cicadas |
| tauiwi | foreigner |
| Te Ao Māori | the world of Māori |
| Te Ao Pākehā | the world of Europeans |
| Te Ngutu o te Manu | the beak of the bird, The name of Tītokowaru's pā |
| te reo | the (Māori) language |
| tēnā koe | hello |
| tīpuna | ancestors |
| toa | warrior, champion |
| toetoe | native, pampas-like grass |
| tohu | a sign |
| tokotoko | walking stick |
| tuāhine | sister (of a male) |
| tūpara | double barrel shot gun |
| urupā | burial grounds |

| | |
|---|---|
| utu | revenge, retribution |
| wāhine | woman |
| wāhine toa | courageous woman |
| waiata | n. song, v. sing |
| wairua | spirit |
| waka | canoe |
| wero | challenge |
| whaea | mother, aunt |
| whakapapa | genealogy |
| whakataukī | proverb |
| whānau | extended family |
| whāngai | adopted child |
| Whanganui-a-Tara | the Māori name for Wellington |
| whare | house(s) |
| whare kai | kitchen, dining room |
| whare karakia | church, house of prayer |
| wharenui | meeting house, large house |
| whenua | land |
| | also placenta |

# ABOUT THE AUTHOR

John Carstensen is a Danish born Kiwi and has also lived in Canada and China. He has spent most of his life in New Zealand and now resides in the seaside city of Tauranga. He is an English teacher by profession, but retired and devoting more time to writing and fishing. His short stories have appeared in various New Zealand and Australian literary journals and magazines. He published a collection of stories in 2019 and is collating more collections.

He brings his research into New Zealand history, his Christian faith, and his craft of writing fiction together in this fascinating historical novel. His protagonist grapples with moral and spiritual issues and, in the course of the narrative arc, develops strong Christian character.

www.ingramcontent.com/pod-product-compliance
Lightning Source LLC
LaVergne TN
LVHW091039080826
845145LV00002B/561